ECSTATIC
from ONE LIE

ECSTATIC *from* ONE LIE

HADYN J. ADAMS

authorHOUSE®

AuthorHouse™
1663 Liberty Drive
Bloomington, IN 47403
www.authorhouse.com
Phone: 1-800-839-8640

First published by AuthorHouse   01/06/2012

ISBN: 978-1-4670-1978-1 (sc)
ISBN: 978-1-4670-1981-1 (ebk)

Printed in the United States of America

For My Friends

"Yet ideas can be true, although men die :
For we have seen a myriad faces
Ecstatic from one lie,
And maps can really point to places
Where life is evil now.
Nanking. Dachau."

W H Auden : Sonnets from China XII

CHAPTER 1

The Burial

"*Not a drum was heard, not a funeral note . . . .*"
*(Charles Wolfe : The Burial of Sir John Moore
at Corunna).*

August. Summer sunshine over the small, uninspiring town of Portminster. It made little difference here in this English town where people lived ordinarily ever after. Although set in Hampshire the bright, warm day brought no extra visitors and therefore trade here as it would to the soft, southern underbelly of the county where Southampton, Portsmouth and, perhaps more than even these, Southsea, would benefit from the increase in temperature. But so, too, to the west would the county town of Winchester, steeped as it was in history : and, to the Queen Elizabeth Country park which sprawled across the countryside north of Portminster and north of the coastal resorts : and to Marwell Zoo, a magnet for youngsters on such a day as this and, of course, the many other tourist attractions of the county. Not so

1

Portminster ; it would merely bask in the sunshine as its residents went about their daily business perhaps only a trifle ruffled by a marginal increase in traffic which had either decided on this more scenic detour to the south and west or perhaps more likely had lost its way off the congested, long, liquorish lengths of the motorways that led to the more desirable destinations.

For John Ellis, the local newspaper reporter, the weather was most welcome only because it meant he could sit outside at The Fort St George whilst imbibing his lunchtime ration of alcohol as he wrote up notes for word-processing that afternoon for the next day's edition of *The Portminster Gazette*. If there was a hack's job in newspaper writing then John certainly laid claim to having the biggest one going for in this locality there was next to nothing about which to write. He would often reflect that the Births, Marriages and Deaths columns or even at times the advertisements were by far the best reading in the paper, the rest of the journal being about as sensational as Cecily's diary in *The Importance of Being Earnest*. Even the title of the newspaper itself had, he felt, been Americanised out of a desire to make it more attractive than it was or, for that matter, ever could be. So, today, he sat with his notebook on the table, a copy of today's edition of his newspaper folded in front of him lying beside his pint of russet coloured, Winter's bitter and the small plate with his cheddar cheese and pickle sandwiches which he was about to devour for lunch.

Today he got through the notes even quicker than usual there being only three items of news, if such a term could be applied to the local library extension, the local majorettes raising money for a dog for the blind and the local squash club's opening of a small fitness room. Nothing there upon which a reporter of over a decade's standing could not pad out to fill any number of column inches as required with suitable photos and appropriate headlines in 15 point *Bidoni or grot sans shadow* or whatever was now available via the computerised techniques of desk-top publishing. His preparation being done, and having no qualms about his ability to complete his afternoon work in the office at a canter, he decided, it being such a beautiful day, he would indulge in a few more pints of Winter's bitter and get suitably mellow before going in ; perhaps, he felt, like Coleridge taking his laudanum, he taking Winter's bitter might lead to him producing copy akin to the epic fragment, *Kubla Khan*—what a sensational piece of writing that would be!

As he finished his sandwiches which he always ate in a most frugal manner and started to drink his third pint which he did in a much more spendthrift manner he picked up the paper and turned to the crossword. Though never an addict he enjoyed the word games associated with the cryptic clues and he believed by his ability or sometimes lack of it to solve most of the clues he could determine how mentally alert or dull he was at any given time. Today would be a good gauge of the effect of the sun and the alcohol on his cerebral faculties. Always he took a little time to get started, to get mentally in tune with the compiler and even he, occasional crossword completer as he was, could sense a change of authorship even in a provincial newspaper like his own. As he started he reflected that such changes occured much more in the nationals and though he had no idea as to who did submit the crosswords to *The Gazette*, he was positive the style had been unchanged for the past few years at least. After turning over the cogs in his brain cells, he did manage to get started and, despite the slightly soporific effect of the beer, he reached almost the point of completion. He was frustrated by a few final clues but sufficiently satisfied that his mental prowess was not unduly diminished given the variables of temperature and volume of imbibed liquid and so he decided one more pint for the road before going in for the afternoon would have no further deleterious effect.

As he strolled along to the newspaper's offices he turned over some of the clues in his mind and an inner glow of satisfaction that he believed came from his skill in mastering them, though which was far more attributable to the level of alcohol circulating in his blood stream, filled him. In this spirit he paused beside Janice on reception who was, as he came in, working on the crossword herself. Well, what does a receptionist have to do when not answering the telephone? he reflected. Leaning over her and noticing she had made but a skeletal start he endeavoured to give her help by offering her the solution to 19 across, "Turn gloomy when a box appears in the study—*Darken*" and 26 down, "Hide chief in town—*Leatherhead*." Janice was not amused. She knew he had been drinking and, she could tell, had drunk a little more than usual; she felt like someone playing *Patience*, who, quite content to while away the time in what was the most fatuous of card games, had the whole exercise ruined by some interfering busybody indicating that a red six went under a black seven or a black ten could be transferred under a red Jack to release more cards and therefore get to a solution much more quickly than the player desired. Angry though she was, John was a likeable rogue and she had a soft spot for him and so she merely rebuffed his offerings by pointing out that 14 across would be appropriate to his day were he not to get in and get on with his work. His tiring eyes glanced onto the grid. "Bungled, being down on a journalist—*Fluffed*"; he took the hint, smiled by way of apology knowing he had made a contribution where it was not wanted and headed in to his desk and his computer.

The afternoon passed languidly. John did not manage to create an opus in the *Kubla Khan* mould as he had earlier thought he might. None the less he created sufficient copy of quality to satisfy his boss and, he knew, the locals who were the only purchasers of this publication. At least he had an audience for his writing. Over the whole of the country, nay, over the whole world, imaginations were being stretched by creators of novels, poems, articles or whatever which, as the pop song said "voices never shared." He was, therefore lucky. His words would be read, marked and maybe even inwardly digested by readers numbered in their thousands. Not very critical or discerning ones admittedly but the fact that they were there kept him in steady employment and in a job that he had grown into and was prepared to accept. Life was all compromise. At university he may have dreamt about being an investigative journalist who would take on a case with the world wide coverage similar to the Pentagon Papers/Watergate but here in Portminster was the reality of the Fourth Estate for most of his kind—a parsimonious position of provincial periphrasis!

At a quarter to six he had completed all he had set out to do and therefore headed home. Janice had long since departed as guardian of the offices and Anita had replaced her on reception. John whispered a "Goodnight" to her as he departed out into the final sunshine of the day. Had he been on the coast he could have walked in the bracing air along the sea-coast and captured the flavour of the summer holiday beside the sea perhaps even enjoying an ice-cream or lounging in a deck chair drinking a Guinness whilst looking out onto the azure main dotted with the coloured sails of yachts and wind-surf boards as the long day closed. Had he been in the heart of the countryside he could have walked beside verdant rural hedgerows sheltering the beautiful myriad coloured blossoms of the country gardens in the foreground of the picturesque thatched cottages warmed by the crimson rays of the sun's dying light. But here in Portminster he had to make do with a walk up the High Street with most of the shops now closed and the day's litter lying in front of them waiting to be cleared and then via streets and roads, dusty but uncrowded and certainly not of any memorable merit to his maisonette about one and a half miles away.

On route was The Fort St George and again, given the nature of the day, John decided to go home and cook for himself was a waste of effort in the climatic circumstances and stopping here to be fed and watered was infinitely preferable. So indeed he did. He did not mind having to wait until suppers were being served after seven o'clock since he would be able to get in two, perhaps three pints by then and he would be able to soak up at least two more with the meal. This would induce him to an appropriate soporific state in which to go home and read and then fall asleep in anticipation of the day to come.

A lasagne and chips, five pints and a *Cardhu* malt whisky later, John took his leave of the hostelry and since the cumulative impression of the lunchtime drinking and this was now having a decidedly wearying effect on him he decided to take the short cut through the neighbouring churchyard whose far eastern wall he could climb and get into the lane that backed onto his own property. It would save him almost one third of a mile walk and the climb was not difficult even in the condition in which he found himself since he had done it in far worse inebriated states in the past.

It was just after eight thirty and the twilight of the day was fading in a thousand absurd postures. The graveyard through which he passed held none of its terrifying ambience at such a time on such a day and John enjoyed at such times reading the carved phrases on the tombstone. There were bits of Latin for the prestigious dead, *Integer vitae scelerisque purus*, hymnal fragments for the devoutly Christian, *In Heavenly Love Abiding*, and various rhymes gleaned from Laureates such as Tennyson on others, *Tho' much is taken, much abides*. Well, John surmised this evening, words do indeed have many uses. As he meandered through the main tarmacaddamed pathway that mazed through the churchyard he noticed the gravedigger over in the far corner by the eastern wall which he would shortly be scrambling over. The man was completing the filling in of a grave that had obviously been used that very day. Even in his alcoholically induced sonnambulistic state John registered that this was rather odd. Portminster might well be a reasonably sized town but working on the newspaper as he did local births, marriages and deaths were something he was paid to register as they might just provide newsworthy items were the births to concern triplets or more, the marriages to be between gays or lesbians and the deaths to be accidental or suicidal (murder or manslaughter being alien to such Hampshire suburban-ness). Not being able to recall any recent deaths or notifications of funerals he ambled over to the scene and inquired of Tom, the part-time gravedigger whose full time job was assistant caretaker of the local secondary school, who had been interred that day.

Tom, not noted for this loquacity, mumbled something about an Irishman who had nothing to do with Portminster but who seemingly had requested to be buried here. "Small funeral it was, Mr Ellis," he added as he finished the mound and patted it with his spade to flatten it down to ground level. Wiping the sweat from his brow with the back of his earth stained arm and thereby leaving a thin brown scar across his forehead, he leaned back on the shovel which he had firmly planted in the ground, using it now in the

9

manner of a shooting stick. He prodded his earthy right hand into his trouser pocket and took out a crumpling packet of cigarettes and a lighter. He fetched out one of the contents of the packet, stuck it between his lips, lit the end and took a massive inhilation of the gases produced with all the satisfaction of a wine taster savouring the bouquet of a rosy Rioja or a classic Chardonnay. "Only the vicar and two attendants, like," he finalised as he thrust the packet and lighter back into his trouser pocket without consideration as to the damage it might do to the few remaining cigarettes in the packet. "No one stayed around. I got back just as they was leaving. Never even offered us a tip. Talk about miserable mourners!" He took another long drag on his cigarette, stood upright, turned round and removed the spade, angled it up on to his right shoulder like an army recruit sloping arms and with a deadpan, "Goodnight to you, then, Mr Ellis," departed off in the direction of the pub from which John had just come. There was no doubts as to his intention at this, the parting of the day.

John paused briefly surveying the flattened earth and thinking of the body in the box somewhere below it. Had he been less tired he would probably have tried to summon up all the relevant pieces of literature he could associate with death but it had been too long a day and he really had drunk too much especially ending with that whisky which he had never really intended to do. He turned and walked down beside the wall about to the half-way point which was his normal crossing station. He needed no climbing skills to surmount what was a roughly built, slightly crumbling, eight foot high, stone wall and he was soon over and down into the lane and then over his own small fence, through his postage stamp of a back garden, into his ground floor maisonette, into the bathroom and then the bedroom and onto his bed. Before falling asleep his befuddled mind linked one of the crossword clues he had struggled with unsuccessfully earlier in the day and the scene he had just witnessed in the cemetery: "Make underground place in Sussex ask questions." The answer formulated itself, "*Interrogate*." It was too late now to pencil it in and help him finish off the few others that he had not completed and anyway the crossword was unimportant. But that grave .... "ask questions" .... indeed he would .... later.

CHAPTER 2

Sidetracked

"He uses statistics as a drunken man uses lamp-posts—for support rather than for illumination."
(Andrew Lang)

Whisky and beer make you feel queer. Beer and whisky make you feel frisky. Only the romantic soul of a misguided poet could have produced such a saying thought John as he slowly came to consciousness with the dawn that had risen sometime before and was now thrusting its rays of morning light through the rapier thin gap between his bedroom curtains. Whatever order the aforesaid drinks were taken in they had, in the quantity in which John had drunk them, the ability to make the imbiber decidedly repentant of his actions. Though not suffering from the proverbial hangover, yet was he feeling the effects of the alcohol intake from the previous day; his mouth and throat were like the inside of a tramdriver's glove, his eyes seemed sealed together by some strong magical wax and he generally felt as if he had hardly slept at all though truth to tell he had fallen asleep on his bed almost as soon as his head had touched the pillow shortly after 9.00p.m and it was now just past 7.00a.m.

He registered first of all the day; it was Thursday. Only two days until the weekend and freedom, provided no major news items surfaced on Saturday or Sunday and that was just about guaranteeable where Portminster was concerned. A normal day then. In early, check any items from over night, research and interviews a.m., write-ups p.m. this was indeed the usual pattern of his working day. Occasionally interviews and research could not be done in the mornings or maybe even drifted into the afternoon in which case he would either work late or phone or fax in material for others to work on. Rarely was he ever on a news item more than 12 miles radius from Portminster, the areas to the north and south of the town largely being covered by larger city newspapers of Basingstoke and Portsmouth. But he did get around at least in the immediate environs and his local knowledge built up over the decade and then some years he had been working here was quite formidable. As he reporter he was sound and efficient and quite comprehensive in his local news coverage. He had gained the respect of the locals and was generally trusted. For a journalist to receive the comments of *fair, honest, without side, genuine, accurate*—all of which terms had been used by readers in relation to John's work—certainly made him a reporter worth keeping at least for the local items such as he covered. In reality his Deputy Editor and Editor, as well as the newspaper proprietor, considered such epigrams as tantamount to saying someone was a nice person with all the implications of such a description. But then, having such a nice reporter on their staff was a good advert in times of controversy and went along with the image that helped them sell and keep up circulation in the area.

Slowly and carefully, then, John awoke and rose and made his way to the bathroom. His ablutions complete he sauntered back to the bedroom and generally tidied up the pile of clothes he had left strewn on the floor and over the chair the previous night. Most of these except for the trousers were for the wash; the trousers he would take to the cleaners since although they were not dirty the heap in which he had left them had rendered any reasonable and appropriate crease about as relevant as a border marking on a map of Bosnia. He put on a new set of smart casual clothes which were fitting with his line of business and decided he would take the car in from the start of the day in anticipation of some traveling to new venues. One of his perks was expenses paid for such trips and in a good week he could, because of the generous mileage allowance paid by the newspaper, add a comfortable fifty pounds or more to his salary. Feeling refreshed from tidying himself and his bedroom up and from seeing that it was another sunny day that had dawned he went out of the house, into his blue 'K' registered *Rover 414 si* and drove the short mileage into work.

On his arrival it was Janice who was back in reception and who greeted him with question, "Did you finish it, then?"

"Finish what?" he enquired, stopping in his tracks.

"The crossword, silly!" she laughed.

"Oh that!" And until he registered what she was talking about he realised he had totally forgotten the closing incident of the previous day in the graveyard on his way home. Suddenly her question had brought it all back to him. *Interrogate. Ask questions.* Yes. Of course. He must do that if only to satisfy his own curiousity. "Why, no!" he replied. "I rarely do. I only do the difficult clues and give the solutions to others to stir things up," he said wickedly.

"You do that alright," she smiled and since the phone beside her rang she picked it up signalling the end of the conversation for the time being. John nodded to her and went on into his office space.

The first thing he noticed on his desk was a yellow *Post-It* sticker. What, he thought, had business done before this new form of informal memo had been invented? But then that question could be asked about all inventions through the ages and, no doubt, answering it troubled those who dealt with the history of philosophy of science more than any others.

Please ring me first thing. David.

He picked up his telephone and dialed 23, the internal extension for David Hart, the deputy editor. As he listened to the tone he hoped that this might be the start of an interesting local assignment and he felt he had done the right thing in bringing his car from the start. His thoughts were brief.

"David Hart."

"John. You asked me to ring."

"Yes. Fine. Thanks for ringing, John. Look, mini-crisis today. Clare Hills rang in. Summer 'flu or something, anyway she's not in and you know what today is, don't you?"

Clare Hills was the reporter who had a brief on local council and educational issues. That part of David's finely refined telephone speak John had no trouble with but as for what was so important about this August Thursday of all Thursdays he was totally without a clue and readily admitted it.

"G.C.S.E results, John. G.C.S.E. results. Pass rates, failure rates, league tables, that sort of thing. Got to show the locals the local comp's doing its job. Must get some facts, figures and do some comparisons. I'm sure you know what's required. Portminster Community College, the local school's usually very good; Derek White, the deputy head there, usually faxes in the results after they come in the morning's post and comments straight off and he's very approachable if you've got any questions. Other schools round about and in the large conurbations to the south are not so forthcoming and you may need to prise information out of them. I want you to handle this. It's a big item and I will want it in Friday's edition to give everyone something to think about and ponder over the weekend."

His immediate boss had spoken. There was no room for argument. This, he knew, would be tedious work and although the other items that might be waiting on his answerphone or scribbled on memos on his desk were probably equally unexciting at least they would offer him the chance to use some words. This would primarily be figures and cliched, quoted comments from dull and deadly headteachers allowing no scope for imagination. No opportunity here to turn the mundane mediocrity of Portminster's existence into the flamboyant, colourful and opulent life style of a Maharajah! But, so be it. The day was to be consigned to drudgery. The car would not be wanted so the few miles on its clock would not be paid for out of company money. He could not have a serious alcoholic liquid lunch or supper for that matter unless he were to go to the pub after returning home with the car. Yes, that was always possible.

So the day was filled with lies, damned lies and statistics. As he gleaned information from a wide circle of schools, the faxes pouring out seemingly never ending reams of paper with the first seven letters of the alphabet and allied percentages of figures, he became amused by what he was compiling into the final article itself. He saw himself as Winston Smith in 1984 manipulating data which would be acceptable to everyone and, above all, gave the impression that the education service was doing a wonderful job. Yet was he also gifted with Winston Smith's insight to comprehend that what was being presented was so obviously fabricated that it seemed preposterous that the public could accept it. This *was Hitler's Big Lie Theory*; this was something which proved Beckett's damning prouncement in *Waiting for Godot* that people are "bloody ignorant apes!" Yet here indeed it was and the perpetrator of it all in this instance was John Ellis, ordinary, or relatively ordinary, citizen.

The first point of contact for the results was the Headteachers. Getting through to them was sometimes as difficult as B B C T V beating I T V in the ratings when *Coronation Street* was being screened. None-the-less, the inner sanctum of the school was eventually reached and the comment on the school's result elicited from he or she who must be obeyed. This comment in all cases hardly varied and was certainly never profound. Like an intoned mantra emanating from some Hari Krishna high priest the replies all stated that the results were very pleasing, better than the previous year's and above the national average. On hearing this for the umpteenth time, John reflected that no doubt some poor journalistic sod not a million miles away in the neighbouring counties of West Sussex or Dorset was undoubtedly getting the same responses from the Headteachers of the schools in his location; and this was unquestionably being repeated nationwide. Here, then, was the first antinomy of the Ellis' law concerning examination results: if all these school produced results above, or in some cases when the Headteachers remembered with advantages, well above the national average, where were those schools or those educational institutions which were below the national average in order for this mystical average figure itself to be below all the schools he (or anyone) contacted?

Having gleaned all these similar statements from the Headteachers, John reflected on the results themselves. Aged 35 he had been schooled during the days of G.C.E. 'O' Levels and had left at about the time C.S.E.s were being introduced. Certainly it was the time of grammar schools and secondary, of selective education and he had been a model pupil of one of the former institutions. In his mind were embedded the figures of 20-25%. Notionally he recalled this was the number of pupils who achieved 'O' level standard, most, but not all of that percentage being educated at the grammar schools. C.S.E.s had blurred the examination graph a little but not seriously with the notion of a C.S.E. Grade 1 being an 'O' level equivalent. Maybe then the quantity of the population therefore who were of 'O' level standard might be more clearly represented by a figure of 30% or so, subject in some cases to the discipline that was being examined. That seemed reasonable to him. However, since G.C.S.E.s, that wonderful melding together of the two examinations had taken place in or about 1987 as far as he knew, this figure of the population achieving what he regarded as the old 'O' level standard had risen to over 50%! A marked increase indeed! Herein lay the formulation of Ellis' second antinomy of the laws relating to examination results: if such an improvement of 20% (in some subjects even more!) had occured within a six year period, why did teachers not wish to be paid by results?

Lastly, as he bedded down this massive four page spread that was about as informative as an organ grinder's monkey, he recalled a feature printed quite recently from Highbury Further Education College in Portsmouth promoting and advertising a new academic award scheme, the national and vocational qualification, N.V.Q.s in education-speak. He got up from his desk at this point and went to get the back issue that contained the information relating to these new courses. He opened the appropriate edition to read the banner headlines putting forward the Government's message relating to this scheme: THE ROUTE TO A 'WORLD CLASS' WORK FORCE. He smiled. Here was his third and final antinomy: if G.C.S.E.s had improved standards (and the increase from 30 to 50% most assuredly proved they had!), why did the government and many educationalists feel a need for yet another bank of qualifications?

He had enjoyed thinking of these things during the boredom of dealing with this task which had taken him almost up until 6.00p.m. Maybe it was just casuistry on his part but he did wish that the population at large were capable of such an analytic approach to this form of data. However, he knew that along with a great deal of other similar material that was turned out the vast majority saw things in the Light Brigade's terms, *theirs not to reason why*! In Communist Russia to have thoughts such as he had and to express them would have been considered to have been a form of mental illness and he would, no doubt, have been exiled to Siberia or confined to a lunatic asylum. Here in the U.K. such thinkers would be considered as eccentric or too educated for their own good or perhaps it would be suggested they were suffering from stress.

John was jolted out of his end of work day reflections and reverie by his telephone ringing. So engrossed was he in these thoughts that it really did startle him. He lifted the receiver.

"John Ellis. *The Portminster Gazette.*" His standard response.

"Cut the formality, John, it's Helen! I'm back!"

The voice was music to his ears. It was Helen, an old flame from Portsmouth, though she certainly would not have approved of the adjective! She had been away working in Germany for nine months with her company.

"Helen! Well, what a surprise!" He seemed temporarily dumbstruck.

"Well, aren't you even going to thank me for my cards and letters? I did so enjoy receiving yours!" she added with withering sarcasm for, truth to tell, John had sent one card to her in nine months.

He was embarrassed and faltered an apology, but he knew her : she would just use this fact to rib him with when their relationship picked up as he hoped it would given that she had taken the trouble to telephone him. It was so good to hear from her. No doubt she had a lot to tell him about her German experience. There was lost time to be made up, too! In order to compensate for his epistolary drought he felt it incumbent on him to welcome her return by inviting her up for the weekend and so he began, "Well, great! How about you co . . . ." but she interposed. "John, do come down and see me this weekend. You must. Now that I'm back I feel quite alone. I will have to rebuild my friendships here at work and in this city. It would be so good to see you after all this time. We've got lots to talk about and we've got to compensate for our time apart."

He was very pleased by her enthusiasm. Her whole tone was sensuous, inviting. There was no way he was going to disappoint her, for to do so would be to disappoint himself and deny his own very natural impulses, but before he could even respond in the affirmative she said, "Now I'm not taking no for an answer. If you've anything planned for this weekend you must cancel it for my sake. You will do that, won't you? Oh, I know you will; I am well aware you can't write," she commented with the barb he knew she would for a while be prodding him with, "but I assume you can talk and we've got a whole lot of talking to do! I'll be expecting you then no later than 7p.m. tomorrow. We can go out in the town and later go for an Indian in one of those super restaurants in Palmerston Road. See you! Don't let me down. Ciao for now," she laughingly said and then added, "or should that be Auf Weidhersein?" and she put the phone down leaving John mouthing a, "Yes, I'll be there; looking forw . . . ." into the phone line at the end of which was now a dormant telephone.

John sat for a while with the receiver in his hand just staring at it. He then replaced it, shook his head in disbelief whilst at the same time mentally reassuring himself that he had heard from Helen, that she was back, that she wanted to pick up where they had left off and that she had invited him to spend that coming weekend with her. He was electrified with anticipation but before he decided to get up, leap about and demonstrate his emotional joy he remembered how that phone call had interrupted his thoughts. He decided therefore to quell his natural urge to share his sexual salvation with the remnants of staff left in the office (for it was now gone 6.00p.m.) and check carefully the article he had put together so that the run could begin that evening. It could be that all his philosophical investigations in the manner of Immanuel Kant concerning examination results had effected his concentration in assembling the montage from all the faxes and comments he had received. He decided it was therefore in his and the paper's interest (there had been cases he believed of some over-assiduous Headteachers suing papers which had misrepresented their comments and/or results!) that he double check the article. This he did and thankfully it did not take that long and he was pleasantly surprised to discover that he had in fact made no errors and therefore was without sin.

Job done, John headed for home after parking his car he decided a visit to the pub was not in order that evening. He had so much to look forward to on the weekend he did not want any experience between now and the time he would head south to take away even by the merest smidgeon anything that would reflect in any way upon the way he was feeling about the forthcoming few days. Rather he decided to check his wardrobe and all the clothes he would take and he even tidied up the interior of the car since they would probably motor about in it a bit on Saturday at least and he did not wish Helen to think he had become an even worse slob in her absence than he was before she went away!

That evening and the next day John was to all intents and purposes oblivious of his work though he had the experience not to betray this to his superiors. He was sufficiently adept at giving the impression his mind was tuned in to *the Portminster Gazette* and everything that appertained to its general welfare and its greater good and glory. But Friday 6.00p.m. was locked so firmly in his mind that if he had a philosophy that day as he had had Kantian pretentions on the Thursday, it was teleologically determined towards that hour, that specific point in time in the history of the universe (there or thereabouts) when he would leave his place of work, get into his car and point its nose southwards towards the maritime capital of England, Portsmouth.

Time like an ever rolling stream eventually brings about by its passing all things that humankind anticipates though it may not always deliver such things in quite the manner in which they were imagined in the mind. But on this particular occasion everything went as John imagined it would and he found himself parking outside Helen's small terraced house in the Portsmouth suburb of Drayton at 6.49p.m., only fifty-two minutes after leaving work.

The week was dead; long live the weekend! All of this and what was to transpire over the weekend that was to come served to blot out, at least temporarily, his resolve to follow up the graveyard scene of two nights before.

CHAPTER 3

A Religious Calling

"The two possibilities are that we may not hear, and the other possibility is that hearing we may not answer."
(R Ferguson : Some Reminiscences and Studies).

The Reverend Robert Fergusson was Pickwickian in shape, size and character. He had come to Portminster from Glastonbury and felt, therefore, it was appropriate that he was vicar of the church and parish of St Michael's for it constantly reminded him of that most famous of English landmarks, St Michael's Tower, the Tor, (sometimes referred to as Gwyn-ap-Nud's tower), under whose shadow he had lived for a good many years along Roman Hill in his church manse that overlooked the road towards Street and the River Brue where, so legend had it, King Arthur had thrown the fabled Excalibur. The memory of such a romantic, mythical area never faded though he had now been vicar here in Portminster for over 25 years and had only occasionally returned to his former parish for church anniversaries or special celebrations.

Now in the eventide of his ministerial career he had a reputation in the community for being a Christian vicar of the old school. He had no car and was content to visit parishioners far and wide by Shank's pony as he would laughingly say and, he would add, he was surprised with all the walking that he did he should still bear the overweight, roly-poly figure that he did; he was certainly no advert for walking as good exercise! He not only visited the sick, dying, the imprisoned in the true spirit of Matthew 25, verses 31 following, but he made a point of seeing all his congregation at home at least some time during the year and sharing the ministry of the gospel with them by his visit and by prayers with the families visited. A great church pastoral worker indeed and this was one of the reasons why the congregation at St Michael's had kept its numbers up, nay even increased them marginally, during times when church-going was rapidly going out of fashion and the Church of England was finding stiff competition with the rise and attraction of the Baptist and Unitarian sects.

This was not, however, the only reason for his success. Though the concept of the sermon might well be regarded as a dying art, here, surprisingly enough, in a Hampshire backwater, was evidence that such a great English tradition was still alive. Fergusson was renowned for his sermons and in this respect would have been more than welcomed by any nonconformist group for he stood head and shoulders in his oratorical ability compared with even the best that certainly their representatives in this county and for a few roundabout could offer. It was not just the quality of the sermon but his manner of delivery. For he conveyed the humour, the jollity, the freshness of spirit that should go along with Christianity and his exhortations rather than being shot through with hell and damnation in order to put the fear of God into his congregation were rather peppered with wit, with jokes and badinage and above all personal reminiscences with which his audience could identify. He was a wonderful raconteur and had a mixture attributes that would more appropriately appertain to stand-up comics and serious actors but these blended together with his anecdotal style gave rise to a well-merited reputation that certainly made the locals bring anyone who stayed with them to hear him and occasionally attracted individual interest from further afield.

He came from a well-to-do family and after public school (whenever he talked about this period of his life he would describe himself as *Billy Bunter* whom he saw as the literary embryonic presentation of Pickwick) and was educated at Bristol and London Universities getting a first class honours in Classics at the former and another first class honours in Divinity at the latter. His training for the church was done at Wescott House, the Church of England college in Cambridge, and his first curacy was in the east End of London. He had, therefore, eschewed a comfortable life and really had become the Christian shepherd prepared to sacrifice himself for his flock. His London years (a good twenty of them) had given him experiences to use in his subsequent brief posting to Glastonbury and thus finally to Portminster. Stories circulated locally of deeds done in the Christain spirit as for example his giving of his heavy, warm overcoat and giving it to a ragged tramp wandering through Portminster High Street on one icy-cold February evening or the time he baptised gypsy children when they had been turned away by all the other local churches because their itinerant parents would not attend church regularly . . . . "suffer the little children." But he was not generally one for ostentation or to court controversy and on recent issues, Aids, homosexuality, women priests, he was content to toe the party line by a mixture of acquiescence and silence—"qui tacet consentere."

Even now he could have retired comfortably for he and his brother had inhereted their parents' wealth and properties and his brother, indeed, had built up a small, but rewarding, hotel business in the Channel Islands. But he was content to serve the local churchgoers and had managed to persuade his brother to offer special deals to the church to allow for ministerial conferences and communicant members of the church to use the hotel facilities on good terms.

Never having married, the rector and the rectory were looked after by an ageing spinster, Miss Simpson; given her generation she was more than happy to be known by this nomenclature alone and there were probably very few now alive in Portminster who would have known her Christian name anyway. She had been housekeeper to the incumbent before the Reverend Fergusson and, indeed, the one before him and she never considered the concept of retirement though she was now certainly into her late seventies. She lived in an annexe to the property and, apart from her cleaning and cooking duties had in the past occasionally done typing work for the rector. With the advent of word-processing and the need for greater administration within the church organisation there was now a small office set up as an extension to the vestry in the Church itself and a part-time secretary was employed there three afternoons a week so such duties were now no longer required of her, a fact for which she regularly praised the Lord for she wanted little to do with such new fangledness! Never once in all her years in this job with the bachelor incumbents whom she served had anyone thought the situation lacking in propriety, nor indeed had they any reason to do so.

As John Ellis approached the rectory on the Wednesday following his wonderful weekend in *Pompey* and a week to the day when he had seen Tom Barber filling in the grave, he knew exactly the reception he would receive. It was just after eleven thirty in the morning and, having completed the interviews and research for his stories for the next edition he felt he had time at last to follow up this small affair which had been at the back of his mind off and on for the past seven days. He felt it would all be a waste of time but he had enjoyed his brief encounters with Miss Simpson and the Reverend Robert Fergusson in the past and had appreciated the Reverend's erudite letters to the press as well as his contributions to feature articles on religion. It would be good to kill this brief time before lunch and then afternoon in the office in interesting company. As he walked up the long gravel drive to the grey, stone mansion which was the rectory and which was bearded on the front and the sides by heavy, and now old, yet rampant ivy, he smiled as he recalled the weekend past, thought pessimistically about the one to come which, being the bank holiday weekend required that he worked, and then considered optimistically the weekend to follow that for he would be going back to Portsmouth then and since both he and Helen had some holiday time to come that particular weekend would be protracted by three whole days making the period of time worth an age without a name!

As he rang the doorbell the sequence of events, at least in all its initial stages were exactly as he had visualised on the way.

The door was answered by Miss Simpson.

She looked at him through her rounded spectacles, observing and identifying who it was like a cricket umpire deliberating on an awkward l.b.w. decision. Once she was satisfied that she knew and was prepared to entertain the caller she said, "Well, Mr Ellis, what may we do for you?" And then, assuming that no caller ever wished to pay his or her respects to her since they were calling at The Rectory and not her separate annexe, added, "It's the rector you wish to see no doubt."

John smiled and nodded his agreement.

"Come in, come in. the Reverend Fergusson is in his study and there's no one with him so he'll be able to see you. Please wait here in the hall while I go and check."

John had anticipated that brief wait in this quite spacious hall. He never failed to enjoy just looking round at the prints that adorned its wall which were all in some way connected with the Reverend Fergusson; a print of Wescott House, his Cambridge College, some rare prints illustrating parts of the city of Edinburgh, the Athens of the North, where his progenitors had lived, some prints of churches in and around the east end of London and Glastonbury, Somerset, where he had worked and even one of St Michael's, Portminster. As he surveyed them as he had done on previous occasions, Miss Simpson came back along the small corridor where the minister's study was and announced in the manner of a headmaster's secretary, "The reverend Fergusson will see you now. This way please," and she ushered him from the hallway, down the corridor and in through the open door of the room of the study.

The Reverend Fergusson greeted John with a hearty handshake and a smile as wide as the skirt on the Southsea-Isle of Wight hovercraft.

"Not come to collect already?" he said as he ushered him to a seat in front of his desk behind which he went to sit. "They're not due until the start of next week."

John was taken aback by this, not knowing to what his host could be referring.

"No, of course not," he went on. "Not your department and anyway they know I always post them off regular as clockwork a week ahead every Monday."

John sat mystified and his look clearly betrayed his inability to register what was being talked about to the cleric. He illogically surmised that another feature article was being written for this newspaper and was about to comment on this when enlightenment was thrust upon him by the Reverend holding up a crossword grid and saying, "Sorry, John, you clearly weren't aware; yes, I compile the *Gazette*'s crosswords . . . ."

"You!" interposed John. "Well, I never knew . . . ."

"Yes me! I do it under the fancy pseudonym of Eusebius now for the past eight years ever since that retired Cambridge don, Frank Raymond Chawner, who used to live in Portminster passed away. He had the job before me." At this juncture he realised he had not offered John any refreshment so he rose from his chair and went to the door to summon Miss Simpson to tend to their needs. True professional that she was she had anticipated these desires and was already on her way from the kitchen with a tray containing a coffee for her employer and a tea (no milk no sugar—there was nothing wrong with her memory concerning the tastes of visitors) for John as well as a plate with six chocolate digestive biscuits. After she had placed the tray on the desk and left the minister motioned John to help himself to the biscuits which he declined but he was very happy to have a cup of fresh brewed tea. "Do you ever do the crossword?" inquired the cleric.

"I must confess I sometimes start them but I tend to use them as brain testers. You know, I reckon if I can work some out the old grey matter must be functioning quite adequately. I rarely finish them and if I do I would never send them off."

"Pity, pity," rejoined his host. "I love playing about with words. I think it helps my sermonising. Hugely funny at times. For instance, here's one: 'He couldn't possibly turn over a new leaf?' Four and three? . . . . Page boy!" and he chuckled with laughter at this very corny joke but his laughter was catching and made even John grin. "Oh, there's some more serious than that, of course; ones that really make you think and are really full of artifice in the clues. But essentially they are all based on puns or anagrams and within those formats there is a considerable amount of humour. Wit, the great bard himself might have called it, and perhaps that is a more appropriate term. Did you know, for instance that 'Woman Hitler' is an anagram of 'mother in law' and 'I'm a rocket pro' can be arranged to spell out 'Patrick Moore'?" he chuckled again and John again found the humour contagious.

As if to feed his loquacity he helped himself to his third chocolate digestive and continued.

"I don't believe in putting in obscure words though unless the grid forces me to do so. Having said that there are some beautiful curious and interesting words in our language are there not? 'Logorrhea' for instance, or 'Machicolated,' 'Subfusc,' 'Zinzulation,' 'Whid'—it's like a foreign language isn't it? All wonderful stuff!" and he picked up his fourth chocolate digestive and having eaten it finished his coffee with an almost triumphant swig.

John was enjoying this. It was not what he had come about but he was impressed as ever by the reverend's erudition and he felt a sense of pride being in the presence of a crossword compiler, a task which demanded a quick witted and intelligent mind and John had always felt that although like Larkin he sometimes felt that he was spending his "second quarter-century/Losing what he had learnt at university" he himself was a person who dealt with the word hoard and therefore had affinity with and respect for someone of his own ilk and, he was sure, his host reciprocated those feelings else he would not be conversing like this. In order to contribute to what, to date had been a one sided conversation, John offered his observation that he had read or perhaps he had seen a T.V. play where a crossword compiler had inadvertently offered clues which, during the second world war had been considered subversive and whom, therefore, the authorities at the time had decided to ban.

"Oh yes," rejoined the clergyman. "I heard about that. I sometimes think that there could be a conspiracy of crossword writers and that members of M15 or M16 or whatever are always communicating with each other through *The Times, The Observer, The Guardian* or, who knows, *The Portminster Gazette* in this way. Remember 'I help the Great Lady'! What more appropriate anagram could there be for *The Daily Telegraph*?" and he burst out in peals of laughter only pulling himself up to say, "But you didn't come here to see me about crosswords, did you? Well, well," and still rosy cheeked and slightly watery-eyed from his merriment he got out his handkerchief from his jacket pocket and wiped his eyes as he continued, "now what can I do for you. What's the business you're on?"

John had himself to pause before he replied because he was desperately trying to work out ways of remembering all these wonderful little anagrams and clues whilst himself being caught up in the humour of it all. Settling down, however, he went on to state the purpose of his visit.

"I just thought I'd come to you to ask about who was buried in the graveyard last Wednesday and whether there might be any news item in it. I certainly wasn't aware of any bereavement of note but you may be able to enlighten me."

Just as John had failed to register the ecclesiast's opening gambit about crosswords so the Reverend Fergusson seemed totally nonplussed by John's statement.

"I'm sorry, John. Someone's misled you somewhere. I haven't conducted a funeral since the middle of July and there have certainly been no internments in the cemetery conducted by any other priest since that time."

"But last Wednesday, as I came through the churchyard, I actually talked to Tom Barber as he completed refilling a grave over in the far corner by the eastern wall."

"Never! There's been some new turfs laid in that corner of the ground and in a few other parts where dogs have got in the done some digging but there's no grave there. No grave."

John did not like to contradict a man of the cloth but he was positive he could not have been mistaken and so he suggested that they both go and see.

"Seeing is believing, eh, John, as doubting Thomas would say!" smiled his host, the Christian reference being singularly appropriate. "'Blessed are they that have not seen and yet have believed.'" He added as if to rub salt into the wound but he smiled so benignly on John as he said it there was clearly no malice or innuendo intended. "O.K. Yes. Why not? It's a nice day and a brief stroll over to the cemetery will be nice constitutional before lunch.

They rose together and before leaving the rectory the minister informed his housekeeper as to his destination though not the purpose of his departure and added he would be back in good time for lunch and was as ever expecting something to satisfy his appetite considering he would now be walking off the coffee and biscuits of which he had just partaken.

They walked the short distance in silence, each savouring the transitional summer autumnal air and, as they entered the graveyard and headed towards the spot to which John had referred, their gait slowed as they both glanced at various inscriptions on the tombstones which they passed. As they reached the spot, John did in fact see no flattened piece of earth but a large area of returfed earth, solidly flattended. He stood amazed, astonished. The Reverend Fergusson noticing this ushered him further down into the graveyward to his right and after about a further 80 or so yards there was another such, returfed spot. From here, the minister pointed to one more green patch towards the edge of the cemetery furthest away from them and said politely and certainly not critically, "You see. Re-turfing, as I said. Someone certainly misled you, John. Your source has let you down!"

Until this time John had not completely divulged all the circumstances of his encounter with Tom Barber but his companion conjectured correctly in his deduction that John had met Tom in the graveyard on his way home via the short route and had been the worse for wear having come from *The Fort St George*. The Reverend Fergusson at this point put his arm reassuringly round John's shoulder and gave him a playful hug. "Ah, John, usquebae, usquebae. You were no doubt inspired by John Barleycorn! 'Kings may be blessed . . . .'" he alluded. "How much did you have, John, tell me that? It certainly played tricks on your mind."

John was still incredulous. "But . . . ." he began, remembering he had downed a few but certainly, in his opinion at least, not nearly sufficient to give rise to such befuddlement, such self-deception. Yet was he here in the company of a divine of all people and had with his own eyes just viewed, nay present continuous tense *'is viewing'*, the evidence which contradicted his own version of events. There was nothing in the reverend's manner to indicate he was lying or guilty in any way of deceit so the evidence was definitely stacked against him.

Still with his hand round John's shoulder, like a pair in a three-legged race, the cleric walked his visitor out of the graveyard towards, in fact, the direction of the very public house on which his recent, minimalist comments could be said to have cast aspersions. At the gateway out of the cemetery, the minister took down his arm, smiled at John indicating almost as if he had heard a tacit confession and had absolved him of his sins and bade him farewell. "'Remember Tam O' Shanter's mare'" he said cryptically and John registered the obscure message. "Do come and see me any time. I enjoyed our morning. You have certainly given me food for thought inspiring me to recall Burns' poem so I will have to use that now for a clue or two. You ought to try my crossword more seriously from now on. After all I've give you a few free insights today! Now don't pass your day sitting *boozing at the nappy, getting' fu' and unco happy,*" he quipped as he shook John's hand, turned and headed back to the rectory.

Despite the parting advice to do otherwise from the rector, John strolled into the pub, salving his conscience by thinking it was now lunchtime after all. As he sat pondering what had happened he had enough of the rationalist's doubting abilities to question the empirical propositions he had just recently beheld. Turfs might flatten a plot but beneath their surface there could still have been digging, deep digging indeed and they may therefore merely be a cosmetic covering for what lay hidden underneath. By way of a synthesis of the rationalist and empiricist philosophies here John made the only conclusion possible, that is that what he did have was evidence of digging and of digging only. In order to take this further he would remain sceptical of the rector's reassurances and contact Tom Barber. A witness as involved as he was would certainly resolve the matter one way or the other!

Having reached this point in his thoughts, John was now able to enjoy the pint that he had just ordered and which Iris, the landlady, had carefully placed in front of him.

CHAPTER 4

Moving On

"*Sir Thomas More: 'In good faith, Rich,
I am sorrier for your perjury than my peril.'*"
(*Robert Bolt: A Man for All Seasons*).

That afternoon John finished his copy quickly and decided to make contact with Tom Barber. Although not having his telephone number and not knowing his home address he rightly surmised that by contacting the school secretary he would get such information since they would know it was being given out to a reputable member of the public if ever a journalist could be so described. He lifted up the receiver and dialled the number confident that the calls on which he was now embarking would resolve the problem of the graveyard once and for all. The telephone was answered by Margaret Borthwick, the senior school secretary whom he knew well.

"Mr Ellis! What can it be now? You had all the exam results last week and term doesn't begin until just over a week's time, you know!" she said jovially once he had announced himself.

"Tom Barber, Maggie. What's his address and telephone number? I need to ask him . . . ." But John was cut short by Margaret's shriek of exlamation.

"Tom Barber! Tom Barber!" she squealed. "You've just mentioned the unmentionable, John! That gentleman, if such a noun applies to one of his species, is decidedly *persona non grata* at Portminster Community College!"

Taken aback, John waited anxiously for the explanation which, knowing Margaret and her less than discretionary mode when dealing with school affairs, would undoubtedly follow as surely as any river flows to the sea.

"Up sticks and left us at the end of last week. Headmaster was furious saying he hadn't even given any intention of applying for other jobs and that no reference had ever been required from our school, let alone him leaving to take up a new post and anyway he had not even given the statutory month's notice! All this to no avail for Tom merely shrugged his shoulders and told him he was going and there weren't nothing he could do about it! Headmaster was indeed chewing the carpet like but, it seems, he couldn't do anything about it anyway and Tom's gone. Certainly had everything worked out; no problems over fixing up removal or anything. Swans off leaving us here short of a caretaker with Ben Whitemore, our senior caretaker as you know not due back until next week just before school starts again. And there's loads to be done, classrooms to clean and set up, labs to be sorted out, stationery to be unpacked and circulated round the departmental storerooms . . . ." and Margaret wittered on giving an inventory of the school jobs which would have served as a definitive, comprehensive and exhaustive job description for a contract of employment that would have terrified any applicant and ensured that the post was never filled by someone other than *Superman*.

While she thus continued John was turning over in his head this extraordinary and, as he mused, rather coincidental piece of news. It was indeed an unusual set of events and it certainly had not circulated as local news very quickly. Had the Reverend Fergusson known? If so, why had he not told John? If he had not known, what was he going to do when the next grave was required to be dug? Why did the school let him go? Why . . . . ? If . . . . ? There were many questions tangental to this circle! However, first and foremost it was essential to discover the new whereabouts of the caretaker cum gravedigger.

Margaret's list eventually dried up and before she could get into her stride of moral comments to accompany the absentee worker, John Quickly interposed his question.

"Where to? Where to, Mr Ellis? Right . . . . let me see. Somewhere in Cambridgeshire I think it is. Hang on a minute," and although she had put her hand over her receiver to silence her in-office conversation John could hear her muffled tones enquiring of a colleague as to Tom's new whereabouts. The reply having been given to her she duly relayed it to John.

"Yes, I was right, Cambridgeshire it is. He's gone as chief caretaker to one of them opted-out schools there. Lexden Village College's what it's called. Seems he's well set up there. House an' all with the job. No need for him any more to be digging final resting places in order to make up a few bob, eh?"

"No, indeed," responded John and added, "Well, thanks a lot, Maggie. I must say this is much more interesting news than those examination results. Hope term gets off all right despite the problems. All the best."

"Well, no rest for the wicked, Mr Ellis, and that's a fact. If term does start on time it'll be a miracle! If you gets in touch with him don't tell him anyone here's asking for him for we're not. Cursing him, yes, and we're sure his ears will be burning because of it, but asking, most certainly not! Goodbye, now. Thanks for your call," and her defiant, resonant tones dispelled any doubt as to her and the rest of the workers' ability to cope above and beyond the call of duty in this particular hour of adversity.

Still making in his mind all sorts of questions, links, guesses, intuitive associations and romantic imaginative leaps of fancy worthy of the most extravagant of Gothic novels related to the Tom Barber disappearance theme, John collected the Cambridgeshire *Yellow Pages* from the stack of other such publications covering the whole of the U.K. and which was the largest collection of books in the newspaper's reference collection for consultation by its journalists and turning to the heading, Schools, sought for the number of Lexden Village College. Once found, before dialing it, he glanced at his watch; three thirty. Yes, he felt, even though it was still the summer vacation it was likely someone was in the school office just as they had been at Portminster. So he dialed, wanting to get hold of Tom and settle matters. After all, even were things to support the Reverend Fergusson's scenario, he could get information about Tom and his promotion and make a few column inches on the lines of local gravedigger makes good. It had possibilities so he reflected whilst waiting an answer to the dialling tone. On and on it rang and he was considering his mission to get to the truth would have to be postponed, for clearly Cambridgeshire schools were not as conscientious as Hampshire ones when at last the receiver was picked up and a wavering, anorexic female voice weakly announced, "Lexden Village College. How may I help you?"

Taken a little by surprise, Tom had to pull himself together, collect his thoughts and get on with the purpose of his call.

"Oh, good afternoon. Yes . . . ." He was faltering badly and really had to concentrate on what he had to say. "I would like to talk to your head caretaker, a Mr Tom Barber, I believe. He's only just recently moved there."

"Oh!" faltered the thin tones of the female answering. "Mr Thomas Barber. Our new estates manager. Yes, he's here. Who shall I say is asking for him, please?"

"Estates manager!" mused John to himself. "'That which we call a rose . . . .'"; this was indeed a flattering title for the Tom Barber he knew. But it was 'Thomas Barber' now; the full Christian name emphasis was equally ridiculous!

"John Ellis. *The Portminster Gazette*," replied John formally as these thoughts flashed though his brain.

"Hold on, Mr Ellis, I'll put you through." It was the last he heard of that almost mystical voice. Perhaps he thought as he now waited for the rougher, Hampshire burrs of Tom's voice, the timbre which he had just heard was similar to that referred to by Tennyson when he wrote the phrase *an agony of lamentation* for certainly its owner had sounded as though she were in pain and even on the point of departing this world!

His brief reverie was interrupted by Tom's, "Hello, Mr Ellis. What can I do for you?" said in a voice of such vastly increased decibels that John almost had to take the receiver away from his ear!

"Well, Tom, first I must offer my congratulations on your new appointment. You certainly kept that move secret alright, even from us dreaded members of the press!"

Tom chuckled. "True, Mr Ellis, but as you knows I never was one for broadcasting my business to the world and his wife! Anyway, thank you. I am quite pleased with the way things have turned out."

Now it was time for John to get down to business. "Tom," he began, "do you remember when I met you in the graveyard just a week ago in the late evening?"

The reply was not instantaneous. Indeed, John felt he registered a note of apprehension in the pause before even Tom acknowledged and assented to his question with a very elongated, "Yee . . . es."

"Well," getting straight to the jugular, "who was it you said was buried there that afternoon?"

Another pause and even a faintly decipherable intake of breath.

"Buried, Mr Ellis? Buried? I weren't burying no one. Surely you remember I was laying turfs where the ground had been dug up by dogs?"

He being questioned had become the questioner.

"What I remember, Tom, is you saying something about an Irishman who had requested burial there and there being only two, penny pinching, miserable mourners!"

"Come, come, Mr Ellis. Begging your pardon, sir, but you were rather a bit 'tin hats' or 'four sheets to the wind' as my old folks, God rest their souls, would have said. You'd come from *The Fort*, hadn't you? And when I got in there after leaving you to toddle off home, even one or two of the regulars remarked on your *advanced state of inebriation,* as they put it, on leaving the watering hole!" At this recollection delivered with a seemingly a romantic, idyllic presentation Tom could almost be heard to smile and John also imagined the gleam in his eye as he was recalling the incident. Still the listener was not convinced, though the weight of evidence seemed most certainly against him. It was at this point, though, that John's lack of conviction was reinforced rather than erased for good when Tom, who had no reason to add to what he'd said continued with, "If you don't believe me, Mr Ellis, why don't you check with the Reverend Fergusson. He'll tell you I ain't been a digging no graves this past month or so. Then again, why don't you visit the graveyard and see with your own eyes?"

Why should Tom even consider that he would not be believed? Journalists had a reputation for incredulity matched only by their reputation for replacing fact with fantasy, but John was the *straight* man in the local press and was renowned for it! Everyone knew him to be scrupulously fair and Tom, poor, naive, uneducated, working-class Tom, would never have the intelligence to consider anything needed corroboration; what you see is what you get, that was Tom. Though Tom never even knew the term, *empiricist* was the only philosophical category which could possibly be applied to him. His phraseology was all too pat. There was, in John's mind, no possible doubt about some collusion between Tom and the Reverend Fergusson in all of this. However, it was important now he reckoned, to give Tom, just as he had given the minister, the impression that he was right and it was his over indulgence which had led to all this unnecessary confusion; he could deliberate on the subtle complexities of the issue later. Getting to the bottom of a cover-up such as this undoubtedly was, though it may well be very minor indeed, was what real journalism was about and it would give him something to get his teeth into while he went about his humdrum existence over the next few weeks.

"No need for all that, Tom," rejoindered John. "I'll come quietly so to speak. I never thought I was on that big a bender a week ago but, it seems there's no telling what the demon drink will do to a person! Anyway, thanks for putting me straight; I think I'll give that new Winter's bitter a bit of a wide berth for a while! Well, take care. All the best in your new appointment," and he added with a touch of ribald sarcasm, "an estates manager is what you are now, so I hear! We really have gone up in the world! You'll have no need now to get involved in excavating on behalf of the seriously animatedly challenged, will you?" he finalized knowing full well that Tom's slow brain would not be able to work this out in the brief time it took to say it over the telephone.

Tom's response was a laugh which registered his lack of comprehension like the inane grin of the inattentive pupil at the back of the class when asked by the teacher what he or she had just said. The vacuity evident was the major premise for the deduction.

"So, goodbye, Tom. All the best. Maybe we'll be in touch again one day. My regards to Cambridge though—I know you're about eight miles down the road from the university city itself where I was privileged enough to study. You're a lucky man being so well placed. Hope you get time out to enjoy the sights there sometime!"

"Goodbye, Mr Ellis. Best of luck with the newspaper. Don't go drinking too much again, will you?" and with that Tom signed off.

John replaced the telephone receiver. There was work to be done on his own account this time. But there was also a weekend and some days of next week to look forward to. This matter was not so urgent that he could not put it off until that was over. What was the buzz phrase so prevalent at this point with regard to such matters . . . . *the back burner*! Yes, this little bit of personal intrigue between himself, the Reverend Fergusson and Tom Barber and the mysterious corpse or non-corpse as the case may be he would put on the back burner for now. It would keep. Helen and Portsmouth must be enjoyed first and preferably in that order!

CHAPTER 5

At Portsmouth

"Lover of England, stand awhile and gaze
With thankful heart, and lips refrained from praise;
They rest beyond the speech of human pride
Who served with Nelson and with Nelson died."
(Henry Newbolt; For A Trafalgar Cenotaph).

That Friday John had left extra early and had therefore made it to Helen's only shortly after she had arrived at home. As the saying goes, they couldn't wait to get their hands on each other : thus the prelude to the evening! Later, there would also be le dernier bonheur du jour!

John was glad that Helen had agreed to drive giving him the opportunity to drink, so they took her rather nippy, navy blue, 'L' reg, Peugot 205 and headed first just up the road to the top of Portsdown Hill and the pub, *The George*, which was situated on the apex of the hill overlooking this great and famous sea port. It was balmy end-of-summer, early-autumn evening and certainly just warm enough for the lovers to sit outside whilst enjoying their first drink together after nearly a fortnight's absence apart. The light was fading from the sky, (the evenings were certainly starting to draw in), and as it did so, so the synthetic lights of the city came on marking the boundaries of the roads and the motorways which stretched across the long plain below and ran to the shores of the Solent. But also the bright, white lights pinpointing the ferry terminals, the naval dockyard (now a mere museum) and the car headlights and orange and red tail lights as they merged as if on a camera timed photograph. This was an uplifting sight and John imagined that had Wordsworth stood here on such an evening instead of upon Westminster Bridge in the early morning he would have had inspiration for writing an even more memorable sonnet than that which he had created about London! In the merchant harbour almost straight ahead in their line of vision glowed the giant, cross-channel ferries, their portholes leaking rays of amber light like so many torches held parallel to the ground. To the right was the Royal Naval Dockyard its perimeter outlined by the strong shafts of clear, white light emanating from the strategically positioned security lamps and the scattering of the beams from these lights seemed to highlight the masts of that most famous of ships, H.M.S. Victory in a St Elmo's fire that sailors would most surely have dreaded. The straight wide avenue of the coastal motorway carving through the south of the city and whose tributaries led off to its suburbs was defined by tall street lights casting continuous tangerine lines either side of blood red streaks like duelling scars caused by the traffic speedily traveling along the highways. Street lighting unevenly illuminated the many roads that criss-crossed like a giant tartan pattern on the floor of the city itself. The Guildhall, having its own searchlight-style illumination (reminiscent of the war and perhaps a left over from that era that had so ravaged such a key naval installation) stood out thrustingly and prominently on this landscape as did the blue, green, yellow and red bulbs that distinguished the seaside resort of Southsea and all its enticing attractions of amusement arcades and its pier. Finally there was the red, amber, green of the traffic lights, colours that marked the city's horizons to the west and to the east. If the sea reflects the colour of the sky, then the sky above Portsmouth at night most assuredly reflects the colour of earth at such a time and its blackness was thus replaced by an ochre halo poised over a city, deserving in John's mind at least, of such canonisation.

As John and Helen drank so they gazed down on this scene like gods observing mankind from Olympus. They did not have to speak, they merely soaked up the ambience of their elevated position in the estival eventide beside this quite attractive of pubs. After about an hour contemplating the scene and making limited conversation whilst drinking two drinks each, (though Helen was strictly observing the no alcohol rule with regard to driving), they set off into the lengthy, luminous labyrinths of the city itself to a newly opened Mexican restaurant quite near the old King's Theatre in Southsea. Helen had discovered it shortly after her return and since both she and John really enjoyed spicy food it was a natural magnet for their particular gourmet tendencies. After starting with shrimp polenta, they indulged in an indiscriminate mixture of chilli, tortillas, enchilladas and mexican chicken with a large side-salad, all washed down by John with a thick, red wine of non-descript bouquet and by Helen with large quantities of *Perrier*. During the meal John outlined his recent experience to Helen who seemed quite amused by it all. She knew John's liking for drink and although she too was somewhat incredulous as to the possibility of him making such a total misinterpretation of events even given his state of intoxication she felt that for him to be seeing some extravagant, sinister plot behind it all was part of the fantasy, conspiratorial world for which journalists were renowned. He had to admit that although there was possibly some intrigue behind the matter it probably had a simple explanation being most likely a request by the deceased or his or her family for discretion and privacy concerning the burial. Helen made him promise at this early stage of the brief holiday that he would not let his flights of fancy carry him away and certainly not allow any thoughts connected with it to intrude on the pleasure they were to enjoy together over the next few days. John had no problem with such a deal and, indeed, the alcohol was already making him mellow and forgetful to the past and only too concerned with the present and future.

After the meal, which like all delicious and enjoyable feasts lasts an age and during which the company and the conversation are as much to be savoured as the food, they drove straight to Helen's house and there indeed were not slow to pick up from where they had left off earlier in the evening. There was no fantasising in their relationship; it was wholesome, full and exciting sexually; being the love shared and indulged in between two mature lovers who had enjoyed other relationships in their past but who now felt quite stable and fulfilled in each other's company. After the protracted pleasure of close, climax upon climax in their copulation their naked bodies were left gently touching as they fell into a blissful sleep akin to an animal pack huddling together for the night for warmth and protection. And to wake up in this position together, the position in which their night's loving had concluded, body beside body, her breasts against his breast, genitalia brushing genitalia, was an erotic dawn that symbolised the renewal of their love. They did not make love that morning but gently kissed and caressed before John slipped out of bed and went to make coffee and toast for them both. He switched on the small, transistor radio placed discreetly on the kitchen worktop and he smiled as the lyrics of Bob Lind's classic, *Elusive Butterfly*, being broadcast on *Sounds of The Sixties* serenaded his work.

"You might wake up some morning to the sound of something moving past your window . . . . It's only me . . . . pursuing something I'm not sure of . . . . the bright, elusive butterfly of love . . . ."

It was appropriate! Being born and brought up in the sixties, John had memories of such hits and something like this had not only a childhood sentimentality for him but he had grown to like the sweet combination of words and music that summed up an aspect of the ephemeral side that there was to love. His mind floated off as he waited for the kettle to boil and the toast to pop up of associated bitter-sweet sixties hits which would make a melancholic compilation for lovers; Dusty Springfield's *My Colouring Book*, Françoise Hardy's *Le Premier Bonheur du Jour*, Cliff Richard's *Many a Tear* . . . . Click! The kettle had switched itself off. Ping! Two slices of khaki shaded bread popped up from the toaster. John was thus rudely jolted out of his imaginings. He proceeded to make the coffee, butter the toast and layer each slice with a thin sliver of marmalade, place all he had done on a small tray and carry it up to the bedroom where Helen was sitting up in bed reading a novel, her dressing gown hanging loosely around her shoulders.

She smiled. "You're so kind," she whispered teasingly as she put down the book and stretched across to take her mug of coffee and as she did so her left breast delicately revealed itself from the long 'v' of the top of the dressing gown as if in sympathy with her sensual tone of voice. John smiled; the eroticism was enough. They would satiate their love again later, probably that same evening and night again, at present they would just enjoy each other's company and the pleasures of the city during the day. They had five more days, all the time in the world!

That day they spent leisurely enough. The weather was fine and after a morning in the main shopping centre and looking for bargains on the thronging Charlotte Street Market they drove into Old Portsmouth and had a light lunch with soft drinks at *The Still and West*. This old pub at the end of the long cobbled street that ran to the water's edge surveyed the shipping traffic of the Naval Dockyard and the Isle of Wight ferries as well the minor craft crossing the harbour from Portsmouth to Gosport from a little further down the waterway. The boats passing across this generally choppy, traffic churned stretch of grey sea water gave the impression of the pub itself moving; like sitting in a railway carriage when the train stationed next to you starts to pull out and suddenly you give credit to

B.R. for your punctual departure only to find you were victim of the relativity laws of physics! Certainly, as John had remarked to Helen when they had first come here early in their relationship, this was not a pub in which to get drunk as the combination of what was imagined in drunkenness together with what impressions were received from the passing sea traffic with regard to the instability of the premises would be a heady combination indeed and one which might lead to permanent insanity! They left there early in the afternoon and then directed themselves towards Southsea where they strolled along the promenade with its imitation Grecian paving and acted like typical holiday makers briefly popping into the amusement arcades to waste some loose change in the machines and even to buy candy floss and later large ice-creams with strawberry and chocolate toppings which flowed down the mountain of piled ice-cream like lava down the side of a volcano. After this, they returned home, fatigued with the business of doing nothing in particular and they stretched out together on the setee and let the early evening T V programmes wash over them. Later that evening they journeyed out over the hill, beyond Waterlooville, and the charmingly named villages of Cowplain, Lovedean and Horndean to one of the country pubs that nestled in the foothills of the Elizabethan country park. Here they enjoyed the more traditional English pub fare before the journey home through the black night, over the crest of Portsdown Hill to survey the city's illuminations as they descended to Lower Drayton Lane and another night of love making, of nestling down together and consumating their day together.

Sunday was just another day of rest in this oasis of time together. After a morning reading as much as they could of a variety of tabloids and broadsheets randomly gathered together and purchased from the small newsagents just along the road from where Helen lived they went over to the stunning harbourside location of the recently developed Port Solent. Here as they strolled round the shops on the Boardwalk, enjoyed afternoon tea in one of the expensive cafes and deliberated on whether to go to the cinema that evening (and in the end decided not to), they indulged themselves in *window shopping* as they surveyed the millionaire class craft moored in the marina and the houses and apartments with their splendid, large balconies overlooking the harbour and which formed an encompassing arc at one end of the fashionable haven. How they both would have loved to live here! Sans all wordly care! That evening they stayed at home and Helen cooked a light risotto which they enjoyed with two bottles of fine *Rioja* which Helen had been thoughtful enough to get in stock.

The next two days until John's departure on the Wednesday were spent visiting, in many cases re-visiting, the many and varied splendid sights of such a metropolis. Southsea Castle, H M S Victory, The Mary Rose as well as the iron-clad battleship, H M S Warrior, the recently completed 'D' Day Museum and, best of all for John, Charles Dickens' birthplace in Mile End Road. This was the house which Dickens had left in his infancy but which he recollected that he had left "in the snow" and where incidents occurred that he related to his biographer, Forster whilst he was working on *Nicholas Nickleby*. There were many other places not visited but to live in such an environment and not at least partake of some of its history, some of its background which so contributed to its overall life and atmosphere was in John and Helen's opinion a denial of one's humanity, of one's brief, passing presence in this world in the guise of human being. But Helen who had masterminded these days reserved a treat for the Tuesday evening. It had to be special since the next day he would be gone, back up the road to Portminster; admittedly not far away but at sufficient distance to part them. She had obtained tickets for a Baroque music concert at the Guildhall by the Portsmouth Sinfonietta. She, herself, adored music and was a highly competent violinist having passed grade eight with distinction when in the fifth form at school and having played with and finally led her university orchestra in her last year of study at Kent. Since coming to Portsmouth she had played in quite a few concerts with the highly rated, local Havant orchestra and played in orchestras along with the Portsmouth Choral union, again an excellent gathering of musical talent with quite a formidable reputation. John, she knew, liked music; he didn't love it as she did but his whole educational background lent itself to discovery and to respecting all aspects of the Arts and endeavouring to understand and enjoy the complexities therein. He would certainly be more than pleased to attend this concert with her and the refinement, the beauty of what they would hear would be an elegant entree to their last night of lovemaking that week.

Sure enough John's delight matched Helen's gushing enthusiasm that evening. As the gentle water-lapping music of the Harp concertos subsided and the high, scarlet notes of the trumpets matched by the lush crimson tones of the horns in Handel's Music for the Royal Fireworks echoed through the interior of this majestic if not magnificent concert hall, John gazed sideways at the wrapt features of Helen and he knew that soon he would ask her to marry him. He remembered how he had first met her quite a few years back now when he had turned out for Portminster Rugby Club and journeyed to Portsmouth for a fixture. After the match she had been at the bar in the company of one of the Portsmouth players. They had exchanged glances and he had managed to muscle in on her conversation with the Portsmouth outside-half, who was then her boyfriend, by talking to him initially about the match in which they had both played. In the frequent excursions of any player after a game to recycle the alcohol drunk in the club down its toilet facilities, John, in the absence of this Portsmouth player, had managed sufficiently to impress Helen to give him her telephone number and after making dates with her following this they progressed to becoming lovers. They had been satisfied with their relationship not wishing to take it beyond this up until Helen's exile on her company's behalf from which she had just returned. It was evident from her communications with him during this time that she missed him and that she loved him and the renewal of their relationship in the past two weeks had made John admit the depth of his desire for her to himself as well. Now, he knew, would be too soon to broach the subject of marriage, but it would be something that would inevitably inexorably come in the near future. He had an overall plan and believed that once married he would come and live in Portsmouth with her and initially put up with the inconvenience of commuting to his job which sometimes had uneven and irregular hours but thankfully not too often. He felt sure that this stage would be reached by natural progression, there was no need to be forceful about the relationship. There was a kind of acquiescence on both sides, and so he felt certain, that this would be the natural outcome of their relationship.

The concert ended, they walked out into Guildhall square to see the floodlights reflected in the large, dark glass panels of the greenhouse-like building on the council offices opposite and the adjacent public library. As a complete contrast and an inspirational piece of fun, they drove quickly down to Old Portsmouth and the commercial docks, not to The Still and West this time but to the less salubrious, cabined interior of The Bridge Tavern, situated precariously as it was on the edge of the dock itself and out of which any inebriate might fall to a watery death or, if luckier, onto the deck of some small, local fishing smack moored at the edge! Just for one pint before heading home, it made a great contrast with the middle-class atmosphere of the concert which they had just attended. The bar here was festooned with the most obscure of foreign notes, strange, empty, fading packets of cigarettes from all the ports of iniquity around the sailing globe and the pub's regulars were local seamen who were unconcerned about the odd trippers such as Helen and John who had stumbled upon their hostelry and liked to see it as a local places of interest. They knew such adventurers did not stay long, did not mingle and were only intrusive by their presence and, since that brought trade and therefore kept such a decaying establishement going, that was as alright by them as it was with the rather disheveled landlord of the place.

The whole evening proved just the entree Helen had imagined it would. Their love making that night was sublime as they moved with musical rhythms together to the point of celestial harmony in the most extended of extended cadences of a climax that was fulfilling and in the end had pause notes leading to subordinate cadenzas of climax that seemed never ending. Harmoniously entwined, body inextricably linked with body, they drifted off into the pianissimo of a fulfilling sleep. Cradled thus together they awoke and indulged themselves in more love making the early morning before getting on with the day which would see their parting at least for another 10 days or so.

The day passed as it had to and after a light supper at about 8:00p.m. John after embracing Helen and confirming that he would be down again a week that coming Friday set off on the brief journey north. He felt pleasantly fatigued and on arrival home made himself a coffee and telephoned Helen to confirm his safe arrival, to reminisce over what had been the most delightful of times together and to reassure her of his love and the arrangements made. He would need to do a lot of catching up the next day; absence from work even for such a brief spell inevitably makes work accrue in the in-tray that is never shifted despite cover staff or temps who may be drafted in. It was, therefore, an early night and an early start for John but in order to take his mind off the delights of what had passed and try to numb his excitement he picked up the copy of his local paper that had been delivered that day, having discarded the other issues which had also been pushed through the letter box since he had forgotten to cancel them, and decided to try his hand at the crossword before falling off to sleep. Immediately memories of his meeting with the Reverend Fergusson and his subsequent telephone call to Tom Barber floated back to the surface of his mind! He had indeed kept his promise to Helen and sublimated these entirely during the last few days; but then, he reflected he had plenty to take his mind of that issue! Well, with the free tips received from the crossword compiler he would no doubt get through the puzzle quickly and be able to fall asleep with a mental satisfaction to replace the extraordinary physical satisfaction he had had over the past nights.

Propped up in bed he folded the paper to form a sufficiently hard surface on which to write the crossword answers into the grid. Slowly he made a start picking up some relatively straight forward anagrams, "clan very" spelling *cravenly*, "in late" revealing *entail* and "miles out try" giving multi storey. But beyond these he was stuck. Despite his brief insight into the humorous mind of the

Reverend Fergusson in these matters he was puzzed by "O" (six letters) and "OO" (five letters) and others, in his opinion at least, extremely cryptic clues. He was on the point of getting angry with himself over the dullness of his brain but his plan of using the crossword as a mental nightcap was working extraordinarily well and he felt his eyes starting to close with heaviness and he just had the awareness to give way to his sonnambulent state and place the crossword and pen aside, switch off the light and drift off into that "season of all natures, sleep."

He woke early, about 6.30a.m. and immediately came to consciousness. Surprisingly his thoughts turned immediately to the crossword he had been working on before he fell asleep and he reached for it together with the pen and in the thin but sufficient light of morning entered *Oxygen* as the six letter answer for the clue "O" which had not occurred to him last night. This was, however, all he managed to do and although he spent his first waking ten minutes or so of this Thursday in endeavouring yet again to get solution to clues, try as he might nothing came. Apart from cursing his own mental inability he decided to turn his frustration on the scapegoat of the compiler, *Eusebius*, but just as he was about to do so he looked at the name above the top of the puzzle and there was not Eusebius, the pseudonym of the humourous priest, but *Edurn, Son of Nud*! That was the reason he was unable to complete; he could not as yet get into the mind of this new compiler! How frustrating! How annoying! He threw down the paper and pen in anger.

As he got out of bed to prepare himself for the day to come he paused abrubtly. Why? Why? Only last week he had interrupted the Reverend Fergusson as he compiled the forthcoming week's crosswords, the ones what should be appearing in the editions delivered to him. He rushed downstairs and picked up the Monday and Tuesday editions and scrambled through the pages to locate the crosswords. Both were by someone who deemed him or herself, Edurn, Son of Nud. It was possible that the vicar had decided to change his nom de plume but unlikely after all these years. So why the change of compiler? Why was the newspaper dispensing with the services of a well-known, local resident whom surely they would not wish to offend and who could hardly have defaulted on his contract to them? Well, here indeed was a puzzle in itself!

John climbed back up the stairs a little weary from what for him was a rather rapid, over exertion in the morning. He got ready for work and savoured the idea of being able to pursue this most recent twist in events in his personal adventure over the forthcoming days. At the end of it all he might have much more of interest and perhaps of fact, rather than mere imaginings, to tell Helen in about tens days' time.

CHAPTER 6

A Death and A Disappearance

"For an eternity of time there had been no Mr Geard of Glastonbury. For an eternity of time there would be no Mr Geard of Glastonbury, though there might well be some mysterious conscious Being in the orbit of whose vast memory that particular Avatar was concealed."
(John Cowper Powys; A Glastonbury Romance)

Immediately John got to his desk he picked up his phone and dialed David Hart.

"Got back alright then? I trust you had a good time?" commented the deputy editor with a knowing smirk to himself as he did so after he had instantly recognised John's voice as he introduced himself. "What can I do you for you then at this time of the morning?"

John got straight to the point. "Why have you changed the crossword compiler, David?"

David guffawed probably so loudly thought John that his laughter must have been heard outside of his office!

"Good grief! What a question! Earth-shattering that is! You go away for three days and waltz back in defiantly wanting to know the reason for perhaps *THE* biggest *MINOR* change in editorial policy! Because we wanted a change, that's why!"

"But I saw the Reverend Fergusson only last week and he was compiling the puzzles for this week's editions! It's all a bit sudden, isn't it? I hope our St Michael's incumbent hasn't taken umbrage; he has been a useful source of news and I know you and others have had him work on feature articles before now."

"Well," came the voice of his boss, "there's another reason for changing our compiler; his identity has become known!" He paused. His tone changed to the threatening but friendly sound of one who wishes not to offend but certainly wants a particular subject dropped. "Look, John, I am sure you've got better things to worry about than our crossword. It's not your department anyway. You can rest assured we made our peace with the clergy so we have not lost the Christian vote! *Alia iacta est*! O.K.?"

"*Consummatum est* would be more appropriate," though John as he went on to say "O.K.," though he was far from satisfied and had already intended to follow up the matter with the Reverend himself later that day. Not wishing to give any hint of what would surely be considered mutinous thoughts or actions, he decided a quip to catch David off guard might be in order so he added, "Before I go though, who is *Edurn, Son of Nud?*"

David was astute to such a gambit."What! A Cambridge man of letters like yourself not knowing that! A character mentioned in Tennyson's *Idylls of the King*, that's who!" and he guffawed again as he clearly had got one over on John who had thought he was going to trap him. "One up to me, I think on that one, John. Hope you've got enough to occupy you for the rest of the day! Goodbye for now!" and he signed off quite cheerily in a mood suggesting he had achieved all he had set out to do with regard to that particular phone call and its line of inquiry.

"Bye . . . ." said John down the dead line in a transfixed fashion. He held this far-away-gaze posture for sometime after replacing the receiver as he mused over his own little piece of investigative journalism. In truth he was not anxious to get on with the monotony of his job for the elongated weekend had totally spoilt him into a lethargy created by impassioned romance and, moreover he was really far too engrossed in his own imaginings to stir himself. However, he had to gird up his loins to face work and with due resolve he swept all current thoughts aside and surveyed the items that were in his in-tray. It was the usual plethora of local trivia dealing as it did with the local supermarket's plans to combat trolleys disappearing, the local opera group's forthcoming silver jubilee performance and celebrations, Portminster Community College's computer registration system for its sixth formers (why this had landed on his desk and not that of Clare Hills', he didn't know!), The Railway Corinthian's (the best of a mediocre group of local footballing teams) new sponsors and other such crucial events that no doubt make up the world for many small, medium or large communities. The world it seems is split up into such microscosms of Coronation Street . . . . or worse!

As ever, John planned his day methodically and even allowed himself a small pocket of time in which he could visit the Reverend Fergusson and offer his condolences. He realised even to himself it all seemed rather melodramatic but it served as a teleological purpose as he went off around his schedule of morning interviews. Despite his best intentions, this morning's work dragged out far longer than anticipated for he was held up both in the supermarket by the exuberance of the manager's delight in the now to be introduced trolley scheme and at Portminster Community College, the deputy head, Derek White, was equally over enthusiastic about the simplest of computer registration schemes which had been introduced for the minute number of students who populated its the sixth form. In both these places once John had got the facts he switched off his concentration and let his mind wander to related topics. In the supermarket, for instance, he surmised as to what customers would do now that they would be foiled in their attempts to make off with trolleys; would they all buy estate cars or *Range Rovers* and merely load trolley plus contents into the back? Or would they defect to another supermarket chain who were not so sophisticated with regard to crime prevention? Perhaps free trolley with a collection of tokens from various stores might be a new incentive for Christmas shopping? Interestingly enough, on his visit to the school he saw a novel but most adequate use of supermarket trolleys in the Music department where, lurking at the foot of the instrument store he caught sight of two such methods of conveyance—from where had they been gleaned he asked himself—stacked with folded music stands; certainly such metallic items were heavy and the trolley mode of transport was ideally suited to getting them to wherever rehearsals and concerts were being held. Here again at the school he reflected how all contact now with nearly all educational establishments was with deputies and not Heads and not Principals. Indeed, heads and principals had not only become remote figures in their own empires—a dubiously appropriate word for the way many regarded themselves and what they had built up—but also to the public at large. Bit like the absentee landlords! The once revered figure of the community, the Goldsmithian educator whom "every truant knew" and who "was kind, or if severe in aught/

The love he bore to learning was in fault . . ." had long since disappeared off the educational map and would now be claimed to have been a fiction created by educational cartographers. Another sociological and political change to be regretted. And so, appropriately in the words of Burns, of whom John had been reminded only the previous week by the Reverend Fergusson, "the best laid schemes o' mice an' men/Gang aft a_gley", so John was late and had to forgo his planned brief visit to the manse. It was on tedious mornings such as these that John was eternally grateful he had read English at university for he would often set his mind to capture a suitable literary allusion to sum up the experiences he underwent. However, he now resolved to telephone the vicar once he had completed his write ups that afternoon and perhaps he could even arrange a proper interview rather than just an ad hoc call and do a little piece on memoirs of a crossword compiler, guide to cryptic clue solving or some such.

It was just after 5.00p.m. when John completed his tasks which he had found more irksome in compiling than usual, again probably because of his recent, brief vacation and its indulgences. He picked up the telephone and rang the rectory's number expecting, as ever, to hear the sweet but ageing voice of Miss Simpson in her receptionist capacity before receiving the rumbustious tones of the incumbent himself. The dialing tone seemed to ring for longer than usual for Miss Simpson was most punctilious about her duties and when it was eventually answered the formal tones of the received pronunciation of some unidentifiable male wafted down the line.

"St Michael's Rectory. Good afternoon."

"Oh, good afternoon," replied John with duly astonished intonation. "Is it possible to speak to the Reverend Fergusson please?"

"I regret to inform you," pronounced this voice as if it were reading a cue card, "but the Reverend Fergusson passed away just after lunchtime today. May I ask who you are, sir, and what the nature of your business was?"

Flabbergasted, John stuttered out his name and vocation but did not embroider any further with the nature of his call, it now seeming too trite for words.

"Thank you, sir," continued the voice. "A fax was sent to the editor of your newspaper and no doubt you will be publishing brief details of the matter together with the funeral arrangements and an obituary in your forthcoming editions."

John had managed now to get over the initial shock and decided to get in at least a few questions before the speaker could sign off with the statutory mantra of reporters.

"Sudden, wasn't it? What was the cause, may I ask."

"It seems a heart attack, sir. No doubt that will be duly confirmed by a post-mortem."

The clinical assurance of this man was infuriating. "And Miss Simpson? How's she reacting? Is she alright?" continued John in his search for something but he knew not what.

"She's as well as can be expected. Naturally she's shocked, being such a devoted servant of the church and minister as she is, or should I say was with regard to the latter, but the doctor is treating her. She is under mild sedation I believe and resting."

It was like receiving bulletins from a hospital. Bland euphemisms obscuring a multitude of emotions. Finally John asked, "And you; to whom have I been talking?"

"The Reverend Charnock, sir. I am the vicar of St Jude's down the road in Petersfield. I was asked to come up and cover things by our bishop, the Bishop of Portsmouth that is. Please do make contact again if you want more information. Naturally your paper will decide as to who does the coverage but we have a release for information for the obituary which we have already sent on appended to the fax which you should have received. Good afternoon, then," and with that the Reverend Charnock signed off leaving John completely bemused.

In this state of lack of belief John decided to go through the motions to confirm this dreadful piece of news. Yes, the newspaper had been informed later that afternoon. A memo was on its way even now to John for a brief meeting the following morning with the editor to appropriate the tasks concerning the newspaper articles on the deceased and naturally John as the local reporter would have to be at that meeting and he would no doubt get an assignment. Secretly he hoped to be able to write the obituary for he had in mind some flowery extracts and some plots to work in with reference to Eusebius but he doubted the chance would come his way as most of that was pre-written and the top and tail was generally added by, at times, junior reporters. No doubt what was currently on file about the Reverend was being checked against whatever the Church itself was supplying and any editing of the main text in the light of this would soon take place. As with many such news items, the only news aspect was in the occurrence itself, its attendant issues and details having been duly forecast, written about, commented upon, packaged and parceled in the due company, in this case newspaper's, manner and given out to the purchasers whose brand loyalty was deserving of such standardisation.

And so everything turned out much as John had predicted in his own mind that it would. The post-mortem confirmed a heart attack as the cause. He, John, had coverage of the basic news story and the funeral which he attended. The obituary was bland spiritually in accordance with its subject matter but failed significantly to do justice to such man who had truly been a loving shepherd in this community. All was over within the week, a temporary minister had been installed at the rectory, Miss Simpson was showing the fortitude expected of her and, to all intents and purposes things were returning to the normalisation so beloved by Portminster, its inhabitants and its environs.

John was glad that his fortnight's absence from Helen was almost coming to an end and that once more he would be journeying to Portsmouth. The recent events had certainly done much to eradicate some of his sense of intrigue over the episodes of the graveyard and the crossword puzzles and clearly the death of the Reverend Fergusson offered this major perspective for him and a chance to reflect so he had decided to concentrate on his romantic future rather than his inebriate past. On the Thursday evening preceding the Friday he was due to go off again he was sitting quietly at home in the early evening letting the dross that was on television wash over him whilst he ate a microwaved chilli-con-carne when his doorbell rang. He was not used to visitors since he did little in the community apart from his work and had never striven to embrace the camaraderie of the office. He got up from the arm chair, positioned his plate with the remnants of his meal at the side of it and went to the door. It was Miss Simpson.

Dressed in funereal black, yet stoical with the fortitude of her age and generation she smiled at John and whispered good evening. John could not help but admire such a figure; it seemed she summed up all that was good about the generations that had preceded his own, the one which was blighted with sixties supposed freedoms and subsequent decadences resulting from such a self-indulgent decade and which, to all intents and purposes, had helped to bugger up Britain! "My Generation," thought John. "My Generation, indeed!" The light was starting to fade from the sky and a chill was setting in the air so John invited her in and at the same time offered tea and the additional benefit of lift home to prevent her having to walk the gloomy pathways back to her annexe after the visit. She declined his hospitality, instead just getting on with the business of her call before departing.

"Thank you for the kind pieces you wrote in *The Gazette*," she said. "it's a pity they never let you do the obituary."

A discerning literary critic, smiled John to himself.

"The Reverend Fergusson was a great man and deserved better. However, before his sudden death he did ask me to give you this and, what with the funeral and all, I must confess I forgot about it. I'm sorry, I hope you understand."

The apology, totally unnecessary as it was given the circumstances, being like a soldier at the battle of Rorke's Drift putting himself on court-martial for feeling tired and afraid, was again typical of the spinster and endeared her and her few surviving kind even more closely to John. She now handed him a rather tatty, brown, envelope which had been badly sealed down and which revealed a torn off scrap of lined paper inside. As John easily opened it to take out its contents he re-iterated his request and having it yet again declined pleaded with her to stay just in case there was anything within the envelope pertaining to its bearer. She paused long enough for him to find the piece of paper contained nothing but the number 2496 written right across it in headline style. He showed it to Miss Simpson raising his eyes to indicate his own lack of decipherment. She glanced at it.

"I'm sorry, Mr Ellis. It means nothing to me. All I can say was that he was insistent you should have it and he gave it me very secretly and even advised that I tell no one else as to its existence. I have obeyed his instructions and that's all I can do, I'm afraid. It's so sad that he is now not around to reveal what he meant but he did say he was sure you would understand. Perhaps," she added cautiously, with a hesitation indicating that she was touching on the territory of the Almighty and the mysterious ways in which he performs his wonders, "he realised you would have to work this out on your own and preferred not to worry me about the matter or let me in on his fears and premonitions. Goodnight to you, Mr Ellis. God bless you."

She pronounced this benediction in the manner of her former employer as she left and went off into the eventide of the day.

John closed the door, went back into the living room, turned off the television, ignored the remainder of his meal and concentrated hard on the figures on the piece of paper. It wasn't a telephone number. Even northern Hampshire had been converted to six digit figures for some time now. Then was it a crossword clue? If it was, it was decidedly cryptic. There was no logicality about the sequence nor about what they conveyed. It was hardly a Biblical reference though no doubt some books of that text would run to Chapters 24 and verses 96 but even if there were only a few John did not have the energy to look them up and since there could well be more than one the decision about the relevant one would make the whole thing a lottery. Perhaps there were no such chapters with 96 verses anyway! Nor was it a hymn tune for John could recall from his own brief encounter with church, church going and Sunday school in his youth, no hymn number getting into the thousand category let alone the two thousand one. Mathematically it was an even number and John was competent enough to work out a set of factors for the figure but there again he came to a dead end. He tried every association of ideas with the deceased vicar that came to mind but the only one that stuck was the crossword one. And then, suddenly, like Paul's conversion on the road to Damascus, John hit on what was being referred to. Crosswords themselves were numbered. For many years now the reverend Fergusson had compiled the crossword and each one would be numbered; 2496 would indeed be very recent, perhaps even his last and in that John would find more of what he was looking for he was certain. He leapt up from his chair intoning inside his mind the exultant Eureka of Archimedes and searched for past editions of the newspaper. Much to his chagrin he had no copies beyond the most recent and those were filled with the crossword compilations of that obscure Tennysonian character. He would have to wait until getting in to work on the next day when he could go to past editions and all would be revealed. He was tingling with excitement reminiscent of his student days when he was looking forward to hearing and interviewing for *Varsity* some celebrity come up to Cambridge for a debate at the union or a guest lecture in some faculty.

After a rather fitful night's sleep full of anticipation John got into work extra early intent on making a start on the crossword and thus his new found search and adventure. He went immediately to where the back copies were stored and went about three weeks back in editions as a starting point finding initially 2496 in the Monday edition. Friday, the Friday he had gone off to Portsmouth for his long weekend, was therefore the day of the 2496 crossword and, as he surmised, that indeed was the last one printed under the Eusebius nom de plume. Quickly he turned over copy after copy to reveal that Friday's edition and then scuttled through the pages to find the crossword he so eagerly sought towards the back of it. *More haste, less speed*, he muttered to himself when he failed to come across it in his first frantic and frenetic search. Slowly, labouriously he returned to the front page of the appropriate edition and turned the pages over one by one hoping to light upon the crossword as he came towards the end. He was to be deeply disappointed for, very much to his surprise, pages had been removed and in particular amongst the missing pages was the one that would normally have contained the crossword. No wonder his initial attempt had ended in frustration; but now this frustration was to be extended! By this time, Bill, 'Ginger', Perkins, keeper of the archives (probably because of his age he was one of them himself), and general dogsbody had come in. John's temper and temperature were both rising given the stalemate of his current position and he shouted angrily across to his aged colleague generalising on the situation in order to elicit a response, "Did you know pages were missing from some of these editions? I thought they were supposed to be a full record of all that we produced for posterity and all that?"

Ginger shrugged his shoulders. "It happens," he shouted back. "Mainly adverts and the like get taken out at times. Nothing serious. All the hard news," he said witheringly, "from you lot always remains. That covers the legalities I think."

Knowing that nothing would be achieved by arguing the toss, John marched off and ranted at Ginger as he passed, "First I've bloody known it to happen. Records should be intact, not in pieces! Bloody slovenly librarianship if you ask me!" but since he did this on the march of his dramatic exit the words were picked up only in patches by the object of his anger who registered the conversation as the doppler effect of a hooter of a passing diesel train is registered.

John went to his desk and angrily looked through what had turned up. He now decided that sometime during the morning he would steal in to the public library which also held back copies of the local publication and get what he needed from there. It was a delay only; an annoying one, indeed, but it would be resolved speedily in time. Contemplating the situation in this light helped him to settle down and get appropriate control over what he had to cover during the morning. His tenseness subsided, calmness returned.

It was 1.30p.m. when he managed to get into the library; half-an-hour and he would have to be back at work. All he needed to do was locate the newspaper, photocopy the crossword and that would be it. He used the escalator to the first floor of the building where the local archives where kept, asked the lady at reception where he could find the appropriate edition of *the Gazette* and waited while she went and retrieved it for him.

"Please return it to the desk when you have finished with it. Thank you," she intoned as she gave it to him.

John walked over to one of the large tables, spread out the newspaper and began turning the pages. Initial frustration generally leads to anger; subsequent bouts of frustration generally lead to melancholy, floods of tears, inability to come to terms with reality, a breakdown even! John was now proceeding into stage two of this disease. Here, in this library edition even of a fatuous, futile, insignificant publication, the key pages—as far as he was concerned—were missing. Was he ever going to find this elusive crossword?

He folded up the text and walked over to the desk. The librarian, who had been seated at a computer desk at right angles to the main reception desk, got up and approached him to relieve him of his package. Downcast, dejected, the sorry sight of the character registered with her so she asked in a routine rather than caring manner, "Couldn't find what you were after then, sir?"

With the mien of a battleship grey sky laden with rain, John languidly responded, "Did you know pages were missing from this edition?"

"Oh, dear," she apologetically offered. "I am sure you appreciate, sir, that once we issue such material, we have no control over it until it's returned and we cannot possibly check everything when it comes back and keep customers waiting for an all clear so to speak. I will mention it to our head of section though but I cannot really see that we can do anything about it."

"No, I suppose not." Weary and yet resigned to yet another cul-de-sac in his quest, John shuffled out of the library scuffing his shoes as he ambled back to work in the manner of a petulant schoolboy. As he made this short journey he reflected on the strange coincidence of missing material from this particular edition of the newspaper and his thoughts started to inject him with a little more excitement and renewed his recently deflated fervour for his enquiry. Someone, something, he surmised had the deliberate aim of eradicating this crossword because of the information it contained. What John had to do was to circumnavigate these interventions that prevented knowledge but now he was faced with the seemingly impossible task of retrieving an old edition of a far from collectable publication.

As he entered the office he decided that his next step would be to ascertain the winner of that particular crossword and see if he or she had kept a copy of their winning entry; it was worth a try. Ignoring his write ups, on getting to his desk he telephoned the finance department and talked to a minor clerk who had dealt with sending out prizes to winners of the variety of mediocre competitions in the publication. A Mr John Green of Petersfield was the lucky recipient of the £25 prize for Crossword number 2496 and John was not only able to get the address but also the telephone number. Consequently he phoned Mr Green who, being a retired naval officer, was at home that afternoon. Yes he had received the prize and was *pleased as Punch* about it for he'd been doing the crossword for any number of years. The money had come in very handy for buying a few bushes and shrubs for his garden. No, he never kept copies. Not worth it. Papers became too much litter anyway. And no, he couldn't remember anything about it. Was now getting into the new boy's crosswords, finding them a bit tough and didn't want reminders of the old ones at present to fog his judgment. Sorry and all that. John was about to suffer a relapse; phase two of the disease was coming back.

In such a state he got through the afternoon writing copy on local charities which were raising money for a minibus for the Hospice which served their area, the local squash club which was going to ban all smoking forthwith and who would refund memberships to those smokers who wished to leave as a consequence of this decision and the local Methodist Church whose minister and congregation had decided to abandon the *New Methodist Hymn Book* and return to the older, traditional one with John Wesley's stirring 1779 Preface and with which most of its ageing members were far more familiar anyway. As he did so his mind gnawed away at how he was going to get that copy of *The Gazette*. Just as he was completing the write up on the Methodists back to basics hymnology, he leapt up from his desk and rushed down to reception where Janice was answering an incoming call. She was astonished by John's sudden appearance but her training and poise let her finish the call and then she turned to him and inquired as to what gave rise to the almost manic, distracted look on John's face. This, for him, was the last chance; Janice usually did the crossword. Had she retained a copy? He waited anxiously, apprehensively, agonisingly for her reply.

She smiled. "I don't keep copies but living at home with my Mum anyone would think we're members of Greenpeace intent on saving planet earth. She keeps everything, duly filed and selected until we've hoarded enough to justify a journey to the appropriate recycling part of the local tip. You wouldn't believe it. Under our stairs is a positive fire-hazard being as it is stuffed with newspapers, wrapping paper, boxes and what have you. The back yard has piles of bottles, separate that is from the masses of aluminium cans—not good for the image, any of that lot! And somewhere or other she even stores carrier bags for the 1p refund on the weekly supermarket excursion! So if anyone's got it, Mr Ellis, we have!" She was pleased to be of service to him for in truth, naive, attractive youngster that she was she fancied this middle ageing bachelor who seemed to her in some ways to be living life on a lonely edge of his personal but never his professional life. Anyway she could endear herself to him might be a gateway to an emotional response on his part.

John's face slowly took on a rosiness and smile unseen since his first internal cries of *Eureka* the night before. Like a valve of an old radio he warmed up, crackled and spluttered back into life. Somehow he felt there was to be no disappointment at the end of this line and yet he must secure his advantage. He checked that Janice would finish at 5.00p.m. He could not get away until shortly after that and so he asked her to wait with the offer that they would go back to his place, collect the car and he would drive her home so that he could get the edition of the paper he so desired. She was happy to oblige. This was, for her, as good as a date.

With the same alacrity as he had rushed down reception so John headed back to finish his work in order to make progress in his own investigations. The schedule he had set for himself and Janice now was going to make him late for Portsmouth and yet, amazingly enough despite the attractions that the weekend offered in that respect, John was so engrossed in this matter he was willing to postpone the start of it. He therefore dialed Helen's number and left a suitably worded message on her answer phone to the effect that being detained at work she should not expect him until a lot later that evening.

At 5.20p.m. therefore John and Janice left for his maisonette. Though increasingly frantic about the time scale, John was polite enough to offer her some coffee at his maisonette before they took the car and drove to her family's residence in a new housing estate to the west of the town. On arrival she invited him in, introduced him to her mother who seemed such an ordinary person John had difficulties in imagining her as some kind of environmental magpie. He was again polite enough to accept a cup of tea which he drank alone while mother and daughter rummaged through the understairs newspaper collection. Eventually they came in together to the sitting room where John was dunking a digestive into the half-filled cup of tea and with the looks of people on *The Antiques Road Show* who had just discovered their old, drab, dusty attic painting to be worth a small fortune, presented the Friday edition to John. His reciprocated pleasure was reflected in the face that he forgot he was dunking a biscuit and so the dipped part being soaked too long in the liquid disintegrated to leave a dry upper part which he now ate and swallowed rapidly and a thick textured brown solution in the cup which he would have to drink a little later and which he knew would be like drinking some vile baby food mix. He put the cup to one side, rose and received the newspaper like a child being awarded a certificate in a school prize giving ceremony. He thanked them profusely as he quickly glanced through the pages and verified that nothing was missing in this case, the elusive crossword was there and he even noticed it was in virginal condition; Janice had clearly not had time to get started on it that day! So pleased that he got what he wanted he returned to his tea, finished it with an unnoticed grimace and apologised but assured them he had to take his leave. They were reluctant go see him to but accepted the inevitable and after he had driven away mother looked at Janice with knowing look that indicated John might be a prize worth seeking and brief though this encounter had been her daughter should make a play for longer, more meaningful ones.

John sped back to his maisonette, rushed in and settled down with the newspaper. Now he had time to do what he had been longing to do since almost 24 hours before. Portsmouth, the tight time scale he was on had disappeared from his mind and he was fully focused on the crossword grid and clues before him.

It took him a little time to get started probably because of his excitement but eventually he penciled in "Play with treacle duff"—*Electra*, "Young William may be of use to campers"—*Billycan* and "Carnival swindled the noble knight"—Galahad. These were highly appropriate to the writer and John could picture the torch-like, beaming features of the late Reverend Fergusson as he contrived such clues. And so he continued. "Grave entry-imprisonment"—*Committal*. "Able pupil loses direction for south coast resort"—*Brighton*. "Terrorist organisation in heads steals copyright"—*Pirates*. "Immoral, dithering, UNO curls us up"—*Unscrupulous*. "Irishman we hear filed wrongly in China"—*Paddy Field*. "In-cave voters rave at do"—*Conservative Party*. "Old fashioned chap's jacket"—*Dolman*. "For every panel there is a crime in the court"—*Perjury*. "one out to find singer with rebuilt ears"—*Searcher*. And on he went though the answers did not come rapidly. As he was drawing to a conclusion he was shocked out of his tunnel vision on this matter by the sharp tintintabulation of the telephone. Annoyed he got up from the chair in which he had been sitting and went over to answer the phone in the corner.

"John! John, what's keeping you?" It was Helen.

Christ! He looked at his watch. Nearly 9.30p.m. everything had gone out of his mind! Imagine forgetting about the weekend!

"Helen! Helen! Oh, Helen! I'm so, so sorry. Something came up. Quite surprising really. I've not long got in and am getting ready to head off. Can't wait to get down there after all this nonsense. I'll tell you all about it when I get there. Promise. Another hour or so. *Burma*," he quipped trying to defuse the situation.

"*Burma?*" responded a less angry but bemused Helen.

"Be undressed ready my angel," elucidated her lover and added before she had time to criticise such schoolboy humour, "yes, childish I know. *Swalk* and all that; romantic teenage stuff. Won't be long now. I'm on my way."

She couldn't be angry with him for she looked forward to seeing him as much as he did her, his recent pastime having but temporarily removed that longing on his part. "Do take care," she said. "It's late now. Just take you're time. I'll be waiting up for you. I've got something ready."

"And some food I hope," interposed John now feeling voraciously sexual for having had a triumphant outcome to his working day he truly longed to cap it by becoming a vanquished victor of Helen in bed.

"And some food," she agreed understanding his wavelength precisely. "I'll see you soon," and she put down the phone.

John, too, replaced the receiver and returned to the crossword. He had completed all but five clues and felt now that his concentration had been too disturbed to try to finish of what he had found was becoming increasingly difficult anyway. He now wished to concentrate on the weekend. He was satisfied he had got as far as he could at present and nothing would be achieved over a weekend which was now to be geared to sexual rather then celebral stimulation. He would come back to it all on Sunday evening, hopefully complete it then and have time to assess the answers and see where they were all leading, if anywhere!

Reflecting on the day's Herculean task to get hold of this newspaper and crossword, John now saw it as among the most precious, most sought-after of his possessions. Carefully he took the folded edition and preserving its current shape in readiness to complete the crossword he took it upstairs to his spare bedroom which doubled as a home office and locked it away in the small, two tier, *M F I* filling cabinet next to his desk which had the now ancient *Amstrad Wordprocessor* on top. Confident that all was safely gathered in, John went to his bedroom, grabbed and roughly packaged a variety of casual clothing, from thence to the bathroom for an equally random selection of toiletries and headed down to his car.

As he drove down darkened road through the tunnel of the night to Portsmouth he decided he would not inform Helen of his current investigation, rather he would surprise her with its outcome once he was satisfied as to where it was and would eventually lead him. Fabricating an alternative cause for his delay was hardly a Titanic exercise for a journalist though he did have reservations about lying to someone he loved and to someone he knew he was going to ask to marry. However, such moral stirring he managed to subdue, justifying to himself that his investigation would be no more than a diverting escapade which would provide an amusing story to be related to her in future and which she could enjoy in the manner of Jane Austen's *Northanger Abbey*, the Gothic imaginings of an imaginative young lady.

As he neared the city his mind moved from the days events and brooded on the future 24 hours. It would be delicious. He was now in the mood to enjoy it all, to drink it to the lees! Nothing could upset him now!

CHAPTER 7

Another Disappearance

"*I am out of place in the capital,*
people take me for a beggar,
as you would be out of place in this sort of life,
you are so . . . ."
(Basil Bunting: Chomei at Toyama).

The weekend had been all both Helen and John had wanted it to be. More and more they were confirming their love and everything on the romantic front seemed to be headed in the right direction. They were to meet again next in a fortnight's time, John insisting as ever that he preferred coming down to Portsmouth rather than have Helen journeying up to the backwater of Portminster. She acquiesced in this arrangement, content it should be so and surmising that John's long term aim was to be domiciled with her in Portsmouth anyway, a city she had come to love and which she truly regarded as her home now. Before leaving John assuaged his conscience over his deceit regarding the story of his delay by buying Helen some expensive, silver jewelry in a small fashion accessory shop tucked away in a back street of Southsea. As he journeyed home, therefore, on the Sunday evening to pick up his adventure where he had left off he felt, indeed, something of the inner contentment of a monk, a soul at peace with life in this world and so he would be in the ideal mood to complete the puzzle, soberly reflect on it and find out its inner meaning as such men of the cloth claim to have done with regard to the mystery of existence.

Having parked the car, he went straight upstairs tossing his holdall of clothes and toiletries casually on to his bed through the open door of his bedroom and then went into the study. He unlocked and opened the filing cabinet, carefully took out the paper and went downstairs. He glanced at the final clues as he made himself a coffee but could not concentrate enough whilst doing this to solve them. Once the coffee was ready he went into the sitting cum dining room, seated himself comfortably in the chair with the newspaper and a pen and started to think long and hard. He was right; he was in the perfect mood to complete everything and, indeed, it was not long before the final blank squares were filled with letters and the whole puzzle was finished. This gave him an inner glow, a self-confident air of satisfaction and he reveled in his initial achievement by putting down the pen, surveying the completed grid and finishing off his coffee. Now came the more difficult but infinitely more intriguing part of the exercise!

He decided the crossword format was not condusive to him making sense of the message for it was unlikely that everything should link together to form a perfect jigsaw; rather there would be some irrelevancies, words used only to fit and complete the grid. These would not be deliberately misleading but he must guard against them. He laid down the paper and went upstairs to get some A4 blank paper. Armed with this he sat down in the chair again and started just copying off the words and trying to think of links as he did so. *Galahad*, connected with the Arthurian Legend . . . . *Electra*, connected with the Greek legends surrounding Agammenon et al . . . . *Billycan* . . . . ? Nothing in that line of thinking! *Searchers* . . . . 60's pop group . . . . no, perhaps the concept of *Holy Grail*-Galahad . . . . ? Too tenuous. *Brighton* . . . . *Conservative Party* now there was something definite, that's where one of their most famous or notorious conferences had been held. John drew a circle round these words and joined them with a set of lines with half-arrow heads like the B.R. logo. It was a start. *Committal* . . . . shades of the prison house . . . . *Perjury*. Yes, another connection to be suitably encircled and joined. Also the clues for those words contained key words—*grave* and *imprisonment* and *crime* and *court*. *Pirates? Paddy field?* Not much there. *Rook? Tree?*

These among the last clues he had completed. It seemed a jumble. It seemed nonsensical. Maybe he was just wasting his time. But wait. Look at the clues again, as well as the solutions. *Pirates*—contained the terrorist organisation, the I.R.A. Connected with Irishman we hear . . . . Paddy, Patrick. Brighton, Conservative Party Conference, I.R.A. bomb attack. *Committal* . . . . yes one man was serving time for the outrage. *Perjury* . . . . had there been lying in court? In those trials, who could possibly say? It was all statement and counterstatement. Back to those clues—*grave*. That linked with *committal* as well . . . . we therefore *commit* his body . . . . etc from the funeral rites in the C of E Prayer Book. John had been sure he'd seen Tom Barber finishing off a grave after a burial. *Perjury*. Both the Reverend Fergusson and Tom had perjured themselves to John at least for both had denied any knowledge of the grave and instead insisted John had got it all confused with re-turfing. What was it Tom had said . . . . burial of some Irishman not connected with the parish . . . . two tight-fisted mourners . . . . ? It all linked together. What was it the Reverend Fergusson had laughingly stated; the intelligence services of countries communicating through cryptic crossword clues. Here, now he was being communicated with. He had to join the searchers and reveal all the intrigue behind this situation. John's brain was a kaleidoscope of ideas.

But no! It really was all too ridiculous for words. If he started to believe all this nonsense it was not any better than believing horoscopes in the tabloids. Certainly there were connections between the words and the clues but any crossword could be used like this to create as convoluted a plot as any cheap thriller adapted for prime-time television. He would be stark, staring mad to believe all that he had just thought. Were he to embark on a search to see what came of all this he would become a victim of his own delusions, he would be sucked into the whirlpool of reality and illusion and suffer from an inability to differentiate between the two. Most assuredly he would become a figure of ridicule as he unearthed no plot, no intrigue, no collusion, just the silly imaginings of a middle-ageing journalist. A kind of journalistic menopause in his career that would most certainly confirm the ending of the same! Helen would laugh him to scorn. The famous McEnroe cry of the eighties, "You can't be serious!" reverberated in his brain and he had to admit it was highly appropriate to what he had considered.

With a long sigh like the sagging supports of suspension bridge he got up, dropping the paper, his notes and pen on the floor and looked at the time. Jesus! It was gone 11.00p.m. and he hadn't phoned Helen to thank her for the weekend, re-assure her of his love and let her know he was like Stevenson's hunter and fisherman—home from the hill and the sea. Was it too late to disturb her? No. He must just give her a call. He did so and apologised again by way of being economical with the truth. He could hear her tired voice over the phone and so kept his message brief, whispering a sensuous goodnight and sweetdreams until about ten days' time again.

He was tired himself. A nightcap was required and he decided a large Scotch to commemorate the weekend and his outlandish imaginings was in order. He had always enjoyed usquaebaugh and liked to buy different malts though he was far too much of an imbiber to collect them. When one was finished he sought out another and any which he distinctly liked (though he had not the most discerning of palates) he would remember to ask for in off-licences and supermarkets and therefore sometimes, though quite rarely, buy the same bottle again. At present he was close to finishing a Laphroaig, a fine malt with a distinct perfume of deep dug peat and which he had come to enjoy. He got the bottle from the kitchen along with a glass and poured himself a large, large measure and sat back down in his armchair to savour and enjoy it. He looked at the fine amber liquid like a highly refined oil clinging to the sides of the glass. The light of the room seemed to be soaked into it and through it giving both an effulgent outer and subduing inner effect to its colour. He drank a large gulp and winced as he swallowed, the liquor seeming to take the skin off the inside of his throat as a grassburn does off unprotected skin in summer though without leaving a scar. Then this pain was followed by the healing process of the inner warmth the liquid provided as it flowed down his gullet and seemed as it did so to intensify its viscosity so that it slowed its passage to the stomach heating the whole body like water through a radiator. It was pleasant. He finished off his first glassful and poured yet another which he started to drink and his tiredness coupled with the power of the alcohol began to make him feel quite mellow. He began to reflect . . . .

The connections he had made may seem contrived, but what of the other facts surrounding this case. His mind wandered through them. Tom Barber? A sudden, surprising, quite remarkable move for a local such as he. The reverend Robert Fergusson? At the memory of the name, John drank another draught and appropriately so given the surname, given the drink! Taken off as crossword compiler immediately after the appearance of this crossword and then suddenly, surprisingly, quite remarkably within a few days of its appearance, dead. And then the disappearance of the crossword itself from the publisher's and from the library's editions. Three vital sources of information put out of reach or at least made extremely difficult to get hold of!

His glass was empty again. He refilled it this time draining the bottle of its contents. A change, then, sometime next week, he mused as he continued to drink and think. Maybe . . . . maybe . . . . The effect of the drink at this stage was now sufficient not to make John drunk but rather to make him bold. Crossword's completed. Links have been made. The Rev is dead. Tom Barber. Lexden Village College. Getting to him personally, face to face, not on the end of a phone, would resolve this issue once and for all. A surprise visit. Get Tom with his guard down.

John was beginning to fight off the tiredness and the alcohol with intense concentration on this issue. Tomorrow he would drive north to the south of his university city and confront Tom Barber. He would take the day off on a sicky, as many of the staff did on occasions though he, himself had never had a day off sick in his life and the thought of pretending in this way to get a day's leave was really anathema to him given his puritanical upbringing. Able to get out of bed with the use of the faculties, however stumblingly and however inadequately meant work. The devil finds work for idle hands . . . . etc. Yet he was resolved and before going to bed he had summoned up sufficient mental strength to carry him through with what he considered the terrible deed.

He slept well probably as a result of the alcohol and on waking at about 7.00 a.m. he telephoned David

Hart's home number to register his sickness. He was no Thespian but he gave a tolerable performance of someone with a mixture of a sore throat and mild chest cold and, anxious to placate his boss who was quite astonished at hearing from John of all people early in the morning crying off sick, repeatedly stated he would take all the medication necessary to ensure he was back at work on the Tuesday. Truly John hated himself for this, feeling even more guilt over the matter than he had done when offering paltry excuses to Helen over the weekend. He started the day, therefore, with a rather heavy heart, needing desperately to expiate this deliberate sin.

The morning was fine, being now well into the light, sunny, bright but low temperatures of early autumn and the drive up to join the M25 and subsequent M11 was surprisingly clear of traffic making the two and a bit hour journey more than pleasant. As he drove John first enjoyed the day for its own sake and heard inside his mind the words of cummings,

"I thank You God for most this amazing
day . . . .
. . . . for everything
which is natural which is infinite which is yes."

His thanks to God in this way was to him like a prayer and did much to remove his anxiety over his early morning sin. God could not be mad at him if he gave him such a lovely day to enjoy like this. As the journey progressed though, doubts crept in about the purpose of his visit. This really was a ridiculous quest; or was it? He had to convince himself in the cold this time, without the aid of last night's alcohol. Certainly what he had conjured up was Machievellian in the extreme but there were examples throughout history of such intrigues and just as it was a chance in a million to win the football pools yet Mr Man-in-the Street on occasions did so, could not he, an ordinary reporter have stumbled on the journalistic equivalent thereof? The car radio, tuned as it was to Classic F M was playing Mozart's *Magic Flute Overture*. Normally car music was like wall paper, surveyed only when first put up and thereafter lived with as background until changed. The musical background in this case to his thoughts, however, seemed remarkably pertinent. Had not the death of Mozart in some ways been contrived by that most secretive of groups, the Masons, who were angry at his revelations of some of their practices in his opera, *The Magic Flute?* Well, perhaps it was an apocryphal story but like many such there was probably an element of truth behind it. And now John was on his way to discover the element of truth behind his. Satisfied with his premises and conclusion, John even had time to consider that after seeing Tom Barber he may get a few hours to travel the 8 miles beyond Lexden and visit Cambridge and

Coleridge College where he had studied before returning. It was sometime since he had been here and it would be interesting to see the changes and re-familiarise himself with the sights.

He had no difficulties in locating Lexden and the school, the Village College as it was named, since it was fairly adjacent to the M11 and well sign-posted. The school buildings were quite compact, the older ones being of a khaki coloured brickwork and being all ground floor set like a college forming a quadrangle around an expanse of grass with a rather poor, cheap imitation of a fountain in the centre. The additional, two newer blocks were set to the side of the original buildings and soared three storeys high and were clearly large and spacious being formed of large expanses of glass set within imitation granite covered breeze blocks with some metallic fronting in places painted cardinal red. Modern steel and glass structures—true glass curtains of buildings. It was in the foot of one of these that John had to go to report to enquiries as the directions in the car park indicated.

On arrival at the school office John pressed a button to ring a small electric bell to catch the attention of one of the busy office staff. A bespectacled, anorexic lady approached him and as she did so John could not help thinking of her as a stick insect and also how frightening it would be to have to make love to someone so flimsy.

"How may I help you?"

The voice was unmistakable. This was the sick, sad tones he had heard over the telephone when he had first contacted this institution. The figure matched the voice. She should be clothed in white samite, there was something mystical, wonderful about this being; the voice, the form . . . . a member of the living dead.

"I'm John Ellis," stated the visitor and, by way of convincing his audience produced his Press Card, though why a *Portsminster Gazette* Press Card should cut any ice here in rural Cambridgeshire he could not imagine. It was force of habit. "I believe a Tom Barber works here. As your Estates Manager?" (He had even recollected the title, though truth to tell it was so politically correct as to be laughable, unforgettable and totally inappropriate!) "I knew Tom in Portsminster and I was passing through so I thought I'd look him up."

The lady blanched, if an already alabaster countenance such as her own could be said to do so, and John instinctively felt something was amiss. She had, however, the presence of mind not to reveal the cause of her reaction at this point. "Tom Barber?" she replied in a voice as soft as the six pianissimos marked in Tchaikovsky's bassoon part in his Pathetique symphony. "If you kindly wait in the foyer, sir, I will see your request is attended to," and she directed John with her eyes to the area through which had just come and in which there were low, soft seats for visitors such as he who would have to be kept waiting while staff were fetched for appointments.

John thanked the lady and went to sit down. As he browsed through the scatterings of old school magazines, statutary Governors' Reports and gazed at the surrounding examples of children's art work mixed in with photos of school teams, music ensembles, sponsored activities etc. he also heard somewhere distant musical refrains of an orchestra. Quite talented it sounded, too. Professional indeed. The atmosphere at this educational establishment seemed calm and condusive to learning and the few children he had glimpsed on errands out of class seemed tidily turned out and were going purposefully about their business. Perhaps such a state school merited a place in *The Good Schools Guide* or whatever; it was certainly preferable to Portminster and to the few others John had visited in the course of his work.

He had not been waiting very long when he was approached by a short, attractive female probably in her late thirties or maybe just into her early forties. She was very smartly dressed in a light grey suit with pastel green blouse through which her white bra was more than visible as her suit jacket was left open as was fashionable, she wore emerald framed designer spectacles, black patent, two inch heeled shoes with small, shimmering brass buckles and she had short, styled auburn hair. A tidy and most neat picture of school elegance.

"Mr Ellis? Caroline Hobbes," she said, stretching forth her hand as John got up and thus greeting him with a friendly handshake. "I'm the Headteacher. Will you come this way?" and she led him to her office down the corridor to the right.

"Headteacher, eh?" thought John as he followed. "Must be serious!"

Her office was what he expected. A computer and keyboard in one corner, a long desk loaded with paperwork, a small trophy cabinet with a variety of shields and cups in varying states of lustration, a couple of bookshelves with National Curriculum folders jostling for position with books on management and teachers and the law. Amidst all this paraphernalia of education was the statutory personalisation of the framed family photograph and a miscellany of paperweights, mugs and writing implements. On arrival she seated herself behind her desk true to tradition and the psychology so necessary to lording it over children and all visitors for that matter! The position of authority and, more importantly, of protection! She motioned John to sit on the low armchairs to the front of the desk and distanced from the seat of power by a small coffee table. As he sat down, from a door at the side, the anorexic being entered with a tray bearing two coffees and a few, wafer thin biscuits.

"I ordered coffee. I assume that's suitable," she said to John and as he indicated his assent the drink was put before him and he added a spot of milk from the jug but no sugar and he declined a biscuit." Thank you, Mariana," said the headteacher to the ethereal being as she set down a coffee on her desk before departing.

Caroline Hobbes wasted no time in getting down to business.

"How well did you know Mr Barber, Mr Ellis?"

John registered the past tense and hoped it was merely an idiomatic phrasing of the question. He did not instantly see the ambiguity in the fact that he was being interviewed and was not the interviewer!

"Not well, no not well. Tom, you see, was a local. Most of the residents of Portminster, therefore, knew him. He had been born and brought up in the district, went to the local school and all that. Had dabbled in county cricket for Hampshire as a youngster, I believe, but some latent eye defect made him give up the game though it was his first love and recreation and he still coached and assisted the local team with preparing wickets using his groundsman's experience . . . . not at Portminster Communty College I might add which has gone the way of modern sporting philosophy, no competition and all that! Sorry if that gives offence," muttered John, realising his possible gaffe. Caroline Hobbes just indicated none taken and John continued, "Some people aspire to return to their schools as a teacher or even as headteacher; Tom's ambition could be summed up in the fact that he was well content with being the assistant school caretaker at his *Alma Mater* and occasional gravedigger at St Michael's where he'd attended Sunday School and where he worshipped with his family. That's about it really."

There was a pause and, John realising he had volunteered sufficient information to date and not wishing to be pressed on this briefest of biographies as to the subsequent reasons for him wanting to call in and see such a nonentity while passing through the southern Lexden territory of Cambridge, added, "I was, as were others, surprised at his move here. What made you take him, may I ask?"

Caroline Hobbes sipped her coffee and decided it was in her interests to explain the situation. "Well," he did apply, "very late in the day for the job as I recall. He came well-recommended, I might add. A first class reference from the local minister and one from a Dr Mike Parsons, Head of Churchill College, an independent school just down the road from you I believe?" In order to stem any question relating to a lack of his employer's reference she continued, "He had asked us not to contact Portsminster's head for personal reasons. We are happy to oblige and, anyway, we have contacts to verify that such a request is not made deviously. He had a good combination for our job. Now being direct grant we have to look after our own playing fields as well as the buildings and Tom combined a knowledge of both even though in the former he may have been a gifted amateur, so to speak. At interview he was somewhat taciturn but Estate Managers are appointed for the ability in the job; their public relations comes from making the pathways neat and the garden gay as the poet wrote and does not require the loquacity and language skills of middle and senior management. So we appointed him and got him up here straight away. We were not to be disappointed in our choice," and here she hesitated, finished her coffee and added, "until the start of last week, that is." Here she paused again.

John moved uncomfortably forward on his low seat to finish his coffee and push the cup and saucer further on to the coffee table and therefore give his undivided attention to what was about to be revealed.

"Yes, he was extremely good. Got the grounds looking superb in such a short space of time as I am sure you noticed on arrival. Got on with the assistants and all the cleaners . . . ."

This hiatus in the revelation annoyed John intensely; he saw it as the gambit of the German philosopher keeping his audience in suspense by a sentence construction which placed the verb firmly at the end so that until this key word was pronounced the reader or listener was unable to question, interrupt or criticise, for he could not possibly surmise exactly what was being promulgated. His attention therefore wandered. He reflected on her Thomas Hardy reference in what she had earlier said and felt he might at a later stage let her know he had recognised it. That would annoy her! Headteachers always liked to feel they could outsmart their audience. With children that was probably possible but it did not always work with adults. They needed, he thought, to rise above child psychology, especially since their dealings were more and more with adults. And her public relations references. *O Tempora, O Mores!* This indeed summed up the new educational programmes; all gloss cosmeticising poor content.

". . . . run off with another woman!"

Caroline Hobbes' voice's intonation was so exclamatory at this point that John was jolted back into paying attention.

"Ran off with another woman?" He heard his own voice rise with an equally high inflection of incredulity. "Tom Barber?"

"See for yourself," responded the lady and she handed him a scrawled pencilled note on a earth-stained, torn off, lined piece of A4 typical school file paper. "This is what his wife found on the kitchen table last Monday morning. He had been working late on a booking for the school hall by an extraordinary meeting of the local Gilbert & Sullivan Society and had told his wife not to wait up as he intended to go down to the local pub after locking up and might well be home late. She didn't hear him come in and on getting up at about 7a.m. had assumed he had risen earlier and was downstairs. A terrible business."

John surveyed the piece of paper.

Sorry couldn't face you. Gone of with another woman,. Planed it all for sometime now our move was part of the plan. Latter ill get in touch an to sort things out. So sorry about the mess take care of the kids just cant help myself. Tom."

The handwriting had about it the neatness and care of the illiterate and the content and presentation clearly confirmed the literary skills of its author. It seemed genuine enough and no doubt Tom's wife, Donna, could confirm the handwriting.

"Yes, a terrible business," continued Caroline Hobbes. "We had to do some very quick manoeuvering on this one. Our assistant estates manager, whom we had overlooked at interview, naturally gloated on the way things had fallen out for us but he was not too proud to take his promotion when we offered it to him. Fortunately one of our governors has property in the village and we assisted Mrs Barber and her family to move into there, temporarily of course for she desperately needs family and familiar faces around her and I know we have supported her application to get back to Portminster as soon as possible into a council house in the first instance. Mr Gosse, that's the gentleman we've promoted now of course resides in the house that goes with the job. But we are a man down, so to speak, and have had to rush out adverts to make up the shortfall for we are being stung badly on overtime payments on all of this the longer we are without the correct complement of staff."

Despite his complete shock at what he had just heard, John still managed to smile at the headmistress' concentration on the cost effectiveness of the situation. Human relationships, it seemed, were subordinate to financial implications. He recalled how a jaundiced bankrupt he had once interviewed had advised him that he could rape, commit adultery, criticise, stab friends in the back, insult all and sundry, destroy and devestate whatever human values there were in marriage and friendship and still be an acceptable member of a community for on such matters people were prepared to forgive and forget; but never, never ever must he beg, borrow or steal money no matter how much or how little for money was the god of humankind and to make a mistake in that field was tantamount to commiting suicide, to being ostracized for life, to making himself the greatest social pariah possible.

The voice of experience! Straight from the horse's mouth that one!

"I'm sure you will respect the information I have given you, Mr Ellis," the headteacher was concluding, aware she was talking to a member of the press and clearly concerned about public relations for herself and for the school. "There's not a lot of mileage in it anyway. These things happen and in this case they were certainly not foreseen."

"Certainly," replied John. "It would hardly be fair on Tom's wife and family for me to use any of what you have said. It might, though, be in order for me to pay her a visit before I return. Someone from the locality may be something that's useful at this stage and I can indicate that the newspaper may be in a position to assist her in her time of need."

"Yes, that would be a splendid idea. It will certainly give a little more purpose to your visit than just seeing the waiting room here and the inside of my office, won't it? Here, let me give you the address and directions on how to get there," and she wrote the address on a yellow post it pad beside the telephone on her desk. She rose to give it to him and as he got up, too, she indicated the directions he should take and informed him that the house was not located too far from the school itself. He took the piece of paper and thanked her accordingly and then turned towards the door in readiness to leave.

She smiled and they left the office together heading down the corridor to the exit and towards the car park. She had decided to accompany him all the way, not offensively in order to see him off the premises but mainly as a brief envoi pointing out aspects of her school on the short route. The possessive personal pronoun endowed the speaker and by due implication the college with the attributes of goddess and creation.

Respectively, a common trait in headteachers! She paused and even asked him to stop and listen to the orchestra whose rehearsal he had heard earlier on arrival.

"Concert next week," she said. "Aren't they simply marvelous? We have a wonderful music set up here, mentioned in *The Telegraph* you know?"

He had to agree it sounded a most formidable secondary school orchestra. She certainly didn't let up on the public relations! They walked on and he shook hands with her before getting in the car to drive off.

"You have been most open with me Mrs . . . ."

This was instantly corrected to the politically correct "Ms," by the redoubtable lady.

". . . . Ms Hobbes. Thank you. I regret Mr Barber has not been a good advert for Portminster but I trust you won't think any the less of Hampshire because of it all," he added somewhat flippantly though the remark was well intentioned.

"Not at all, Mr Ellis. Goodbye now," and she marched away back to command her school while he went off to see Tom's wife before leaving Cambridgeshire.

It was, indeed, not far from the college to the small, semi-detached house where Tom's wife was temporarily domiciled. As John parked, got out, walked to the door and rang the bell he noticed the dereliction of the garden, its flower beds, hedges and fences and knew that Tom would have been outraged by such an unkempt exterior.

Donna answered the door and look querulously at John. She appeared aged and haggard her long, black hair usually so clean and fresh when he had caught sight of it before now hung lank and greasily down past her shoulders and she had made herself uglier by pushing it back on either side behind her ears like a tied back curtain effect. She might, had she been called upon by John in Portminster have at least recognised his face even if she had not been able to put a name to him, but here she was like Ruth amid the alien corn, she clearly only expected strangers.

"You don't recognize me, Mrs Barber, I didn't think you would. I'm John Ellis, I work on *The Portminster Gazette* and I knew Tom." This time he did not produce the press card for fear of frightening her. "I had called over at the school to see him but Ms Hobbes, the headmistress, briefed me on what's happened. I'm really terribly sorry.

I came to see if I could help in anyway. Ms Hobbes told me you naturally want to return to Portminster and I thought I could assure you that, discretely of course, I may be able to ask the editor to do some leaning on councilors connected with the housing department to get you back."

"You'd better come in," replied the lady to all this not indicating in anyway whether or not what he had said had registered at all.

He stepped over the threshold and she ushered him into the sitting room. It was quite well furnished considering the circumstances though it indicated no attention to detail, no pride that is seen in even the most sparce of houses. She pointed to one of the two armchairs and John duly obliged by sitting down.

"Would you like a cup of tea? It's no trouble to make one," she asked indicating her sense of hospitality had not disappeared.

"No, no thanks. Just let me know, will it be alright for me to act on your behalf when I get back, see what can be done?"

She sat down in the armchair opposite. "Mr Ellis! Oh, Mr Ellis! Yes, I remember you now, vaguely though, to be honest." In a tone of total dejection and resignation she continued, "I don't mind, Mr Ellis. Tom's walked out after eighteen years of marriage. He's got all the money from selling out house. Cleaned it all out of the bank he has and we were going go use that to settle here long term we were. So, what have I got to lose? There ain't no other way I am going to get back to living with my folks except by the help of those kind enough to take an interest. Police aren't bothered. They're not fussed about chasing missing adults. All that will happen is Tom'll be registered on a missing persons' list."

She seemed very matter of fact about it all and offered this collage of information without any thought as to confidentiality.

"O.K. Fine," said John. There was a long pause. She was clearly not going to say any more and although there were many questions he wished to ask he felt the circumstances for doing so were all so wrong he would give himself a guilt trip he could not possibly assuage were he so to do. He therefore rose. "I'll do all I can," he murmured in as reassuring a tone as possible. As he went towards the door a howl of anguish came from the chair where Donna was sitting. He turned to see her contorted features, flooding rapidly with tears of pent up emotion. He immediately went over to her, knelt down beside her and put the clichéd comforting arm around her shoulders.

She buried her face in her hands sobbing wildly but what she had to say was as coherent as it was true.

"Oh, Mr Ellis! Mr Ellis! Something's wrong, something's dreadfully wrong! Tom, why Tom, he's too shy even to look at another woman. He'd never have done such a thing. Even bringing us here was wrong. He knew it and I knew it but 'twas if he had to move, as if something forced him to. He never confided in anyone much but if he talked to anyone it were to me. We only ever talked about simple things, the shopping, the kids, family an' the like. Then, of a sudden, 'Let's move,' he says. When I pushed him on it all all I ever got was, 'It's best, Donna. It's for the best, you'll see.' He was a simple man, Mr Ellis. He even left every aspect of housekeeping to me. Wouldn't even care to spend his own money; I even always had his cash card. He was more than happy with that arrangement. Still got it. He only got to the money at the end by going in to the bank personal like and drawing it all. That's how he was. He'd never have had the ingenuity to have an affair and be able to keep it secret! Something's wrong! I know it is! You knew him, Mr Ellis! You must know what I've said is true. Something's happened to him. Something serious!" and her voice trailed off into the hands in which her face was buried and her sobs engulfed her and the urgency and frequency of them seemed to applaud in support of everything she had uttered. All this had indeed been said with the accompaniment of staccato sobbing, crotchety breathing and sharp and flat intonation throughout and therefore it had taken her sometime to get through it all.

John was pretty much useless in a situation such as this so he did the only thing he felt was right in the circumstances. Saying nothing, he got up went to the kitchen and made a pot of strong tea listening to the incessant crying of Mrs Barber as he did so. He poured the brew into a large mug, added a touch of milk to give it the colour of mud and a couple of heaped teaspoons of sugar to make it palatable and returned. All sorrow such as this eventually subsides and in Mrs Barber's case it was no exception. The tears had ceased to flow and the sobs were less convulsive though the face was still buried in the hands when he returned.

He knelt beside her again and proffered her the mug steaming with hot tea so that the dampness of the steam poured on to her already damp hands but the latent heat of evaporated water indicated to her a significant difference and one to which she felt necessary to respond. Slowly she raised her face from out the shell in which it was set, took the mug and whispered a soft, "Thank you," sufficient to indicate to John that he had done the right thing.

As she sipped at first and then drank the tea, she re-iterated her argument in its simplest form. "You knew Tom," she said. That was the premise. Then, "Something's terribly wrong." The emphatic conclusion. She cared not that this was an enthymematic argument for she was totally convinced of its conclusion and felt the possibility of contradiction to be impossible.

John had to admit that though he had not known Tom as he would a close friend or colleague, Mrs Barber's prognosis of the situation was absolutely valid. But his conclusion was supported by many factual premises whereas Donna's were built largely on emotional ones. He, however, dared not reveal these to her.

There now fell a silence between them, John not knowing what to do next but feeling it would be wrong to leave without being certain Mrs Barber was settled into some semblance of normality. During this time Mrs Barber did in fact return to this state quite naturally, getting sufficient control of her emotions to be able to face the world and its troubles with a degree of equanimity once more.

Once mistress of herself again she turned to John and apologised. "Well," she said, "I'm glad I acted like that in front of you and not some others around here. You cannot be said to be a complete stranger, can you?" She smiled weakly like a leaky torch bulb and wiped her face with her hand smudging the drying tears onto her cheeks and reddening them as she did so. "I am glad you called," she continued. "I would be grateful if you would do all you can to help me, not just for my sake but for the children, you know?" she added meekly.

"Sure," said John. "You are alright now, aren't you?"

In truth he was anxious to get away. Such situations were beyond him and he felt dreadfully uncomfortable and at the same time despised himself for feeling this way because of his inability to cope.

"I'm fine," she uttered and then corrected herself seeing the look of mild incredulity in John's face. "Well O.K. that is. The kids'll be home from school soon. Got to keep up appearances," and, as if to link the statement to the act, she pushed her hair which had stuck to the evaporated tears on her face from the side of her angular cheeks and they dropped lank and stringy down the side of her features doing nothing to flatter her!

She saw him to the door, John looking anxiously back at her throughout the brief journey like Orpheus intent on checking Eurydice was following him. At the door, he paused briefly before leaving and reiterated he would do all he could to help. As he wished her well she left him with the simple but haunting phrase that was to remain with him through all his journey home and even beyond that most amazing of days.

"Something's wrong, something's dreadfully wrong."

She had probably said it to many people over the last week but they had, no doubt viewed her as an emotively disturbed Cassandra. She knew instinctively that John was not like all of those, he believed her and he knew that she knew he did! It was a burden he had to bear from now on while he continued with his investigations; it would be an albatross around his neck until he actually did discover what in fact was wrong.

He got in the car and sped off. He headed straight for the M11 and M25 route south. He never even contemplated a trip up the road to Cambridge as he had done on the journey up even though he did have just about enough time to visit there had he wanted to. He wanted to get home, get away from this shambles of a day and give himself time to think calmly and reflect on his experience. And so he just drove on and headed inexorably south.

CHAPTER 8

A Visitor

"O that he had never come! That he had left me at the forge—far from contented, yet, by comparison, happy!"
(Charles Dickens: Great Expectations)

John arrived back in Portminster early that Monday evening but he was so nervous he wasted the rest of the day in inactivity and subsequently had a restless night's sleep. It was as if his brain were having a continuous panic attack and he could not separate out all the ideas that were jumbled up inside it. Eventually it would reach hyperventilation point and everything would calm down so he would be able to get a perspective on it all but that would take time and one of the remedies to help him get there was to get back into work so that he would achieve a routine to focus his concentration and let the activity subside.

He therefore breezed into work on the Tuesday morning having forgotten his poor chest condition and sore throat from the day before and the first thing he found himself doing, therefore, was explaining away his total freedom from the symptoms that had kept him off for a day. A 24 hour bug became his excuse but he knew he did not convey this convincingly and that most of colleagues (David Hart, indeed, had come to this conclusion after having John's phone call 24 hours earlier) decided it had been too much of a dirty weekend that had driven him to a state of inertia. He was quite happy they should think so for at least it meant they had no concept as to the real reason.

There was also a mixed element of excitement and anxiety in the atmosphere in the office that day and John discovered quite rapidly that this was due to confirmation of the fact that the large *Portmouth Evening News* group was now actively planning to take over *The Portminster Gazette* and this naturally had implications about the whole future for all the staff there. John's official letter detailing this was awaiting him on his desk in a brown manilla envelope marked *Private & Confidential*. There had long been rumours about this and certainly the take over made a lot of economic and journalistic sense. The large organisation turned out different editions of their publication for the various Hampshire areas in which it operated in and around the city itself so moving its pincers north to snap up such a trifle as *The Gazette* was inevitable.

"*Staff will be interviewed and notified as to the tenure of their positions within the new organisation once final details of the purchase have been settled later this week . . . .*" read the letter.

John's attitude was ambivalent to all this. If he was kept on it might mean an early move to Portsmouth and a different, more exciting position; if he were made redundant he would receive a reasonable settlement for his decade plus of service and he would be able to scrape a living by freelancing until he were able to achieve a new position. He might even have a career change, retrain for something maybe? He would wait and see. Being single and comfortably off and without the worries of negative equity so prevalent at the time, he certainly did not feel as threatened as many of his married colleagues. He did, in fact, sympathise with many of them given the current economic climate.

The activity around him and that now lay before him by way of work started to have the antidotal effect to his composure that John had hoped it would have and before long the work of the day had completely absorbed him so that he was not thinking about anything but completing it according to routine and then resting at the day's end.

On the way home just after 6.00p.m. therefore he even felt sufficiently disposed to call in at *The Fort* for a drink before ambling home to cook himself a light evening meal.

This he duly did and, having had two pints and two pints only, he completed his day by rustling up quite a tolerable "cheat" paella as he called it, which he ate whilst watching an episode of *The Bill* on Television. After this he washed up, switched off the television and settled down with some blank paper and a pen to make notes and try to reassemble a plan of what he should now do in the light of the events of the previous day.

It did not take him long to work out that all avenues to direct information had been effectively cut off and that he had to now try a new, probably roundabout and therefore protracted method of investigation. The only piece of information that could help in this was the name Patrick Field which he had deduced was the directive of the clue "Irishman we hear filed wrongly in China" and its solution *Paddy Field*. If this was the person who had been buried so secretively then it could well be he was a member of the I.R.A. (a hint found in another clue) and establishing that fact would be difficult, but not impossible.

There is a freemasonry in all walks of life, none more so that in the collegiate structures of the ancient universities. It was John's good fortune he had attended one of these institutions and could now draw on this most powerful of resources. Only one other of his university friends from Coleridge College had gone into journalism, Trevor Whilde, and he, in fact, had gone back to his native Ireland

and, apart from freelance work for features in the daily and weekend broadsheets and colour supplements about the politics of that country, he also had a retainer from *The Times* working as their correspondent in Dublin and all stations south. Trevor, being Irish and, indeed, holding an Irish passport, had always jokingly claimed a relationship with the great Oscar Fingal O'Flahertie Wills Wilde, suggesting the spelling of this surname was sadly due to his own mother's dyslexia! Trevor had been a riotous student projecting his Irishness in drunken revelries which had to include the singing of "We're all off to Dublin in the green, in the green," and after this exciting rendition in the early stages of drunkness he invariably ended up with the more melancholic lament of "Mounjoy Jail" as the onset of inebriation made him grow more morose. John had enjoyed his company and they had often got legless together in the many and varied public houses of the university city. They both worked on *Varsity* often vying with each other for coverage of certain articles but despite this undergraduate rivalry they had always remained friends throughout university and even on parting after graduation they had stayed in touch. Over the last four or five years though, apart from the exchanged Christmas cards they had not corresponded. It was now time John considered that he rekindle the flame of an old friendship.

He now, therefore, took himself up stairs and into his bedroom cum study where on his ancient and ageing Armstrad he started to create a letter to Trevor with due journalistic imagination in order to elicit from him any thing he could possibly dredge up on Patrick Field. The basic scenario involved him getting a new appointment in features research with *The Portsmouth Evening News* due to their take over of his provincial publication. He created two imaginary Celtic figures, Sean Duffett and Brian McBride, to go along with Patrick Field who was, for all he knew, another figure of his imagination. He added a variety of touches about the security of a major naval basis such as Portsmouth and the proximity of Aldershot and the Royal Aircraft Establishment at Farnborough to act as corroborative detail giving artistic verisimilitude to what would otherwise be a bald and unconvincing narrative. He hoped in fact on reading it through that he hadn't overdone it all. The final touches to surround his inquiry involved a longish introduction regretting their mutual lack of communication in recent years together with some reminders of their undergraduate follies and also hoping that he might get over to Dublin's fair city sometime to renew their friendship and re-establish it with copious pints of *Guinness* and bottles of *Bushmills Whiskey*. Now all that was left to get Trevor's address.

Squeezed onto a shelf to the left of his computer desk was a miscellany of publications including the red spined annual editions of Coleridge College, Cambridge, Annual Reports sent to all members of the College society. John regularly received these towards the end of each year and generally only gave them the most cursory of glances though occasionally there was humour of a sort to be found in the amazingly florid prose passages stretching over quite a few pages eulogising achievements of former and present students and sometimes even longer purple prose passages covering the obituaries of the recently deceased great and good collegians and endowing them with attributes which they probably rarely showed or more likely never ever had! The smaller entries were mere tokens indicating the professions of students and occasionally (when submitted by the student himself) an address for contact; these addresses gave a world-wide network to anyone wishing to follow them up. John recalled that soon after he and Trevor had gone down, Trevor had, in fact, inserted his Dublin address inviting any contemporaries to correspond or visit as they wished. Now John took the first half dozen of these reports off the shelf and he started to flick through them. He smiled as he passed obituaries to the college cat, details of doctrinal theses on such vital issues as Chinese combs and Leibnitz's windowless monads, massive outpourings about the number of London Lord

Mayors and Senior judges the college had produced and eventually he found the Trevor's entry and the required address. Having run off the letter and checked it he now quickly arranged for this machine to produce a stick on address label for the envelope into which he now sealed the letter. He was quite pleased with the night's work and felt more in control of the situation that he had felt twenty four hours or so before. He decided to put it in the newspaper's mail the next day; he wrote so few letters that he did not feel any guilt about occasionally getting his salary subsidized in this way by the cost of a first class stamp or so. Satisfied with himself, he went downstairs and to his disappointment remembered he had finished off the bottle of *Laphroaig* and only had some *Metaxa* in stock with which to congratulate himself and which would act as a night cap. Well, this had to suffice, so he poured himself a goodly measure and headed back upstairs for bed.

The Greek brandy had had the desired effect coupled as it was with the deflation in his over excited state from the previous day and the restless night's sleep that that had produced. The last thing he remembered before falling asleep was the wind getting up outside and he saw this as the inevitable prelude to a blustery and rainy night.

At about 2.00a.m. he heard what at first he thought was a patter of heavy rain been blown hard against the window pain. John loathed his sleep being interrupted in any way. He could manage on 7 hours or slightly less but it was essential that that was restful sleep as far as he was concerned,. He tried to ignore this and concentrated on getting back to sleep; such concentration never helps and, in fact the same sound occurred again two times and forced him out of the arms of Morpheus and he turned over and just forced open his eyelids peering into the darkness of his room. It was that blue-black colour of the night, the colour of the ink he had used in his pens as a schoolboy. It was strange how he recalled those bottles of ink at this point; blue, blue-black, black, red, green in the squat Quink jars or in the more medicinally looking Stephens bottle. He even smiled at the latter thought and his brain in this no man's land between sleeping and being fully awake even recalled the rugby song about calling the bastard Stephen because that was the name of the ink, not Quink! But yes the room was decidedly blue black, blackness he remembered only existed in those caverns as in the Cheddar caves, miles underground when they turned off the lights and that really was a frightening, suffocating black. Thus his thoughts were randomly spread when he heard the sound again and this time it seemed to be followed by some banging on his door. He now got up, sleep was wearing off and nervousness was making him more aware. He peered through the rapier of a gap in his curtains and saw that it was in fact not raining outside and that therefore the rattling on the window pain must have had another cause. As he came to this conclusion he thudding on his door occurred again. Dirt being thrown, perhaps? He tried to stand at an angle looking through the gap in the curtains without moving them to see below as to who was banging on his door at such an hour but no matter how obtuse or acute his angle in relation to the gap he could discern nothing. The banging continued and he now summoned up sufficient courage to go quietly down stairs and stand by the door as it was thumped yet again.

"Who's there?" he asked first of all in such a whisper that seemed as if he really didn't want to be heard. Getting no reply, he raised his voice reiterating the question and this time heard the muffled reply of a voice he fortunately recognised for the caller was naïve enough merely to reply, "It's me. It's me!"

Those words, uttered as they were in a soft, but anxious, Hampshire burr, indentified none other that Tom Barber. John unhesitatingly dropped the catch on the latch, pulled open the door and viewed in the dark the disheveled but unmistakable figure of Mr Barber himself and urged him to come in. Tom was initially hesitant but John grabbed his right arm and pulled him into the small well at the front of the stairs just inside the door. This action he was almost instantly to regret for in doing to he discovered immediately the reason for Tom's hesitancy; it certainly was not politeness but rather the fact that Tom was begrimed with dirt and mud obviously having been like King Lear at the mercy of the elements for sometime and John had now got a fair smattering of this on himself. More of the awful appearance was revealed as John closed the door and turned back into the lobby now switching on the light for the first time. Indeed, Tom Barber whose occupation invariably meant he was tanned by the elements of earth, air, fire and water seemed now to have evolved into an integral part of a swampy geographical land mass and as he stood, head bowed within the house, he was oozing out over the carpet and enveloping his surroundings as if to increase his surface area. John already smeared quickly pushed Tom up the stairs and into the bathroom where he told him to get stripped and washed and merely discard his clothes on the floor. Tom slowly and seemingly painfully obliged and as he did so John went about repairing and cleaning the area affected by the visitor getting it all back to some form of presentability and acceptability. Tom's clothes he gathered into a black, polythene refuse bag and tossed this outside the back door of the kitchen to be added to the rubbish for the bin men and be put out for them later. After Tom had bathed John got him some of his own clothes to put on, ushered him downstairs and seated him next to the gas fire. He then made a strong, hot cup of tea and served it to him whilst he finally cleaned up the bath and himself. All this he did without initially thinking about Tom and the relevance and possible consequences of his visit.

Having achieved this state of normality it was now just after 3.00a.m. that John sat down opposite Tom armed with two glasses and the half-full bottle of Metaxa. He poured out two large measures, offered one to Tom, took a sip of his own and waited for Tom's explanation which he decided to elicit by the opening, joking gambit of the question, "Well you seem to have got away from your new woman, Tom; she-devil, was she?"

Tom grimaced partly in response to his first gulp of the brandy and partly in response to the question.

"Weren't no other woman, Mr Ellis. I did get away though. Away from those devils who were holding me." He started wildly on recalling this and rapidly finished his first glassful of the liquor and stuck out his glass for a refill like a snout demanding more payment from a detective before giving him some more revealing information. John duly obliged.

"I'm a dead man if they catch me now, Mr Ellis, and knowing them, catch me they will." He paused and drank again from the replenished glass.

This vague use of the third person plural was irritating to John but he felt provided he kept his patience, Tom would reveal all. Tom stared at John and realised he couldn't be making much sense so decided to begin at the beginning and hope that would suffice.

"I lied to you about that turfing. There was," (even he knew the difference between the past and the present, so he adjusted this testimony), "is, I should say, a grave where I you saw me that night. You saw me mounding it up and levelling it off and later I planted turfs by way of concealing it but that's a bad move for earth needs time to settle in graves. You'll find its a bit concave there now and will become more so as the earth subsides." He said this with the due professionalism of his craft and with an expression of guilt at having made such a bodged job of the matter. "It were an Irishman as I said. I was told by the Reverend, God rest his soul," and here he seemed to shiver in sympathy with the recently departed, "to prepare a grave that day and not mention it to anyone. He also told me not to return too early to fill it in as those who'd be attending didn't really want to be seen. All this was a bit strange and it was made more so when the Reverend swore me to secrecy on the matter and we even prayed together about the affair with him saying he hoped we were acting right and proper in all this connivance. Well, I was a bit intrigued by it all and I did come back just afore the two gentlemen in attendance departed. I had a good look at them and even saw that they for into a lovely Rover car, new registration 'Six' series I think. Anyway, I finished my job and thought nothing of it til you came past and I just passed the end of the day with you as I would with anyone not thinking about what the parson had said and what I'd sworn to. The next day the parson phoned me early and asked me to come over."

Tom was now well into his narrative and he had forgotten about the brandy which had seemed, in part to spark off this need to talk.

"The Reverend was there and with him was these two men, in fact their car from the previous day was now parked in front of the manse. They said they were from the government and they explained carefully that it was absolutely essential I reveal nothing about them or the internment to anyone. I was quite frightened by this and certainly too frightened to say I's mentioned anything to you! They explained that to cover up the situation I would need to get on with re-turfing and then they indicated they were going to make it really worth my while to keep quiet about the whole affair. That's when they said they could arrange for the job up in Cambridge. Well, I'd always wanted to do groundsman's work as well as caretaking and this seemed ideal though I was none-too-keen to up sticks from Hampshire. They were so forceful in their promises, saying they would handle the application and all that I just let them go ahead and, sure enough, it happened. It all just seemed a formality like and since they were as good as their word I was happy to let it all happen!" At this point Tom seemed quite pleased with his story and with himself and he went back to the alcohol and drank again, liked what he tasted and finished his second glass and again offered it to John for a refill, though this time not so much in a demanding manner but more in the unspoken appreciation of what he had drunk and therefore just wanting some more of the same! John obliged again, this time emptying the bottle as he did so.

"At first it was alright up there, Mr Ellis," Tom continued, "though Donna didn't seem to settle too well. But then you phoned and I must say I felt a bit guilty when you did though I'm sure I never gave you any clues as to what had really happened. However, it seems these government people found out someone had been making enquiries and they approached me again." Tom was becoming anxious again as his narrative came more info the recent past and he quaffed another large measure of the brandy to calm himself. "They have contacts everywhere Mr Ellis. There ain't nothing they don't know or can't find out. It seems you never know when they are listening in to what you say or watching what you do. It's terrifying, it really is. Like the Mafia they are," and he shivered with anxiety yet again and took the last large draft of the alcohol getting sufficient courage to continue. "They told me that clearly I was not safe there and they would arrange a disappearance for me on the pretext of an affair. They wouldn't listen when I ridiculed them over such a thing. Me? An affair! I ask you! That would never wash I told them but they wouldn't listen. So yet again they were true to their word and they spirited me away up to some place in the Lake District where they said I could stay until things settled down and they had decided what I could go on to do and where I could go. Ah they were too clever to leave me alone there. I had a nice room an' all in a big, secluded country house and they said I could do gardening or whatever I wanted to keep myself busy but always someone was watching, always someone outside my door, always someone never far away. 'Twas like prison despite the pleasant surroundings, I had to get away. I had to do something. Three nights ago I managed to scramble out my bedroom window, shin down the drainpipe schoolboy fashion and headed off and I can only assume no one followed me though I'm damn sure once they discovered my departure all hell was let loose! I headed for here. I don't know if Donna's still at the school but anyways I wasn't going to visit her for that's the first place they'd look. I remembered your call so I thought I'd come and let you know everything. You're a newspaperman. You can reveal my story and help me out of this mess!"

Tom came to a halt. He hadn't pleaded. He just said things in such a matter-of-fact, believing kind of way that

John could even forgive him the naivety of thinking he wasn't followed and of now having implicated him most assuredly in this business though he was implicated in it by his own choice anyway. He looked at Tom's empty glass and at his own; seeing he had a small drop left in his own and Tom's was completely dry he took Tom's glass and gave him his own urging him to drink as if by way of reward for his story and also as a sign of reassurance that he had done the right thing, he had come to the right place and he would get some help to try to extricate him from what seemed a nightmarish scenario. Tom at first went to decline the offer but being sufficiently aware to see the manner in which it was offered he buried his misgivings, took the glass and said, "Thanks, Mr Ellis. Your health!"

My health, indeed, thought John, given the circumstances.

Tom finished his drink and for a brief episode of time there was a silence between them. John realised that Tom must be tired and he himself was starting to feel the effects of the disturbed night's sleep despite the racing excitement of all that Tom had said. Moreover, he had work to go to in the morning! He therefore now suggested Tom use his bedroom since it was likely he would sleep the longer of the two and he would make do on the downstairs setee. Tom, being weary as he was, was not going to protest over this, so duly wishing each other goodnight they each went to their respective beds and both were soon fast asleep; in Tom's case due to his exertions over the last few days and in John's case due to the earliness of the hour and in both their cases due to the cheap, Greek alcohol.

John re-awoke at about 7.00a.m. and despite the night's events he did in fact feel quite refreshed. After getting himself ready for work he looked in on Tom who was sleeping like the proverbial babe and no doubt would continue to do so for some time to come. He decided to leave a note for his guest to the effect that he stay in the house until John came home around lunchtime. He also indicated on the note that by this time he hoped he would have set in motion sufficient activity to extricate Tom from the bewildering set of circumstances in which he found himself. It, therefore, was absolutely imperative that he should stay put. John wrote the message twice in red using a large felt tip board marker pen on two large pieces of white A3 paper and left one in the bedroom beside Tom and one at the foot of the stairs assuming that if Tom missed the former which would be difficult but perhaps not impossible, he could certainly not avoid the latter. John also added just before he departed his office number should Tom be anxious about contacting him on waking.

At work John first found an ominous second brown manilla envelope marked *Strictly Private and Confidential* and this, indeed, was a letter summoning him for discussion with his new employers that very afternoon. The letter politely informed him he would be welcome to bring either a union representative or a colleague to the interview which would be in the Editor's office at 2.30p.m. It was, he thought, all rather sudden but then the initial letter had said words to the effect that initial interviews would be held later in the week and technically Wednesdays p.m. came into that category. In considering the letter and the current events John realised he might kill two birds with one stone and so got on the telephone to David Hart.

"I wonder if you'd like to be my accompanying colleague at my professional development interview this afternoon?" asked John after the initial exchange of brief pleasantries.

"I like the euphemism," said David. "Why, yes, I'd be glad too." Then, sensing this was not the complete object of John's call, he added, "Anything else I can do for you?"

John paused slightly collecting his thoughts so as not to betray the situation completely to his superior.

"Well, yes. What are you doing at lunchtime today?"

"Heavens!" shouted David down the line, "now you're propositioning me! It won't help at the interview you know!" He laughed at his jest and the forwardness of his joke.

John remained placed. "No, come on. Be serious. Something's come up and I wonder if we could chat about it privately over lunch at my place. I've got some beers in the fridge and there's plenty of cheese and salad stuff or microwave stuff if you prefer something warmer. It is something I'd like to talk about in private and it could be important."

"Sounds wonderfully vague and yet intriguing, though still smacks of propositioning! Yes, O.K. I can be free. I do hope it will be worthwhile. I'll come round at 12.30ish if that's alright by you? Actually it will help us concentrate our minds on the more serious business of the afternoon if nothing else and we should get our act together for that I suppose."

"Great. Yes, just after 12.30 should be fine. I'm off out shortly but will make sure I am *chez moi* by then. Thanks ever so much, I do appreciate your trouble in all this. See you later."

That morning seemed quite interminable to John though he did not have far to travel in the town to cover his local stories. By coincidence he arrived back at his maisonette at exactly the same time as David was arriving and both tried to out do the other by literary allusions, David's quote about John "coming more carefully upon his hour" probably having the edge of John's "ill met by moonlight."

As they entered all was quiet as John ushered David into the sitting room and as he settled himself went through the formalities of asking what he wanted to eat and subsequently got his requirements, beer and a light salad from the fridge. John himself had no appetite being full of anticipation of getting Tom to reveal his story to David and then discussing how it should all be handled. He even imagined it as a small scoop and minor triumph not only for himself but for his newspaper and that might have favourable repercussions that very afternoon! He left David to make a start on his meal whilst heading off upstairs to see Tom whom he supposed was still sleeping off the exertions his experience.

For the first time now he saw that one of his notices was not at the foot of the stairs where it had been left. This led him to believe Tom had got up and seen it and either disposed of it or taken it back upstairs. On he went up the brief flight of stairs, round the landing at the top and gazed through the open door of his bedroom revealing the room to be totally empty and as he entered it showed no signs of anyone having ever been there but himself. Even the clothes he had loaned to Tom in the past twelve hours were back in the drawers or on their hangers and only forensic science would ever prove they had been worn by someone else.

John was angry, frustrated and exasperated and rushed downstairs into the living room his features clearly revealing his anguish. David looked up from his meal and, being astonished by the now rather harassed appearance of his colleague who had gone quite cheerily out of the room only minutes, nay seconds, previously was nonplussed.

"I'm sorry, David," muttered John answering the question that had not been asked by David but had been implicit in his look of surprise. "Everything's gone wrong. There was someone I wanted you to meet. Had an interesting story in fact but it seems he chickened out and has gone off." John was still anxious not to reveal anything about his personal pursuit and investigations for fear that he would look ridiculous. Indeed, he had so little proof of everything that some might suspect he was on the verge of a breakdown and this was the last thing he wanted anyone to consider given his present situation. But as his thoughts moved to the word, proof, he suddenly remembered the black bin liner he had filled with Tom's sodden, filthy smelling clothes; that would be lying out in his back garden where he had thrown it and it would give him something which to show David and from which he could start to reveal his own story.

"But hang on a minute!" he shouted to David as he rushed out the back to retrieve the only tangible evidence available to him at this stage.

No man could have looked on a vast desert so awestruck as John looked on his small back garden having opened the door out on to it from the kitchen. True there was no infinite stretch of khaki sand as far as the eye could see revealing nothing except the possibility of mirages in the offing but what was there was as pitiless and cheerless as such as view. There was the brown creosoted fence on three sides with a small latch door leading out onto the lane running at the back of the houses. In the middle lay square of green grass autumnally thick but short. Down the sides ran one yard wide earthy borders with statutary rose bushes. In front was a small paved area which had a rotary clothes line, hardly used and therefore rusting, set at the concrete-grass border. To the right was a metal dustbin, the edges of its black liner lipping over its brim under the lid. There was no separate bag of clothes. In desperation John went to the bin and removed its vulcanised rubber, black-green moss tanned, cracking lid to show only the littered remnants of his daily living.

He replaced the lid and looked around again in disbelief that was now turning to the fanaticism of the avowed believer. In this case he was coming to understand that it would always be thus. Every bit of proof he thought he had had to date had been whisked away, covered up, eradicated usually on the point of him revealing it. What had he left now? A crossword? A letter to a friend for more information? This was his last lifeline. Would that be expunged as well? He would have to wait and see. Resigned to this state of affairs he returned yet again to David who had started to eat during this second brief absence of his host. Once more he apologised and was alert enough to explain away wasting his colleague's time and even joked about things saying at least David had got a free lunch for his trouble. David registered his friend was subdued and crestfallen at the outcome of events but decided not to press for any revelations which might further embarrass him. Instead he chatted over the programme for the afternoon ahead of them, agreed basically on a wait and see strategy and after a cup of hot coffee each they made their way slowly back to the office.

The meeting with the editor and the managerial staff of *The Portsmouth Evening News* group was to be as short as it was to be decisive. There were a lot of buzz phrases bandied about—*lean and mean, mid-ninties profile, Strengths, Weaknesses, Opportunities, Threats, part of the learning curve, mid-career change and development*—but at the end of the meeting what was abundantly clear was that John's services were to be dispensed with. He could not complain about the terms offered; they were generous in the extreme and involved an immediate lump sum payment in addition to redundancy pay, three months' notice with due salary and protection of pension accrued to date together with the guarantee of excellent references etc. and even opportunities to get priority treatment on any submission of freelance work for features. Though a little bit shocked by the suddenness of all this, John had previously run over in his mind such a scenario and therefore he did not really require time to consider it all. This was just as well because the rider affixed to the package was that although he had been offered three months' notice he should leave with immediate effect. This was indeed startling and for a moment he hesitated on the brink of declining the package and seeing what the consequences of such an action would be. However, discretion being the better part of valour, John caved in, shook hands and went away to clear his desk though he had little thought as to what he was going to do at least in the near future.

Some people are motivated by success. They achieve something and they feed on their achievement thereby becoming avaricious for more. It seems for such characters there is no law of diminishing returns as there is in the economic world; indeed, nothing succeeds like success and for them nothing exceeds like excess either. John had never been motivated in this way. In fact he had never really been ambitious in any success orientated way. He had certainly a lot to be proud of: excellent 'A' Level results, a scholarship to Coleridge College, Cambridge, a first in Part I of the Tripos and a 2:1 in Part 2 as well as quite a few writing awards for local reporting in his modest journalistic career. Generally though he was content and strove to do no other than his best at what he did and, to that extent at least, he could be deemed successful.

Now John felt motivated, but not by success but by its opposite, failure. This feeling, so outlawed by modern psychological thinking in terms of a motivating force, can be, and in many cases is, a much more powerful spur to achievement. As John walked home with the debris of his career gleaned from off his desk and pushed into one cardboard box and squeezed into his brief case he knew he had come to an end but was equally sure he would make a new beginning. So, the new conglomerate dispensed with over a decade's experience in a matter of minutes! So, all attempts he had made so far to get at the truth of the mystery surrounding the burial had been thwarted! He now had one valuable asset which would assist him in the future—freedom! Freedom to operate at least for a few months in exactly the way he wanted to. No constraints except perhaps financial ones but even those were not too severe or at least they wouldn't be in the first instance though he would have to take due care as not to beggar himself on his mission. He was resolved. He was determined. As he walked on it seemed every step he took built up the resolve, raised his determination.

And so he got home. He just laid the box and briefcase at the side of the stairs and decided he would duly deal with the contents later, it mattered not when. He went into the kitchen and looked for some drink. No spirits left. Why, oh why, had he not replaced that whisky? And the *Metaxa*? Well that reminded him all too consciously of the night before. Only two cans of some supermarket branded beer in the fridge. Well, they would have to do! Maybe he would go to the pub later or even call in at an off-licence. He took these out and went into the sitting room. Sitting in the chair he pushed open the ring-pull on the top of one can having placed the other on the floor beside his seat. Meekly, almost apologetically, the beer fizzed into a large tear of froth where the opening had been made. He sat and look at it and then raised the can to his lips and first sucked in the froth and then guzzled down the beer in large gulps. It was cold and rather tasteless and lacked all the warming and medicinal powers of a spirit. He finished the first can, discarded it at the side of the chair and started on the second one. He just felt he had to drink, it didn't matter what. The mechanical process and the fact that he was consuming alcohol were sufficient reasons separately and together for his action. As he was half-way through his second drink, he suddenly stopped, put down the can and after a short pause just broke down into tears as he tried to come to terms with all that had happened so far and tried to convince himself yet again that here was a new start, not an end. Now more than ever he desperately needed an anchor in what was truly the greatest storm he had encountered in his life so far. And only he was going to be able to provide that anchor for himself.

CHAPTER 9

An Interlude

"They flee from me that sometime did me seek
With naked foot stalking in my chamber:
I have seen them gentle, tame and meek,
That now are wild, and do not remember
That sometime they put themselves in danger
To take bread at my hand . . . ."
(Sir Thomas Wyatt: They flee from me . . .)

Being unemployed was worth a feature article in itself if John's experiences were anything to go by. There were the circumlocutary details to be completed for the Job Centre to claim the dole and for the D H S S to claim the income support to which he was entitled though his claim to that particular department came to nought. Provided he turned up at a set time every fortnight and autographed a piece of paper then within two days a predominantly green and orange cheque with shades of faded pink and blue superimposed in the middle on the top plopped through his letter box duly typed up to pay him a derisory sum in the region of £90.00. But that was the routine side of things and just part of the system; an incidental to be put up with, to go through the motions of. Hardly arduous though certainly boring.

Days were filled with lethargy. Out of habit, John still got up just after 7.00a.m. and then meandered through his morning routine of toiletry and breakfast. Although having nowwhere particular to go he would find himself ambling about town in the morning generally ending up in bookshops or the library where he might browse through the computer index of books just trying to locate obscure titles he remembered from his past at school and university. It was interesting to find that the library often failed to have copies of books that he considered interesting, important and, above all, simply a good read; perhaps they had gone out of print, been stolen or it was just that the library's resources never stretched that far despite the fact that this was an index which covered all Hampshire public libraries. He also found himself now doing the shopping at times which he considered odd for he had tended to squeeze in this aspect of his life on Friday evenings after work or Saturday mornings when not away. Again, it was merely to kill time or was it that time was killing him?

What he found interesting was the number of other people around during the day. Didn't they work? Didn't they have jobs to go to? Surely the nation's unemployment wasn't as bad as it appeared to this journalistic observer on the streets. But then John realised he had to categorise people. There were the pensioners, of course, permanently, but not always happily, freed from the chains of labour. This group, however, by no means accounted for the masses in which he found himself. Shift workers of course . . . . but shouldn't they be in bed? Ah, no, there were those in that number who worked long shifts only three days a week and therefore had the other four days of the week off. Teachers, of course, never seemed to go more than a six week stretch without a holiday, that often being a half-term lasting at least one week. Policeman, fireman, health-workers too seemed to have jobs involving a fair amount of flexibility in their hours. Flexi-time working and studying seemed to account for another slice of the pie-chart he was assembling in his mind on this issue as he found himself engaging in conversation with these denizens. The concept of a flexi-time student was one that he thought worthy of research sometime and he was rather horrified in his initial forays into further and higher educational studies to discover that so many courses had become modular and degrees were therefore now available as if from a menu list, a holiday brochure, or a home shopping catalogue to be taken as and when required and plopped into the shopping trolley of experience. And of course, the final percentage was inevitably the group to which he now belonged, the unemployed.

In the sense that John's initial depressive reaction, despite his resolve, made him waste the first week or so of his new found freedom in this rather desultory manner, he did take wise precautions in other ways concerning his present state. On receipt of his pay off (which was surprisingly instantaneous given the circumstances) he paid off the outstanding balance of his car loan. He also paid a lump sum off his mortgage thereby reducing it to a repayment his current fortunes could bear and accordingly made an agreement with his building society to that effect. He set aside part of the lump sum in a high interest deposit account in order to have something for the future and made arrangements with his pension fund to keep some kind of contribution going so that it would not just stay static whilst he was out of work.

There were two other fronts about which he was particularly concerned. He judged that Tom Barber had been correct about the powers and knowledge of those with whom he had dealt. He had no doubts in his own mind that he now faced these redoubtable opponents whoever they were and was being watched. He even suspected that his rapid departure from *The Gazette* was, in part at least, occasioned by his involvement with the late Reverend Robert Fergusson and now also possibly the late Tom Barber. It was therefore, in his own interests to keep as low a profile as possible over the forthcoming weeks.

He had to give the impression, he felt, that he was tamed; that he had cast off his doubting Thomas approach and now believed that there was nothing to be investigated in any shape or form. This was not too difficult for, in truth, the only bait he had out at present was his letter to Trevor Whilde and he must have patience and wait for a response. He would not telephone him for he even imagined that his line might be tapped. And so he went about to all intents and purposes giving a creditable performance of one who was unemployed and did not quite know initially what to do with himself.

The other issue in his life was Helen. Redundancy was a severe blow to the scenario he had planned for the two of them and he even had difficulty in summoning up courage to tell Helen of his circumstances. But tell her he did and she was naturally consoling. She suggested he come and stay with her temporarily but he felt that was not a wise move at present. He suggested that he postpone the weekend they were due to have together shortly for about another two weeks and then, once he had got used to his new found freedom and had at least set a few personal applications in motion and maybe even started some research for possible feature articles, then they should get together again. And, he suggested, he would come down at that time for at least a week or more and perhaps she could get a little time off work and they could have a mini-holiday such as they had enjoyed not so long ago. Helen was not at first convinced that they should cancel what they had already planned, and being the loving and partly mothering type she was keen on giving him some tender loving care since she felt so sorry for him, but eventually she did accept his need for space given his circumstances and said she would look forward to their future time together with even more relish. He was glad they had agreed so amicably over the situation and he, too, looked forward to the feats he had planned after what would by then he quite a long famine.

Thus his days were spent in diversions. The bookshops, the library, the park, the town centre, the shops, the local swimming pool and leisure centre with its *Aqua Springs* spa and saunas became part of his daily or weekly itinerary. He had enjoyed rugby as a schoolboy and as a student and for a brief period after leaving college but had never taken sport too seriously and when the rugby died away he never actively sought to replace it with anything. Now he had time to consider. He had dabbled in squash and bought some kit wherewith to play the game since he found the local leisure centre ran leagues for people who were free during the day and when the courts were readily available; moreover this off-peak time was charged at an off-peak rate and therefore it was not only chronologically convenient but financially convenient as well. It also helped him meet new faces and gave him an insight into the world of people who had part-time, job-sharing, flexi-time or shift work commitments. So, too, the spa and saunas charged a cheap rate for those who used the facilities in the mornings and he was happy to do this for he would take a book to read with him which he would get through in the time out of the pools and the heat. It was the sauna which he most enjoyed in all this leisure time now available to him. There was an exquisite sense of pain in soaking up the heat and literally soaking it out again. Breathing in the dry air left a burning sensation in the roof of his mouth and at the back of his throat not leaving him parched in any sense but rather mildly scalded with a lingering, ashen taste. The sweat dripped from his brow at first and down his back from the nape of his neck, it then beadily bubbled from the pores in his arms and later flowed from his chest and stomach and the tributaries from these areas came to a confluence beneath his navel and around the base of his spine and soaked into the wooden boards staining them from a dull white to a rich toffee colour beneath him. The salt droplets from his legs, meanwhile, caught in his hairs and sat on them shining like dewdrops caught in a spider's web in the early morning light. The sauna seemed to concentrate his mind. He never attempted to treat it as a contest by timing himself and his durability for to do so would be highly dangerous. Rather he treated it as a cell, his own prison, in which he could think intensely and intently on anything which troubled him and, hopefully, come to some resolution. It was these sauna sessions indeed that pulled John back from the brink of morbidity and self-pity and helped him focus his resolve on how he intended to act depending on what he did or did not find out from Trevor Whilde who was across the sea in Ireland.

For about a month he lived out this existence and became accustomed to it. He did look at topics that might be worthy of research for feature articles but nothing really caught his imagination. He backed off from pursuing the flexi-study student enquiries not just because his initial finding proved so horrendous to him but also because he at one stage contemplated doing research and wrote to Portsmouth University to discover what opportunities there were there to do so. On receiving their brochures and after further talks with their literature department he felt that there was hardly any rigour demanded from them and he would hardly achieve much more than he had when he had received his first degree some 12 years since. It seemed to him he had had the best of education and what was currently available was a poor imitation of what had gone before and he felt disillusioned by it all. Another area he embarked on was part literate, part sociological.

He was intrigued by the decline in the mining industry in the U. K. and, although it was an area he knew nothing about, he thought an anthology of extracts from literary texts in praise of and detailing the sociology of what was becoming an extinct industry was in order. He therefore re-read Lawrence and dug up copies of Llewellyn's *How Green Was My Valley*, Jones' *Bidden To The Feast* and other such texts and wrote off to the N. U. M. about what he was doing hoping they might fund the publication of such an anthology under his editorship. Alas the eighties had not only hit at the membership of the unions but also as a consequence their financial resources and this was to be another avenue of disappointment.

He even briefly took to writing semi-comical, satirical verse on the more outrageous items of news such as the increase in home-brewing at the expense of the public houses, British Rail's absurd reasons for train delays, Essex girl jokes, Irishmen who claimed their personalities suffered because they had the mickey taken out of them at work (and were awarded compensation for such a frivolous claim) and many others. This package of doggerel he sent to *The Portsmouth Evening News* suggesting that they incorporate a comic poem once a week on a news topic just by way of entertainment value. He added that he was prepared to write to a deadline and pointed out there could be a Christmas anthology of the verse which would be a good stocking-filler and from which they could glean extra revenue. His ideas were rejected.

He had not got beyond these avenues when it came time for him to visit Helen again. He was now more than prepared to do so as he felt that not only had things become tedious but he had, indeed, frittered away his initial weeks of freedom and he knew he would get renewed strength and encouragement from Helen and would return with a much more positive attitude. He had not heard from Trevor and he decided just to leave things dormant on that front because the less he troubled it, the less he would be troubled. He also decided not to tell Helen about what had transpired; the less she knew the better and he certainly did not want her dragged into that particular mire. Before setting off south he had to complete forms for his absence with the Job centre since the week he was to be away coincided with his signing on day and such a clash was catered for by appropriate elephantine paper work from this particular circumlocution office.

And so back to Portmouth for a period of ten days inclusive! Helen had managed to obtain leave for two extra weekdays but for the rest of the time John was left to his own devices. He confessed to Helen how he had wasted this first month in cul-de-sac pursuits and she was able to see reflected in this his depression. She comforted him in every supportive way she could and certainly proved to be a healing balm at this particular juncture. She gave him his self-confidence back and reassured him that they still had a more than meaningful future together.

From the balmy end of summer days, times had moved on now into the first cold blasts of autumnal October. Helen had rejoined the local orchestra and was enjoying her musical activities again. Thursday was rehearsal night and that evening John went to watch the local clash of the Titans in County rugby between Havant and United Services. They agreed to meet up after there respective engagements at the New Inn, Drayton later that evening.

John arrived at the match shortly before kick-off. The floodlights gave the pitch an eerie appearance as it lay bare before the thirty players stampeded out over it. The tufted grass appeared stiff and yellow in the blaze of light and the spectators huddled behind the sets of rails either side of the arena looked like a barely discernable, ghostly crew on deck about to witness a flogging. Their breath hazed in front and above them as it condensed onto the frosty night air and obscured their faces from recognition. The match was for John what he would describe as the unacceptable face of rugby football. It proved, as many local derbys do, to be a bloody, bruising battle made up of many professional fouls, a large percentage of which the referee was unable to discern and therefore penalise. The literal heat generated from the play delayed the ground from being frost covered as the evening temperature plummeted towards zero and, at the end, as players and spectators departed, the pitch resembled a mixture of oxtail and pea soup in a white frosted, square bowl. This heat, too, steamed off the forwards and rucks, mauls and scrums had the appearance of Turkish steam rooms or New Zealand's Thermal activity centres during the course of the game. The metaphorical heat gave rise to punch ups, brawls and free-for-alls that would have done credit to any John Wayne movie. Since the friction was caused by six of one side and half-a-dozen of the others there was no way the referee was going to give anyone their marching orders. What was in its history inaugurated as a running game became a kicking one and perhaps justice was done in the score line which was drawn by Havant being awarded the match for having got five of their points by a try. Thus John's evening; numbed by the cold and by the quality of rugby football he had endured.

As for Helen, enjoying the warmth of a school hall for a rehearsal of Dvorak's Serenade for Orchestra Opus 78, the evening was much more comfortable and enjoyable. This languid, mysterious and almost menacing Czech air put through a multitude of variations in quite exquisite scoring was a delight to play. Dr Malone, the conductor, was sensitive for the need to keep players involved and did not over fragment the work by stopping and starting, criticising, running through in sections and generally punctuating the flow of the melody and the chance to play for the players. Like a good referee he allowed things to progress and only reined things in when, in the orchestral management sense, musicality necessitated. The standard of musicianship in this group was high, anyway, players only getting in after quite demanding auditions and the general approach and ability therefore was a professional one. As Helen played she made a mental note of ensuring John would be down for the weekend of the concert in just over a month.

And so they met and exchanged comments with each other on the way their evenings had progressed. Though diverse in pursuits, yet were they joined in conversation and interests and each respected the other's territory and space and this accounted for what was now cementing into a lasting and loving friendship between them.

John during these ten days did indeed have a most relaxing time. It allowed him to forget the strains he had been under and to take stock for the future with the support of the one he loved. On days when left to himself he wandered around the locality soaking up the atmosphere and the area he so liked as if it were a medicine of which he was in need. He went for long walks in the Queen Elizabeth Country park and reflected on the Quaker colours that were starting to usurp the autumnal almonds, rusts, saffrons and ochres. He observed the trees being stripped naked to face the blasts of winter and the tar coloured and textured leaves gathered at their bases waiting to melt into the brown bowels of the earth. Many trees now looked like candelabra against the slate coloured sky. The pathways through the forests were damp stretches of mahogany coloured earth still scattered with a crazy paving of leaves in places, but not yet the muddy, chocolate highways they would become as Autumn inevitably melted into Winter. The hillsides were still a rich green made bright by lingering dew and would remain so as a backcloth, steadfast against the seasonal changes.

Other days were spent on brisk, bracing walks along the sea front. As the hovercraft now splashed into the oyster coloured seas the very spray seemed to freeze into the air and like Jack Frost's fingers turn all around to ice. Boats, ferries, ships now chugged and buffeted through leaden waves in the Solent, pushing out spume like snow before a snow plough. Here again the colours had changed. Neutral tones new abounded where the Jackson Pollock splashes of colour on surf-boards, deck chairs, swimming costumes had been only a matter of months before. The amusement arcades, the ice-cream and sweet stalls, and parts of the pier now boarded up like buildings waiting to be demolished. Yet even these would be resurrected within about six months; a reasonable gestation period.

Despite the dying of the year and its attendant sadness, John came out of his depression and realised that for him, too, a period of renewal, of taking stock would have to take place before he made progress. A part of him had died; long live the new part! Helen was solace as were his own thoughts. As his brief sojourn came to an end, although he had not settled on any specific new policy with regard to his future he had resolved to be more decisive about it. The days of *Waiting for Godot* were over, finished with. Helen could see the change in him even within this short period and she was glad he was back to being his old self again and she was convinced as was he that all would be well.

Thus, having arranged to see Helen again in a fortnight's time, he returned to Portminster bouyant with hope, if not with plans for the future. On driving into the town he decided, after having parked his car at home, not to go straight in but to have a few pints down at *The Fort St George* to celebrate his future. On entering he saw Janice who worked on reception and who had so kindly got him the copy of the sought after crossword edition not so long since. He smiled over at her just as her male companion returned to sit beside her bringing her a drink. She glanced back but in a cold stare of acknowledgement and recognition, nothing else. He received a much more decidedly backward look of contempt from the boyfriend who joined her and John noticed she was busily explaining things to him the minute he reverted to looking at her. John was not naïve; he had known that she had fancied him in the past when he was working on the newspaper and he had more than an inkling of how she had felt when he had asked that one particular favour of her. But that past was over. Clearly it was well and truly over for her as well as him. No doubt his esteem had fallen not only in her eyes but also her mother's now that he was to be numbered amongst the umemployed! *Persona non grata*; not a very enviable state to have assumed.

He smiled rather bitterly to himself while he awaited the arrival of his pint of ale. But he would not allow such maudlin thoughts to get him down. He took his pint of Winter's best brew, held it up to the light and relished burnished, coppery tincture. *L'Chaim* he said to himself. To life! And he downed the draught within about seven seconds, a time worthy of any rugby club bar superstar! He ordered and then drank another, more slowly this time savouring the taste as the liquid languished on his taste buds and slaked a true beer-drinker's thirst. This had set him up fine. He now headed home.

Inside the front door on the carpet lay scattered 10 days' post. A jumble mainly of circular letters dealing with all variety of items from postage stamps to central heating and double glazing. It was, after all, getting closer to Christmas and everyone was out to maximize sales. John picked them up and went into the living room where he started to discard them as he surveyed the irrelevance, to him at least, of their contents. He had got through half a dozen or so when he came to an envelope he certainly did not want to discard. It was long, contained certainly a substantial letter, had an Eire stamp and was post-marked Dublin. Well, this was worth coming back for.

Before settling down to read its contents, John shuffled through the rest of the pack of envelopes and, as expected, found there was nothing else worth keeping. He picked up this bundle of rejects and took them out to the bin in the kitchen. He then rang Helen briefly to inform her of his safe arrival back home and promised her he would keep his spirits up until next they met. Moreover, he assured her, he would prove he had done so by having some good news for her. Thus satisfied, he gave the letter from the Emerald Isle his undivided attention. He settled into his chair, switched on the gas fire, tore open the envelope and drew out the enclosed several folded sheets of A4 and began to read.

CHAPTER 10

A Letter

> "Death has no right to come so quietly."
> (Elizabeth Jennings: Sequence in Hospital)

The letter was dated ten days previously and therefore must have arrived one or two days after John had left for this recent sojourn in Portsmouth. He also noticed Trevor's address had changed and he used that fact partly to account for the fact that there had been quite a considerable delay in replying. After noticing and reading these preliminaries John read on.

. . . . Yes, thank you for reminding me about the green Chartreuse. Before Dave Burnside's 21st and since, I have not dared touched the stuff. All I can say is that it added a nouvelle cuisine touch to the vomit! That green sauce surrounding the usual pieces of carrot and meat was certainly distinctive! But you are hardly one to talk! What Chartreuse did for me, I seem to recall Crone's cider did for you, though without the culinary effect aforementioned. In terms of apres pissed smell, give me the liqueur anytime! Can I see you blushing now? I don't think

you dared go back to The Granta after that particular night. Have you, indeed, ever been back since?

Actually, even better than our escapades, you must remember 'Noakes the Throat'? Not just college yard-of-ale champion in something like 20 seconds or so but also King Street Runner extraordinaire! Just a few seconds over nineteen minutes for that amazing feat though I believe it had been beaten—quite recently in fact! Well, all records are set to be broken. But what about the night he was so pissed at college dinner that when he got up to bow out to the principal to exit he crashed lifeless onto the floor. A real dead faint! Pandemonium in college hall at such a refined event as college dinner. And a mediocre story like that got quite a few column inches in 'Varsity'. What was the headline again? Something involving Vino Callapso if I remember! Well, we were always hard up for hard news were we not? Legend has it, you remember, that he also turned up twice to take his driving test as an undergraduate in an appalling state of inebriation. Then there was the evening when he was accosted by The Master of The College, who seeing his alcoholic state remarked, "Drunk again, Mr Noakes!" and got the reply, "So am I, sir. So am I." Knowing Noakes, I am sure that story is not as apocryphal as it sounds. And now, I noticed in the last Annual Report, he's been elected a Fellow of the Royal College of Physicians and has received some honour in America's Safety and Health Hall of Fame! 'How the whirligig of time brings in his revenges'!

There must be something Freudian or whatever in the fact that whenever we recall undergraduate days it is stories of being arseholed that immediately spring to mind. Next to those, of course, it's stories of sexual encounters. I always remember making love in a punt to some leggy bit of skirt from Newnham; it was a weird experience—flat bottomed boat, flat bottomed tart (as I recall!) and liquid River Cam underneath. Perhaps it was just a wooden, Heath-Robinson prototype of the waterbed! Anyway, I thought this was terribly with it until a few weeks later having to read the only writer more tedious than Henry James, John Cowper Powys, there was a description of such a scene in his novel 'Wolf Solent' or 'Weymouth Sands' or was it one of the others? They were all so much the same and so esoteric but according to that mindless Prof Williams these were the English literary equivalents of the works of Tolstoi! Not fair on Tolstoi in my opinion! But, sure enough, there it was in that text; to think that an arid, dreary writer such as he should have 'been there, done that' to use the modern parlance . . . . or perhaps as all writers he just had a good imagination. The best fillies were from Girton, though, were they not? I am sure you recall the two college balls we went to there! Just like the rugby song . . . . 'fucked them in the parlour, fucked them in the halls' . . . . lovely, randy, blue-stockinged, no knickered lithe young things! I wouldn't mind seeing that college's annual report now and seeing what those ladies are currently up to. I am sure you'd like to find out what's happened to delightful Davina—her of the quotable quote—'Who says size doesn't matter? It's got to tickle your tonsils or you might as well not bother!' Since you scored a hit with her we all knew you had no worries! Do you ever wonder what she's doing now. "O Mistress mine, where are you rooming?" Bet you're blushing now! . . . . Having said that, does size really matter? Surely it's the motion in the ocean that counts! Well, I like to think so! What does that say about me then?

John enjoyed reading all of this even thought it was by way of preamble to what he really wanted to learn. He was not blushing but he certainly was smiling at these reminiscences. Nostalgia is important to everyone, not least the educated. There is no reason why the intelligentsia's, if that's the right word for them, recollections should necessarily be of higher order than anyone else's. It is rare for anyone to be like Wordsworth with his memory of the daffodils or the solitary reaper; those sorts of reminiscences are the exceptions, not the rule. Rarely is it such aesthetic or artistic moments that are remembered but invariably those connected with the sins of gluttony in all its forms and perhaps even more often than that, carnality. This is probably not Freudian, as Trevor had surmised, but simply due to the fact that, though man might well want it otherwise, the basic fact is we are animals and therefore primarily emotional and not reasonable. So John read on . . . .

. . . . Well, enough of the wilder side of our undergraduate days. It seems one of the entry qualifications must have been that students are only admitted providing they subscribe to the philosophical doctrine of psychological egotistical hedonism! But we did enjoy the groves of academe too. I still value the fact that many of the lecturers may have been eccentrics but they were experts in their field. Remember Elmer Lewis who wouldn't let anyone into his lectures unless they were wearing a gown? Incredible traditionalist—took some stick. Having said that his lectures on seventeeth century literature and background were exceptional! I've still got my notes, though I must confess they are little use to me now. Then there was Anthea De Mauriçon who wouldn't allow anyone in who was wearing trainers! Too boorish she would say! Actually her Lit. Crit. lectures were genuinely inspirational. At the end of the day, it's things like that that stick in your mind as well as the sex, drugs and rock 'n' roll. 'Intellectual discipleship,' my school headmaster used to call it; as a rebellious sixth former I thought it was all so much hot air but I have to confess it was part of what I have come to remember and admire. I doubt if these new universities will be able to generate anything like the fun we had in learning with the new breed of students and for that matter, lecturers they are recruiting. "O Tempora, O Mores!" Yes, I was among those who got my Latin 'A' Level to

get into Cambridge though you'd hardly need it to recognise a quote like that . . . .

It was interesting, thought John, as he read that Trevor should have come to conclusions about education that he had himself. But then, on further consideration was this really as interesting as all that? Surely not. They were, after all, products of good schools and a world famous university. Like sexism, it had been inculcated into them. It was natural they should be scornful of the present and what it offered. Part of that very education itself had rubbed off in their condescending attitude. The greatest liability in education is education itself. John remembered his English teacher telling the class this and then proving his point by asking any member of the class to recite the alphabet backwards! There were no volunteers. And since that time John had only met two persons who could do so; a divine young lady who worked in insurance and who told him her grandfather had taught her to learn it that way and a rather dull, E F L teacher John had interviewed and who had so learned it to impress his foreign students! It was his, and Trevor's, education that was getting in the way of allowing them an objective view of the world as it stood now.

These thoughts John layered on top of the understanding he was getting from the letter as he read it. All this, which he enjoyed, was inconsequential but, he knew as with his own epistle, Trevor would get round to the key business sooner or later. And so he read on . . . .

. . . . *My work in Dublin and it environs over the past decade or so seems miles removed from all that sweet enjoyment now. Although I've enjoyed my news getting and feature writing, mainly in the world of politics as you know, I often wish I'd gone into Arts reviews of Sports writing where I could really use the power of language. There's been some beauties recently by journalists in those fields—cricketers described as wearing cemtex pads when they keep getting l.b.w. decisions against them, opera singers described in terms more relevant to Sumo wrestlers, works of art seemingly more at home in a fast food restaurant than an art gallery—all good stuff and certainly a tribute to the literary ability of the writers. My prose plods and anything good I write seems to derive directly from that past master, Swift, perhaps appropriately so in that I'm in Dublin. I did even quote him when I last wrote about the Tory dealings with the Irish parties over here though I did not acknowledge as such by inserting the appropriate inverted commas and probably no one recognised it and so gave me undeserved credit. You know the piece from 'Gulliver's Travels'—"Perjury, oppression subornation, fraud, panderism and the like infirmities were amongst the most excusable arts they had to mention . . . ." Sums up most politicians most of the time and why try to be original when it's been said as effectively as this?*

And writing about those things brings, of course, the I.R.A. to mind.

Felicitations, by the way, on your new prospects with the Portmouth Newspapers Group. They've got a good reputation and I know they're getting someone good in you! Those names you sent me! Brian McBride—no! There was a minor politically active McBride in the north, Belfast to be exact, but he was a businessman dealing in shoes and carpets and apart from some possible dodgy deals with one side or the other in which he and his private plane were involved there's nothing on him. He's retired now but still lives in the south of the city but has no known connections and has not had for some years now. Sean Duffet—no! Common name a bit further south and some family connections but the only ones I discovered of any import were footballers (association, not Gaelic); quite good footballers, it seems, but certainly not political—except when they were playing sides from the north or from England! But ears pricked up when I mentioned one, Patrick Field! Seems there is mileage in that one though I must say, despite my good contacts here, the trail went very quickly cold and dead on him. This leads me to believe you may have something hot on your hands with that one!

As I said, other than determine you have got a biggish fish in your county with him I've not been able to find out much more but, to alleviate the disappointment that is now running through your mind, I have made contact with a very good friend of mine in London and he has suggested that you make contact with him and he may be able to help you. Believe it or not he's from the other place (so this is not entirely due to the old school tie brigade) but don't hold that against him. His name is Dr Kenneth Churcher and he runs a social work agency in London. But—Cave Canem! This is in fact a genuine agency which also acts as a cover for government undercover work mainly for the D H S S, Inland Revenue and all that, infiltrating as it does the world of the great unwashed, you know! Churcher's quite a sharp cookie as well though in appearance and manner he gives the impression of an intellectual snob. If you get nothing else he'll give you a splendid lunch very much in your style since it will have lots of liquid of the strong and vintage variety to wash it down and his conversation is excellent. Be prepared by swotting up on all your poetry and drama—he is awash with quotes and literary allusions. The agency's located fairly centrally as I recall but he'll give you address and directions once you contact him on 071 404 3031. I have had some dealings with him in the past—even passed on information to him about agency workers heading his way so he owes me and you can remind him of that. He said he would get some research on Patrick Field going when I contacted him—just before word processing the epistle off to you—so by the time you get to him he may have more relevant news and something for you to follow up further.

So there you are. Now you owe me, too. I expect, therefore, not to be out of touch again for another 4 years or so before you write to ask me for a favour. Rather I'd like to hold you to your promise of trying to get over here. Can't you swing an expenses trip on your new job—tell them you're actually going to meet this Patrick Field or some such thing? I know there's still a recession on but I would have thought it was possible. There's plenty to do and see over here—The Irish Holy Trinity of Guinness, Murphys and Beamish for example! And, don't forget it's in Dublin's fair city where girls are so pretty! And if those items don't appeal (and if they don't you must have changed from the John Ellis that I once knew!) then this land's the home of Yeats, Beckett, Synge, Joyce, Swift and my great ancestor, Wilde himself . . . . to name but a few! Well, that's the commercial break . . . ." If you ever go across the sea to Ireland," "I'll take you home again, Kathleen," and all that. I do hope you'll make the effort and I naturally wish you lots of luck with your research.

I doubt if I'll be over there at least not in the near future. I have a lot of work here and, though it's not exciting, I enjoy it. Then again I'm far too fond of this country, "my home, my native land," and all it's got. I had my three years exile and it was a good exile but it wouldn't be the same to come back not even for a short break. We do, indeed, "remember with advantages" . . . .

John realised he was nearing the end of the script for this was the maudlin Trevor coming out now: the one who had gone beyond the wild exuberance of Epicurianism and was now filled with Cartesian doubts. The one on whom alcohol was beginning to take effect and who realised he had drank too much and was heading for bad case of scrambled brains, unhealthy sleep and surrealistic dreams . . . .

. . . . *when we think back to our past. Was it really that good? Oh I am prepared to say it was—indeed, I've more than done so in the earlier part of this correspondence—to join in the philosophical conspiracy of minds that says it was. And, if we all do it, and we most surely do, then it was so, was it not? But in reality what did it all amount to? Three short years filled with some making new friends, some reading and writing, of frequently getting pissed and rather less frequently, of shagging? Not much different from the rest of our lives really! But that's hardly original thinking is it?*

Anyway, John, do stay in touch this time. It was good to hear from you. I do keep tabs on things through the annual report but even more so through the Cantebridgian and Coleridgean grapevines. Do get yourself over here. I trust you have remembered all the words of those good (and bad) Irish songs, I taught you. That will stand you in good stead when you step on to these emerald shores. Do keep me informed as to how your inquiries work out. If you get some good stuff I wouldn't mind sharing your material. We always got on when we worked on 'Varsity'. No need to change the habits of a lifetime. "Floreat Coleridgea . . . . Souvent me Souvient . . . . In Fide Fiducia . . . . Finis Opus Coronat . . . ." or whatever. "Facilis est descensus ad averni," more like . . . .

And there he signed off. It had been a long read but a good one.

It was much as John had expected and, indeed, apart from the tendency towards a philosophy of melancholia towards the end, not unlike the epistle he had sent to Trevor. He had enjoyed this brief trip down memory lane and, in fact, it reminded him of other events not mentioned by either of them in the course of their letters. University life had been fun; looking back on it now it seemed truly to be a land of lost content, a highway he would never traverse again. But apart from this indulgence in nostalgia, John was also extremely pleased that the object of his quest was genuine. Clearly Patrick Field, this mysterious person who had been interred close by, was someone to be reckoned with and the activity surrounding his burial clearly had significance. He resolved to telephone Dr Churcher the following day and arrange to visit him as soon as was convenient. He had let the trail go cold for long enough and it was time to pick up again.

When he dialled the number that next morning he got the standard agency reply issued by the received pronunciation of a female of indeterminate age and looks on the other end. To all intents and purposes it could well have been a recording!

"Churcher's Care Incorporated Agency. How many I help you?"

"I'd like to speak to Dr Ken Churcher, please," rejoined John quite confidently yet holding the key page of Trevor's letter in front of him for a kind of reference or prompt, should he need one!

"Who shall I say is calling?" came back the standard question.

"John Ellis."

"Is it in connection with anything in particular, Mr Ellis?" demanded the voice.

"No. He is expecting me to call sometime. He should recognise the name."

"Thank you. Please hold and I will put you through shortly."

As the voice thus signed off it was replaced by play over music, in this case John recogised as Vivaldi's *Four Seasons*. Quite an up-market piece of piped music to play to callers, thought John as he listened to the sharp staccato of the strings imitating rain lashing down upon the earth. Certainly somewhat high brow for the clientelle that a care agency would get. None the less it was considerably preferable to the usual single note versions of *Frere Jacques* which were so common with many other companies. His listening was interrupted by the plum-sounding, superior, languishing, Oxford-educated tones of Dr Churcher who greeted him quite warmly.

"John Ellis. Trevor's undergraduate colleague. How nice to hear from you! Trevor said you would call. How are you?"

John was pleased that he did not have to introduce himself. Dr Churcher had done his homework and sounded much as he had been led to expect he would.

"I'm fine, thank you, Dr Churcher. I was . . . ."

"Oh, Ken, Ken, if you please. I stand not on ceremony!"

"Yes. O.K. Ken. I was wondering when it might be convenient for me to come up and see you on the matter I wrote to Trevor about and which I believe he briefed you about."

"Yes. Yes, indeed he did, and most intriguing it is, I can assure you young man. I have already got some more information for you and it would be best that we met to discuss this perhaps over lunch rather than as disembodied souls at the end of telephone lines. I might add it is not the sort of thing we should, in fact, discuss over the phone anyway. How are you fixed for later this week then. After Wednesday seems quite clear from me at present—at lunchtime that is anyway."

John hesitated. He did not want to give the impression that due to his unemployed state any time was convenient. He was, after all, conscious of his pretence to Trevor which, no doubt, would have been passed on to Ken Churcher.

"Hang on. I've got my diary here." And he pretended to take time to look it through in order to confirm an appropriate date. This was followed by a further fiction. "Wednesday would have been O.K. Thursday's out I'm afraid but Friday should be acceptable. I can make it up there for about 12.00-12.30 and as long as I can get a train about fourish in the afternoon to get me back here by sixish. That should work, shouldn't it?"

"Friday. Right, I'm putting it in now and I'll tell my secretary. Get up here about noon. We'll have a chat and there's a lovely brasserie just across the road where the company's got an account so we can indulge ourselves. And, it will be Friday after all so no worries about work the next day—or that afternoon for that matter."

"Right, then, Friday it is. Now can you just let me have a brief outline as to how to get to your offices? Trevor said you would in his letter to me in which he only gave me your phone number incidentally!"

Ken Churcher gave the address and directions as a child who had learned Tennyson's 'The Brook' by rote, no doubt having had to do so many times before. Then as a valedictory he signed off with Macbeth's injunction to Banquo, "'Fail not our feast.'"

John put down the receiver and hoped that these last words were not ominous in anyway.

Between now and the Friday of his proposed meeting he had to occupy himself meaningfully given his resolve to Helen in his recent trip to Portsmouth. So indeed he did. He had, in fact, been thinking about what avenues he might explore in the journalistic field and he now felt he had at least three good ideas worth taking on and trying to sell to the company which had been so dismissive of this services.

He therefore spent the next days contacting first Andrew Pollard, a local historian who had produced copious books about the development of Portminster and its surroundings. In discussion with Andrew he agreed to adapt parts of his books for a series on local history for the newspaper. So too, he contacted Christopher Springville, another splendid, somewhat ageing local Hardyesque figure who knew every nook and cranny of the surrounding countryside, its walks, its wildlife and its flora. Here again he saw a market for popularizing local walks of interest; these could provide useful travel articles and could develop into a little series certainly in preparation for the spring and summer months. Finally he thought he would do some independent literary research into writers who had lived in the area by way of complementing the historical items from Andrew Pollard. To this end, he wrote to his old University requesting use, should the need arise, of the University library facility where he knew he would be able to obtain copies of all that had been published up until quite recently at least.

Whilst engaged on these topics he first wrote and then phoned The Portsmouth Evening News at his old offices and arranged for an interview with Kevin Conker, the local features editor, to go through his plans. Going back to his old workplace, although he had hardly been absent for very long, was something of a traumatic experience but he handled it well and was well received. Kevin thought his ideas had promise and therefore engaged him intially for a brief series of local history articles to run on a weekly basis for six weeks in the first instance in Thursday editions whilst at the same time asking him to complete at least three trial pieces on the local walks idea so that these could be assessed by appropriate editors who dealt with travel, holidays and tourism to see if they could be used and developed. He admitted he had nothing to offer as yet from only the most cursory of searches on local writers but would hopefully be able to get back to the publication on that matter. Details of payments and contracts were to be worked out before the first publication and, of course, with regard to the history articles some remuneration would have to be given to the original author, Andrew Pollard. John was buoyant at these new prospects and was sure that financially things could be arranged to everyone's satisfaction. It seemed that he had served his time in purgatory and that although this was not anything like full-time employment, it was an opportunity to use and extend his journalistic talents as he had wanted.

Optimistic at the turn of events he contacted Helen and enthused to her over the phone about his success. Anticipating further success from his now imminent London trip he indicated that he would come down again at the end of the fortnight and they would duly celebrate. He felt he was now laying the foundations of his new, successful future and was keen to pursue it.

Heady with his recent efforts and excited with anticipation of the forthcoming day's events, he arose early on the Friday morning keen to get an early train to the capital even if it meant arriving early and having to wander around until the time he was expected. As he finished his coffee, he heard the dull thud of the flap of his letter box as the postman delivered the mail. He decided to see what had arrived before setting off. There was a lovely, art-designed card from Helen sent with her love and congratulating him on his new found success. She always knew how to make him feel wanted and how to boost his confidence. It was so sweet of her! There was the electricity bill and here, with the Coleridge College crests on the envelope and a Cambridge postmark was the Annual Report from his college. He opened it and discarded the envelope glancing briefly through the contents noticing the odd entry about former students making it to Lord Mayor of London and a couple of passing obituaries on High Court judges and Nobel Science prize winners in a very hurried manner now knowing time was getting on and he should be getting on his way. The usual content, he mused. Still, a good publication should always clearly consider its audience and in that respect this magazine should be no exception. He thought initially of taking it with him as some something exciting to read on the train! However, he felt that it would best be left until he returned for such reading was ideally suited to having a laugh and a reminiscence before bedtime. Anyway, he always bought a broadsheet newspaper to read on train journeys which were for him most infrequent and he was not about to alter the habits of a life time! He therefore left it on the table, its dull burgundy cover melding in with the matt rosewood surface on which it was placed.

And so he headed off to the station to catch, along with other commuters, the 8.15 train to London which would get him there comfortably by 10.00a.m. and allow him time to cross the capital to the offices of Churcher's Agency. He boarded the train and was lucky enough to get a seat, this being towards the end of the commuter period and therefore the workers being a smaller group who could afford to start work at 10.00a.m. and did not have to be in a 9.00a.m. or earlier. Quite a pleasant class of commuter with whom to journey. John, having purchased *The Times* was avidly reading it as the train pressed on towards Waterloo, its London destination. As he read he decided he might even have time to have a bash at the crossword. Even if he could not do this on the way up, then it would be worth keeping the paper to have a go on the return journey though he wondered if his lunchtime imbibing might not make him very fit for such an exercise then.

Had he more avidly read his college's Annual Report before disgarding it and leaving it at home in favour of this daily press he would have found a stop press obituary to a close, former collegiate friend of his. Free-lance journalist Trevor Whilde, aged only 37, had been found dead at his Dublin home only a matter of a few days before the publication went to press and was issued; a full and appropriate obituary would appear in next year's edition.

CHAPTER 11

In London

"*I have heard that something very shocking indeed
will soon come out in London.*"
(Jane Austen: Northanger Abbey).

John detested London. He had not been a frequent visitor to the capital recently as he was in his younger and undergraduate days but whenever he approached the city and intense loathing grew upon him and filled him with disgust. Whatever he was heading to do in the city was not the problem; the international rugby at Twickenham, the Test Matches at the Oval and Lords, the plays at the National and the Barbican, the concerts at the Albert Hall and the Royal Festival Hall, the musicals in theatreland, the Tate and the National Galleries, the Tower and The Houses of Parliament or just the lunch or dinner invites such as he now headed for were pleasant in themselves and to be enjoyed. But they were escapism. They blanked out for the time of their duration the awfulness of their environment.

It was this awful environment that was now starting to impinge on John and make him feel uneasy as the train covered the last few, slow, laborious miles as it decelerated on its journey to Waterloo. As he looked out of the carriage windows first he saw the decaying, early century brick terraced rows of houses with the odd shored up public house and run down shop interspersed amongst them. The seediness of each of these areas seemed insidious to him and must, he felt, have a damning effect on the poor inhabitants. These building slowly gave way to the blocks of flats built in the late fifties and early sixties. Tall, erect, grey buildings, slotted with windows which peered out to give a panoramic view of windows in similar tall, erect, grey buildings. There were patches of grass between some of these towers which only estate agents would dare to call lawns and which only the colour blind would call green. Then there was the occasional shock of colour of a cramped, tarmaced play area populated by small groups of children with their parents helping them on the swings or the slide but above all ensuring they did not stray from the demesne, a cautious precaution for so much of the area looked the same it was a wonder even adults recognised their own homes let alone their small children. Stuck in the middle of such hives of habitation were the large, elasticated buildings of the new pubs, stretched long and low as a contrast to their surroundings and with defiant neon lights emblazoning their names in the vicinity. And also the small, compact, breeze-block battleship-grey shops which sold little more than cheap trash, unlabelled groceries and tabloid newspapers.

These ugly sights were cordoned off from the trains by yards of rail-track, fencing and occasional brickwork. Everything on or adjacent to the railway seemed tainted with darkness. Bricks that had been red had aged to a flakey matt blackness, fences which may have been fawn or sienna from creosote were now decidedly swarthy, grass and weeds were peppered with charcoal and all of these therefore complemented the inky cinders between the tracks themselves. The sleepers supporting the rails on which trains ran were like sagging, fat, ancient cigars and the rails themselves apart from having one last vestige of a gleaming, silvery strip across the top from the constant friction of the historical trains and carriages which crossed over them were rusted on the sides to the the colour of faeces.

Now as the train neared the heart of the city itself so stations flickered in front of the windows and large office blocks in cascades of glass thrust themselves towards the skies as if they were desperately searching for a way out of this human, malformed jungle in which they had been set. The livid, tinted glass reflected similar neighbouring monstrosities and nothing of what was going on behind

195

these eye-like fronts could be discerned in any way. Everything closed, everything sheltered, everything hidden, probably because what it would expose about the humans who inhabited such an environment would be worse than the environment itself.

And then a small oasis of air and light as the train crossed the bridge into Waterloo station itself. But this blackened strip of iron shooting across a grey, sluggish river which seemed to carry more assortments of litter than river traffic was hardly out of character of all that had preceded it. And so the train nosed into the station beside the platform for the disembarkation of the passengers.

Alighting on to the large, slabbed paving of the platform the lights, all on, made daylight, which was just about filtering through the grimed dome of the building, brighter and this made John blink as he walked towards the exit where stood a guard. The uniformed official was a gesture only: passengers flashed tickets before him which he could not possibly discern and certainly made no attempt to. It was as if, thought John, anyone mad enough to have traveled to this hell-hole of humanity for a day or longer, could not possibly be denied. The old joke to the traveler—"Thou disna want tae go tae London; thou has tae!"

Once through the small arch which sectioned off this platform, John ambled out onto the open concourse of the station itself. It was like a cathedral which had been de-consecrated first by being sanitised by fake marble flooring and then cast in the mould of a public convenience with coloured tiling on almost any surface which would bear such defacing. The small stalls selling newspapers, trashy novels, expensive sweets, fruits, drinks and sandwiches were like the money makers in the temple who were driven out by Jesus. They would not be driven out here. This was a monument to late twentieth century capitalism. Exploit every area of space going to customers who would be so hungry from interminable waits that they would be driven to purchase whatever was available at whatever exhorbitant prices. Only the very top of the building lay left unchanged though the red sandstone of which it was built had been cleaned up to accompany the cosmeticised effect of the whole. In the bars piped music played, on the platforms undiscerable announcements were made over rasping tannoys and the arrivals and departure boards clicked over providing a solid ground bass for the overall cacophony.

John headed to his left following the signs marked *London Underground*. Then going out from the mixture of natural and synthetic lighting he headed down white, neoned tunnels adorned with all manner of adverts. Then on further, down windy, winding, dirty, aluminium escalators fatigued with the weight of passengers, following signs marked Northern Line, the black strip on the liquorice allsorts map of the lines that were carved out under this metropolis. And at last out onto a draughty platform with black, gaping mouths at either end and a thronging thread of people along its edge awaiting the arrival of the next train.

John remembered, quite appropriately he observed, a long forgotten crossword clue. *On the Paris Underground a dwarf we hear finds time for music.* Metronome. The Reverend Fergusson would have liked that one. Here in these man made burrows under the earth, people became gnomes. As he waited along with others for the next tube train he observed how they all seemed cowed and hunched. Then, when the train arrived and they had got on and those who were lucky enough to get seats found them, so they sat hunched and cowed behind papers or carrying cases or books or children even! Sitting or standing like plastic gnomes in a garden, they were silent, patient figures just letting life pass them by as they were transported to a destination. They could just as easily have carried fishing rods as anything else! Those who stood stared into nether space, holding on to one of the hand rails above or at the side of them to give them some sense of stability in this grimed and dusty carriage which bore them forward. Despite the closeness of contact between individuals in such conditions few spoke or even acknowledged the presence of others unless they were in family or friendly groups before having embarked. Occasionally the train would slow and stop in the tunnel and through the windows almost opaque because of the dirt layered on to them John could see in the barely one candlepower light the coils of cables like black serpents snaking their way along the cavernous, tomb-like, dark bricked arched walls which the trains passed through. Then the gush and rush the stations, ablaze with light and again large, panoramic adverts many of which were out of keeping with the surroundings. Each stop was accompanied by the sucking, sliding sounds of the doors opening and closing and the compressed air being expelled, the departure and influx of passengers and then on again. A never ending journey like Charon's to and fro across the River Styx.

John had to change at Tottenham Court Road and cross over to the Circle Line heading east to get to Chancery Lane from where he had been told to walk to his destination in John Street. Here again he followed a labyrinth of white lit corridors and multi-coloured posters interrupted by musicians busking for money at regular intervals. The raucous quality of the sounds from flautists, violinists, guitarists, accordionists, singers, echoed round these tiled, arched warrens and were certainly appropriate to such a Stygian underworld. And so on to the stop at Chancery Lane where, after a journey up a decaying, wooden slatted escalator, (slatted with as much dirt and filth as strips of wood!), the likes of which John thought had all disappeared, he pushed his ticket through the automatic machine, reclaimed it at the other side as it spat itself out, and went up a set of concrete steps into the London air.

The only good thing that could be said about where he was now was that it was on the surface of the earth and not a few hundred feet or more below it! Large, nineteenth century buildings formed wall like barriers down the sides of the heavily traffic streets. The car, bus and lorry fumes circulating invisibly in the air had certainly had a more discernible, deleterious effect on the buildings themselves; their stone and brickwork looked like charcoal smeared sketches as if the rain and the wind had mixed with a black pollutant and wiped itself indiscriminately over their surfaces. Obviously quite grand residences in times past, they were now converted into offices on all floors from one upwards and ground level had been transformed into reception areas for the offices themselves, or wine bars, sandwich bars, confectionery or newspaper shops. There was the occasional London pub left over from a the turn of the century but these were often tatty and run down and the wood and brickword surrounding their windows and doors looked as if they had been constantly gnawed by rats.

John turned down Theobalds Road soaking in all this cosmeticised dereliction and decay as he did so. We all get used to our own dirt, he thought and smiled thinking that was possibly an orginal idea though it might well have leanings towards the writing of Beckett. He, however, could never get used to this aspect of London. An aspect made worse in recent years by the addition of beggars onto the streets of the capital. It had always had its winos, its meths drinkers, its derelicts but now it had an invasion of cardboard city dwellers, dole wallahs, new age travellers or whatever whom John found occasionally frightening and certainly menacing. He remembered years ago when his parents had taken him as a young child to France how he had seen a few beggars on the streets of Bordeaux. He had been intrigued by such a sight and his parents had quietly explained the situation to him outlining in simple terms the welfare state that prevented such sights in the country of his birth and upbringing. Joining the EEC seemed to have brought this unwanted factor over from the continent, he mused, though he knew in reality that it was not the U.K. despite or perhaps in spite of its social set up that had created a situation here that would hardly be rivaled in the main countries of Europe but which might still be equaled in cities in Portugal or Greece or the very south of Italy.

From Theobalds Road then second right into John Street. John had remembered the directions well and certainly this was a little quieter than the turmoil of Grays Inn Road and the Theobalds Road he had just left. But the buildings were similar if a little more respectable. Long terraces of nineteenth century housing with half a dozen steps leading up to the main entrance and which arched over large basements. Again, the majority of these buildings were now offices, quite elegant ones, in fact, and the front doors with their drawbridge of steps and metal balustrades gave quite a nineteenth century feel to the street. The road stretched out into the distance quite straight with the high, three storey terrace buildings on either side. About 400 yards further down, after a crossroads, John noticed some trees lining the avenue and emphasizing this part of London had, and still kept to a certain extent, a quiet, more serene aspect than the mainstream areas of the city. There was only one pub which John passed on the right hand side as he sauntered towards to offices of Churcher's Care Incorporated Agency. The Slug and Lettuce as it was called had a somewhat nonedescript brown façade with mullioned windows and seemed quite large and respectable and in keeping with the quieter, calmer atmosphere of what once might have been regarded as a suburb of the city.

Two hundred yards beyond this was number 21, the object of his journey. John went up the steps and glanced at his watch as he did so. It was just gone midday, a trifle early perhaps but he hoped that would not matter. The door before him was painted in a conservative blue gloss and to the right of it on a large brass plaque was engraved *Churcher's Care Incorporated Agency* and a large symbol, the company logo, of a pair of cupped hands. There was an intercom system for admission, a necessary precaution for security in nearly every building in London. John pressed the button and a voice crackled, "Yes?"

"John Ellis to see Ken Churcher," said John quite boldly into the microphone.

"Just push," crackled the voice back as a long, drawn-out buzzing sound was to be heard emanating as if from the door itself.

John pushed and the heavy door eased open. As he entered it swung back and clicked to lock itself as it closed. There was first a small entrance foyer with a glass paneled door in front of him painted in a shade of fawny cream with a shining brass handle. He pushed this open and came to a narrow corridor to the right of which was a flight of stairs carpeted in a dull grey, rather threadbare carpet. To his left was another fawny cream door probably leading into an office and down the narrow corridor was located the reception area in a room which would no doubt have been a pantry in the original house. He walked towards it and greeted the long, dark-haired receptionist seated behind a conventional office desk topped with word-processor and telephone. It was indeed a very small office space, hardly enough room to swing a cat would have been a highly applicable phrase to describe it.

"Mr Ellis? Do take a seat. Dr Churcher has been informed that you are here."

John saw that to the front and right of her desk were squeezed two small, low armchairs so he thanked her and sat down. She got up from behind the desk and asked him if he wished for a drink. He now noticed that directly opposite, again squeezed into the only available space was a drinks dispensing machine which she was now about to use at his request.

"Coffee, thanks. No sugar," he replied as he looked around trying to take things in.

She gave him the coffee and then pointed to a small paper rack containing some magazines and two of the day's broadsheet publications indicating he may wish to read whilst waiting. He smiled but showed her that he had already devoured *The Times* on the way up so he was quite content to drink the coffee and relax.

Over the next twelve to fifteen minutes as he waited there was a small stream of people let in and out by the lady on reception. They came to the desk, signed a paper and then were given a large, blue, Barclays Bank cheque and departed. Perhaps because they were in London in the borough of Camden, a large number of these were Afro-Carribean, some wearing the distinctive dreadlocks and orange, green and yellow colours John associated with Rastafarians. Others were white Caucasians, and there were also a few Asians who were dressed in the distinctive, colourful silks of their native attire but all seemed to John as if they were refugees from the dole queue, something with which he was unpleasantly familiar. The place almost smacked of a dole office in that there was signing on the some benefit being handed out. The receptionist seemed to recognise most of them and on occasions had time to have a little chat with them which they seemed to enjoy.

As he finished his coffee and speculated on what was happening before his eyes a tall, smartly dressed gentleman approached, held out his hand and greeted him.

"John Ellis! Ken Churcher. Good to see you. You come most carefully upon your hour!'"

John rose and grasped his hand. It was a firm, meaningful handshake and immediately put him at ease. Here was someone he would get on with and could relate to.

"Now then," said his host, "we've got time for a quick look round the old business before heading off to eat. I doubt if you know what happens in Agency work so it'll be a good insight for you. something you might be able to use in the journalistic career of yours. No doubt the sights you've see already are a bit mystifying, eh? Well then, let's go."

Together they exited along the corridor and almost immediately came to a door on the right which opened up to a set of winding stairs leading to the basement. As they went down this flight of steps, their was the unmistakably soft, purring drone of computers and, sure enough, the basement had been transformed into an array of machines operated by ladies each peering intently at flashing, green V D Us and pressing grey keyboards and printers churning out masses of the blue cheques and other assorted items on appropriate computer paper.

"Time sheets entered, cheques printed out for payment," commented Ken Churcher with the parsimonious phrasing and articulation of Trevor Bailey on Radio 5's *Test Match Special*.

Seeing his guest slightly mystified he added more expansively," 'The great Unwashed', very few of whom you've seen upstairs whilst waiting, work for us; care work in council homes mainly though some aspire to private work and even social care and counseling. They complete a time sheet for hours done weekly; we process it and they collect their cheques to cash at the Barclays Branch down the road on Fridays. Special arrangement. And before you ask about bank accounts, BACS, income tax and all that just ask yourself if the type of human flotsam and jetsom such as you've just cast eyes on would even have a bank account or want to have one!"

As they turned to head back up the stairs, Ken took a more confidential, intimate tone with John. "It's partly a cover, of course. The type that works for us needs keeping tabs on, you understand. ' . . . lean and hungry look. Such men are dangerous . . . .' and all that! Oh, most of them are harmless enough and highly suited to their work but there are others who will be the first to lead anti Poll Tax riots, anti Criminal Justice Bill marches etc. Having them on our books gives us some records on them and is always useful."

They marched on up the stairs this time heading to the very top of the building. "They're all so unintelligent, of course, that they don't realise that we've probably got more information on them than would be held on computer were they to have a bank account or whatever. Most of them don't even see the subtlety, if it can be called that, of the company's name: Churcher's C I A! The Whitehall boys aren't too keen on the American implications, of course, but that's their problem. We've been going quite a few years now and have been known to have provided the right sort of information to those who are in need of it."

By this time they had reached the highest floor of the building, beyond the third storey into a self-contained flat perched on the top just like a small penthouse.

"We'll here we are," said Ken, opening out his arms in a gesture of spreading largesse. "'Earth hath not anything to show more fair!' It's quite a nice view of the tops of the dwellings in this area and the place which I had added on when I first invested in this building is quite a sun-trap, isn't it? I lived here initially as I built up the firm but now I let staff use it, by arrangement of course. Some of the girls come up here to sun themselves in summer! It's been more than useful for a few of them to bed down during train and tube strikes during the years though it's a bit cramped when more than two get in it."

John surveyed the scene across the London roof tops. A sea of aeriels like Giacommeti figures thinly etched across the sky, defunct brickworked chimneys topped by sooty, cracked cowls, sky dishes like silvered Grecian shields, miscellaneous, tangled cables and wiring all set against a sea of ebony tarmac with the occasional island of a gabled garret's triangular spearhead thrusting above the oil-slicked calmness. It certainly was a view of London he had not seen before. Having taken in his fill they headed back down with yet another quote starting off the monologue from Ken and John reflected that Trevor's comments on this aspects of his character and others were well founded.

"'Nay, we'll go together down sir.'" They went down to the floor below, the true, original top of the building and poked their heads inside an office. There were rows of ladies behind desks with the usual computers and telephones and most of them here were actively engaged in using the latter. "Most of the rest of the building's like this," remarked Ken. "These are the girls who get the contracts and assign the workers. It's a predominantly female world. Only three men, not including me I might add, out of a work force of thirty seven. No one can say we're a sexist organisation, at least not in the way that term is usually bandied about. Right, now, you've see all there really is to see of us 'warts and all' so let's just pick up a few things from my office and head off to enjoy some Epicurean delights! And, to sort out the main business that brings you here."

They continued down to the first floor and entered his office. This part was preserved something like the original must have been. There was a fine Victorian marble fireplace, high windows arched by a deep pelmet and with long flowing, deep crimson curtains trailing down to the floor. The stuccoed ceiling had a small chandelier in the centre and there were two, expensive, leather arm chairs either side of the fireplace. Another period chair was set behind Ken's large, inset leather-topped desk. The only definite twentieth century accourtrements present were as tasteful, wooden four-drawer high filing cabinet and a computer and two telephones. The room was bounded at one end by a set of sliding doors, gently curved and finely paneled that led through to a large room which fronted the building and in which was set a large oblong rosewood table and chairs. Again this had a similar high window and the room was decorated in a complementary fashion to Ken's office.

"Inner sanctum, here, John. My office, of course, and what I call the board-room next door. Main meetings go on there. Preserved a bit of class here. In the rest 'the old order changeth, yielding place to new' but here I've kept the standards of the original to a certain extent. Certainly a pleasant working situation. Couldn't really stand all that formica-type furniture the rest of them put up with."

Ken unlocked a drawer in his desk, reached in and grabbed a cheque book and multifarious plastic cards in a small wallet. He stuffed these into his inside right pocket of his suit jacket, relocked the door, stuffed the key into this trouser pocket and then smiled at John and muttering the Italian, "Andiamo," he beckoned John to follow him to have lunch.

"Not coming back here after lunch," he added and just before they exited the building he popped along the corridor and left this same message with the young lady on reception.

They crossed the road and just before they turned down a narrow side street Ken reminded John that just down the road from where they were was Doughty Street, the London home of Charles Dickens. John was only sorry he had not had time to visit this place, owning that to be honest he had not known of it, but his host remarked that the place kept odd hours of opening anyway and he wasn't even sure whether it was in fact open to the public at this time of the year with Autumn now diminuendoing into winter. They passed a few small but crowded pubs and a few wine bars equally crowded as well, crossed a small pedestrianised square with one solitary, silver, stark birch tree set in its middle and at the end of one of the four streets which led off it and down which they journeyed they came to a restaurant, *Brasserie du Coin*.

"Not an original title, bit like my company's," remarked Ken as he led John inside, "but the food here is good and the wine most excellent! Moreover, I run an account here and it's a bit like those 'varsity days when I stuck things on the old buttery bill and then was both amazed and choked then I couldn't afford to settle what was due at the end of the term! Slight difference now, though, as I wangle most of this against tax! So, with due licence of my hyperbolic quote, 'Let us drink til we roll on the tables in vomit and oblivion!'"

It was clear he was well-known here and frequented the place for the waiters showed due, but discrete, familiarity and had no problems in ensuring he was ushered to a table, menus and wine-lists being hastily rushed across almost simultaneously with their being seated. John was studying both but was prompted into acquiescing with Ken's order on behalf of them both which involved a pate starter, followed by beouf bourginon with quantities as desired of an Australian Shiraz to wash it all down. It was a heavier lunch than John would normally have had but he was in no mood to argue and he knew that once they got started on the eating they would also get started on the talking and he would get at the heart at what he was here for.

And, sure enough, the meal underway, the conversation became much more serious. Ken was forthright enough to be a little more explicit about this role and John found this in itself all quite fascinating.

".... they even had the gall to visit a mere acquaintance of mine that I'd mentioned to them in passing as a fellow student when they went about checking up on me during the recruiting process at Oxford," he recounted, referring to the secret service side of the civil service cum government for whom he had worked in this company manager's role for more years than he cared to remember. "Sounds all cloak and dagger, doesn't it?" he asked but then appended, "But people forget that down the centuries the seemingly most innocuous of persons have had fingers in the spying keyhole, so to speak. Marlowe, of course, years back but also more recently people like Greville Wynne and Anthony

Blunt of course. There's a lot of us around, mainly making contacts sometimes by accident as happens frequently in my line of business, sometimes by design and reporting back to some rung above us on the ladder. Now it seems you have come into this system, definitely by accident, if what I hear is correct?"

John was not sure he had "come into this system" as Ken had stated, nor was he sure he wanted to, but he acquiesced and then went on to give the briefest of outlines as to how he had stumbled across a character he assumed was one, Patrick Field, but being sufficiently vague as to show uncertainty about his own knowledge and blessed with sufficient personal acumen to realise that his host would only be getting from him a confirmation of what he already knew and, no doubt, could embellish even himself.

Satisfied with what he was hearing, Ken then went on to hint to John about the nature of what he was getting himself into.

"Yes. It seems even our I.R.A. cousins want to know more about the whereabouts of this Mr Field. They have not explained to me why and they are probably a bit suspicious in getting information from me thinking it might be a bit of second-hand, deliberately misleading packaging. However, I have indicated, without being specific, the nature of my source and, it seems, the said gentlemen would like to meet you in connection with it all. Now, this meeting we are having today is for me to be sure of you, which, I must say I am. Then I must get back to them for them to advise me to advise you of what arrangements they wish to make with regard to a meeting, which I assume you want to go ahead, do you not?" At this point he quaffed empty his fifth glass of the Shiraz, poured himself another, and, clearly thinking over what he had just said, commented, "You know, when put like that it always sounds so Goon-showism, doesn't it? Very much my era that comedy programme, you know but a little before your time. No doubt you're *Monty Python* bred and born but they derived a lot of what they had to offer from the zany comedy of Sellars, Milligan, Secombe et all, I can tell you. There was an episode in one of their shows I recall that had a seemingly never ending sequence of lines with characters giving asides commencing, 'Little does he know that the little I know that he knows . . . .'etc. You know the sort of thing—what we've just engaged in! Ah, 'nature is creeping up,' as the artist so rightly said," and he started to drink from his sixth glass.

"I certainly would like to meet them," enthused John, "if only to clear up the matter. I assume you would not advise me to meet were it to be dangerous and, of course, I'd be happy to report back to you as the rung up the ladder from me, so to speak."

"On no, not dangerous, at least not in the fatalities stakes that is, my dear fellow," waxed Ken. "But it would be a good idea were you to report back. You've got to try to get some information out of them for the information they want from you. At least that's what I'd like you to do, though do tread carefully. Whoever you do meet, and I have no idea of who it will be, must be handled with care. You are an amateur going into a pretty professional business, though I am impressed by the way you have handled yourself in this business so far. Mind you I have never known Trevor to sell me a bum steer." Seeing John's eyes register the full meaning of this brief statement, Ken added in confirmation, "Oh, yes. Trevor was recruited as well. He does his job perfectly. He's got the ideal cover and, his background, being Irish and all that, was and is naturally, exceptionally useful."

John smiled. Perhaps it was the wine. He could not possibly keep pace with his host but, all the same, he was well into his fourth. But he preferred to consider this smile as one that gave him the status of being allowed into a new society or sect. Nothing exceptional that is but like a married man who after many years of being faithful commits the act of adultery and, having done so, knows that he shares a secret with himself and the lady whom he has comprimised and has joined a new world but is not in any position to boast about it, much as he would like to.

It was therefore the smile of knowledge, the polite grin of satisfaction and personal recognition and John liked what he felt.

By this time they had finished their meal but a bottle of Shiraz at least two-thirds full was still left. John agreed to one final glass of this whilst his host was happy to finish off the rest but, though pressed, John declined a sweet though suggested he would like a coffee. Ken, who had decided on a sweet for himself to soak up the wine he was still to drink, insisted that with this John must have a brandy for he did not wish to be seen drinking alone even though it was at the end of the meal. John acquiesced yet again but it was an easier acquiescence than at the start since he was now approaching that mellow stage that comes with drinking alcohol before the onset of tiredness.

Over the fag-end of what had been a most pleasant lunch, Ken indicated to John that he would contact him very shortly after following things through and would give him all the details of what he was to do and where he was to go next and any final tips that he may need before the meeting which would hopefully resolve all things. John was quite excited and would dearly have loved to carry through things there and then, the alcohol giving him a will and desire which made him get the time and place of events slightly out of perspective.

After the meal Ken walked with John back in the direction of the offices and then set him on his way reminding him of how to get to Chancery Lane from where they were. They shook hands and with a variety of prolonged and less than sober farewells which were accompanied by reminders of keeping in touch together with expressions of thanks emanating from John, they parted in opposite directions: John to get the train before the rush hour home and Ken to report back to those on the rungs of the ladder immediately above him before going off for a pre-arranged golfing weekend with friends in Essex.

As John headed back through the streets of London and on the underground to Waterloo, the harshness of the city had receded as he viewed it now, through the rose-tinted spectacles of inebriation. Everything seemed more pleasant to him even though the cinereous gloom of the late Autumnal evening was creeping in and in some areas the street lighting, obviously with timing slightly askew, was switching itself on causing penumbras in places and thus making everything much more shadier than it had been when he had first arrived. But the fall of evening and dark hides things too and the seedier, less salubrious, squalid aspects of the city which John had felt so intensley in his soul in the early part of the day were now being camouflaged as the time and its hues blended with the place. Despite the bright lighting in the underground and on the main line station, there was now no daylight to boost its power and so it was more akin to the directed illumination on a stage or within a house and that left corners, niches, cavities and recesses impenitratively dark.

John was able to catch the 4.20 train which was a slow one, stopping at many stations before the halt at Portmisnter where he would alight. After boarding the train he felt for his newspaper and realised initially to his chagrin that he had left it somewhere in the building in John Street. Or had he had it on him when they left the building and went to the brasserie? His mind was too fuddled, too addled to work it out and once the train was underway he fell into intoxicated unconsciousness so the issue became totally unimportant anyway. He was therefore robbed of bidding farewell to the ugly, unpleasant, urban pageant which had so disturbed him on entry that very morning.

He came to rather than woke up as the train was winding its way south through the rural landscape of north-east Hampshire. The light in the sky had faded fast. It was about 5.30 p.m. and they were within thirty minutes or thereabouts from stopping at Portminster. Through the grey windows of the dimly-lit carriage John saw the sky-grey-cobalt tinged verdure of the countryside dotted with huddled cows and sparse spinneys with trees lade bare of their foliage for the onset of winter. It was not an endearing sight but it was a natural one. 'If winter comes, can Spring be far behind?' he mused. Even in an unforgiving, bleak landscape such as this there was hope. He recalled the man made landscape of the morning and shuddered as he started to recollect the day, its happenings and its implications. The sleep had not made him any less tired being as it was induced rather than natural. He struggled to shake off his tiredness and prepared for the deceleration of the train into his station.

By the time the train pulled in it was a little after six o'clock although it had been due in earlier. For what had seemed an interminable time it had loitered outside Portsminster awaiting a change of signal which had eventually come and ushered it into the station. John alighted and, having given up his ticket to a seemingly sonnambulant collector at the exit, headed off on the walk home, about one and a half miles from where he now was. The darkness of night was now fully roundabout and the street lighting arced orange beams onto the pavements. There were few people about this being the time when most are either getting ready to go out for the evening or deciding not to and turning to *The Radio Times or T V Weekly* to enlighten them as to what entertainment lay in store for them if they were to stay at home. John decided he would spend some time at his local and then go home for a relatively early night. He therefore turned into *The Fort St George* when he got there and got stuck in to a few pints of Winter's Special Brew. He chatted to Iris, the barmaid, and her husband, George, with whom he was familiar and recounted vaguely his day in London which had so fatigued him. He did not feel hungry enough to have another meal but he rather foolishly indulged in crisps and nuts to soak up this evening's alcohol intake and eventually felt not exactly queezy but certainly quite bloated.

At about 8.30p.m. he took himself off home and meandered around the house getting changed, making an evening cup of coffee and settling on something to read to take to bed to act as the final sleeping tablet to go with the alcohol to get him off to sleep. Nothing could be better he thought than the college annual report which he had received that very morning and which he had forgotten all about.

Now in bed, the table lamp his only light, the cup of steaming coffee placed on the bedside table beside the lamp, he propped himself up a little wearily on his pillows, opened the book and started to flick through reading whatever took his attention. He smiled as his eyes caught sight of publications by college luminaries such as *The Contemporary Crisis of Culture, Leibnitz's*

Monads: A Dualistic view of Reality, Truth, Virtue and the Meaning of Beauty in the Operas of Gluck and other such crucial contributions to world literature. There were the usual reviews of the college year, its sporting and artistic achievements, the usual list of the eminence of former college members who were now careerists in the most important of ways and then finally the obituaries. The first one of these, quite long and interestingly written was sadly for Peter McAllen, the college chaplain throughout John's undergraduate days. Though in no sense a practising Christian himself he had known Peter quite well since he was strongly associated with rugby and squash at the college and was certainly a member of the good drinkers league! Peter had a generous allowance and was well known for his love of port which he distributed freely to parishioner and non-parishioner alike despite admonitions from the senior college staff in relation to his expenses. Interestingly enough, this love of the good life was mentioned within the obituary and John was pleased to think it had not been overlooked. Another lesser collegian, John noticed had received the dubious honour of being described as 'managing to maintain a reasonable academic standard' whilst at the college. Damning with faint praise if ever there was thought John as his eyes began to feel heavy and he knew he was heading into the arms of Morpheus. And what a thing to write in someone's obituary!

John stretched out and took a last swig of coffee and replaced the mug on the table. He flicked through some other pages and started to read about some octogenerian who had recently passed away and finding it tedious and knowing that if he was now not careful he would fall asleep with the light on he went to put the book onto the table and as he did so it slipped onto the floor and opened itself up two pages further on. He leant over the side of the bed now really quite drowsy and picked it up his eyes catching sight of Trevor Whilde's name as he did so. At first intrigued he lifted it up, sat up again in bed and made once last effort to concentrate.

What he read shook him to the core. Sluggishness, sleepiness, seemed to fly away almost immediately. He dropped the book and swept it over the side of the bed as if brushing aside an unwanted insect or piece of dirt. His eyes stared wide, no longer heavy. He was terrified. Fear kept him in a state of readiness and alertness all through that night. He was certain that even had he had to take a breathalyzer test at that moment he would have passed despite the drink he had taken into his body during the course of the day and the evening. His thoughts were clear and as the long night passed and another grey dawn surfaced on planet earth he was well aware he was in Ken Chrucher's words and amateur who had already, by accident and not by design, entered a profession. But there was no way out now. Alia Iacta Est.

Sleep eventually came to him but only later on the next morning when sheer fatigue was no longer hostage to the previous night's alarm.

Chapter 12

In The South

> "*I have seen them at close of day*
> *Coming with vivid faces*
> *From counter or desk among grey*
> *Eighteenth century houses.*"
> (*W B Yeats: Easter 1916*)

John woke up just before one o'clock. He felt as if he had not slept at all not so much by way of weariness but by his general feeling of nausea. He had a headache, something which he rarely suffered from and decided to take some disprins for it. He got out of bed and his foot trod on the open copy of the college *Annual Report*. The reminder of it gave him the impression he had stood in dog dirt and this made him feel even more queezy. He went downstairs, searched around for the disprins through numerous cupboards before discovering their whereabouts and then got a glass, poured in about ¼ pint of water straight from the tap and popped in three tablets. They fizzed, spurted and spun on the surface of the liquid like a speck of sodium thrown in a tank of water.

He pulled open a drawer, withdrew a teaspoon and stirred the mixture to a flaky whiteness and then gulped it down. It was like drinking a suspension of chalk and water for the undissolved particles stuck on his tongue and were not washed down with the rest that had dissolved. He quickly poured himself another quick swill of water and drank this to wash away this sediment.

Slowly he ambled back upstairs. He was in a quandary. He wanted to contact at least one of Trevor's relatives to offer his condolences even at this rather late stage after the event but he did not know any and trying to trace them other than by writing to the address he had for Trevor would be an impossible task. No doubt, *The Times*, the paper to which Trevor had most contributed would have printed a brief obituary of sorts or at least mentioned something in the Births, Marriages, Deaths column of the newspaper but he would have to search through a few editions to check that. And, moreover, he thought, given his recent problems with such research and the events that he had been associated with, perhaps even triggered off recently, there could be no guarantee that it would be reported in any way, shape or form. He was now only too aware that his involvement must be known about and it was only a matter of time until all was revealed to him and his usefulness may be dispensed with. Strangely enough, the manner that dispensation might take was not at the heart of his worries. What was there was the fact that something might happen to him and he would never know what he had stirred up or been involved in. He recalled the comic epitaph for a virgin, "Returned Unopened", and felt with regard to this mysterious character, Patrick Field, and his internment, he did not want such a vacuity about his own knowledge inscribed on his tomb or urn or whatever! It was strange, he reflected, that it was merely his involvement by asking questions that had brought him to this pass : he had gained no answers so why should he feel at risk? Why, indeed, should he even be at risk?

There was, he concluded, no point in contacting Ken Churcher. There was absolutely no doubt in his mind that he would know by now about Trevor's decease though it had seemed when he had talked to him only yesterday that he had no knowledge thereof. John tried hard to recall details of the conversation with Ken on matters relating to Trevor but what he remembered was far too indistinct and too vague to be conclusive about whether he had any insider knowledge or not. The drink had been a good deadener on that score and probably on others. Anyway, the serpent was more subtle than any beast of the field, and Ken Churcher certainly could be identified with such a creature. John had no illusions about that man and his role. He was probably stitching up someone—maybe himself—or something even as he was having these thoughts about him!

John looked at the time. He realised half the day was gone and still suffering from a headache and still not feeling quite himself he accepted that he might as well waste the rest of the day as well in idleness. So he got dressed and meandered around the house passing the time until evening in a manner akin to an animal grazing. He had nibbles of food, just sufficient for nourishment, spent sometime on his computer, sometime reading the local paper (which he now had delivered and which usually arrived within 15 minutes of school closing being pushed through a letterbox by some schoolgirl or schoolboy who was more willingly involved in such a task than in any commitment to education!), sometime in general reading connected with the tasks he had taken on in relation to free-lance journalism and sometime in watching the moving pictures on the T V screen without really taken in what he was watching.

At 7.30ish he decided he would wander down to the local for a few pints and for something more substantial to eat. He was, anyway, in the need of company and he felt that a suitable intake of alcohol would ensure he slept that night and get back to some semblance of routine the following day. If John had any hobby it was pub going and, in particular, this pub going. The atmosphere in *The Fort* was generally most congenial and it preserved a touch of rural ambience of the origins of what was now among the most non-descript of towns. Inside, the cosiness of the bar, (snug was such a good word now out of fashion and used to describe such a place) was marinated with the flavours of smoke from cigarettes, pipes and cigars of all shapes and sizes, the aromas of beers, spirits and wines and the horseradishy savour of the many of the clientelle. The gloom of the lighting, the low ceilings with black beams suitably decorated with horse-brasses, the fading prints and framed photographs on the walls, the red-patterned, ash dusted pile of the wall-to-wall carpeting and the solid but fake, Victorian tables and chairs which furnished the bar all added to a feeling of safety, concordance and pleasantness for its frequenters.

John was well at home here. He not only got on with the landlord and bar staff but also with other regulars who were always willing to acknowledge him and make conversation even if the level was hardly inspiringly philosophical. The evening that stretched before him was not, therefore, significantly different from ones he had spent before in this hostelry. Drinks from the bar, a light pub meal to be washed down, exchanges with the landlord and landlady (the only ones on duty this evening) and even a brief smile and a chat to Janet who this time had turned up with two other female friends and therefore did not seem indisposed to acknowledging John and asking him how he was and how things were going for him generally. Alcohol is a depressant but even if it did not exactly cheer John up this evening it certainly helped him come to terms with his situation and most definitely eradicate all traces of the alarm from the previous night. Thus John reached that mellow, satisfied stage when even if everything in the garden does not exactly seem rosy, at least there was a sense of resignation and satisfaction within him. Thus armed with the philosophy of sufficient unto the day is the evil thereof he retraced his steps homeward and had a sound and satisfying night's sleep partly due to the alcohol and food, partly due to his inner sense of calm if not well being and partly due to making up for the terrors of the previous night when he was more akin to the fearful and despairing quester in Browning's *Childe Roland to the Dark Tower Came*.

The next few days passed well for John. Nothing untoward happened though there were times that he felt all that had passed sitting like Nemesis on his shoulder about to strike him down at any moment. These thoughts were thankfully momentary and did not lead to any breakdown, hyperventilation or panic attacks on his part. Looming larger in his mind was the anticipation of the call from Ken Churcher, the summons which would indicate his entrance in to play his key part in the drama into which he had inadvertently stumbled and from which he seemed unable to extricate himself. But here again, this thought, though dominant to the other, only occasionally crept up on him as he went about his daily business of putting together work for The Portsmouth Group of newspapers to which he was now in a part-time sense at least contracted.

There were times he became a little melancholically philosophic and thought that all of life, and his in particular, was akin to and Escher sketch, a double illusion, like the *Waterfall*; that what he was encountering was not reality but more like a dream, and yet it lacked the criteria whereby it could be designated a dream and therefore had to be accepted as reality, or at least a representation of it. However, he shook himself out of such moods by thinking forward to the coming Friday when he would be visiting Portsmouth again and his lover, Helen. He occasionally telephoned her in anticipation of his visit and this helped him keep up his wilting optimism on such occasions.

It was early Wednesday evening before the Friday he was due to travel the brief journey south. He had had a fairly routine but busy day and had concluded another two items in the local History series for the newspaper as well as researching further the flora and fauna walks series he was hoping to get accepted for next summer. He had just placed himself in front of the television armed with a mug of hot coffee and switched on to view the news at six o'clock when the telephone rang. Something suggested itself immediately to him that this was the phone call for which he had been waiting with such dread; his entrails ran cold as he lifted the receiver and immediately heard the hail-fellow-well-met tones of Ken Churcher. The conversation started, as ever, with a quotation.

"I have 'good news from a far country," stated Ken without any introduction, fully confident that his audience was John and John only. And then he continued, "Friday's the day. All's arranged for then. If you've anything on, cancel it, my good friend."

John immediately thought about his trip to Portsmouth but hoped that perhaps things would be sorted out during the day on Friday so that he could get away in the evening. He was to be slightly disappointed.

"Seems they want to meet you in Poole, Havenpool to the Hardy connoisseur, Sandbourne way, Corvsgate, Knollsea, Anglebury and all that, I'm sure you remember from the Wessex Novels . . . .," prattled on the caller. "They want to see you at dinner at the Harbour Heights Hotel 7.30p.m. for 8.00p.m. O.K.?"

John decided to get into the monologue and stuttered, "Well, I was going to Portsmouth that evening, girl friend, you know?" and, strangely enough as he said this he started questioning whether or not be should raise the topic of Trevor before the conversation was over.

"Well," rejoindered Ken, "you're not that far away there. I should imagine you'll conclude dinner by 10.30 or 11.00 at the latest. Jaunt back along the M27, you'll be tucked up in bed just after midnight! Remember the prostitute joke? Lovely girl—always in bed by midnight or else she goes home!?" and he gave a little laugh as he did so.

"Yes, I suppose you're right," replied John, "but how do I recognise who I am supposed to meet? Who do I ask for?"

"Not good grammar from a Light Blue!" mocked Ken before getting a little more serious. "All you have to do is introduce yourself at reception. Whoever is to meet you, and I certainly don't know who comprises your reception committee, has arranged everything. You will be taken to meet your hosts. Drinks and dinner will be served and no doubt the conversation will be interesting on both sides if not good! I doubt if they are expecting you to pay so just go and enjoy the view too as it's set on the slopes backing up off the shore line. You can contemplate in the manner of Arnold's Dover Beach if you wish!" Then, as if by way of calming what he knew would be jangling nerves on John's part, he added, "Look, you will be meeting and talking 'in the public haunt of men'. There's really no need for any worries on your part. Believe you me you are a small fish in a very big sea and thereby you do not merit much interest. But what you may tell them may elicit information for you, for us, and once you've extracted that and re-contacted me then you will be satisfied along with the rest of us!"

John was concerned but his adrenalin was now flowing with the concern of excitement as much as anything else. Not to be outdone by the pedant on the end of the line he replied, "'Present fears are less than horrible imaginings!' Yes. O.K. After all it was me who instigated the whole business and I should, therefore, see it through to a conclusion. Only one small favour . . . ."

"That's the spirit," said Ken. "Fire away . . . ."

". . . . since I intend to go on to my girl-friend's after this august event I don't have to contact you, or better still, you won't try to contact me about what went on until I return back here after the weekend. Let's say Monday evening?"

Ken hesitated momentarily. This bargaining, concluded John was not in his script.

"With the proviso that if what you do learn is really pertinent to the safety and well being of the state, which I very much doubt, you will contact us immediately?"

"Agreed," concluded John. All the while at the back of his mind there had been an urge to ask about Trevor but even now, at signing off time, he held his peace and did not ask. "Fine, then!"

"Yes, fine," concluded Ken. "Enjoy the meal. I won't say enjoy the company, that would be stretching credibility and my generosity of spirit too far. Anyway, we'll meet again, 'this parting was well made,'" and with that insiduously ambiguous half-quote from Shakerspeare's *Julius Caesar*, he signed off.

Certainly John did not like that. It left a bad taste in his mouth. He mulled the whole quote over in his mind and it disturbed him, unedged him somewhat as he added his own stress to it . . . . "IF we DO meet again, why we shall smile!/ IF not, why then, this parting was well made!" typical, he thought, just when he was beginning to revel in the exhilaration of what lay ahead, pedantic, poseur, Ken Churcher, had to go and throw a spanner in the works. However, he managed to shrug this off by contenting himself with the knowledge that despite the tintinitis that had rung in his mind urging him to ask about Trevor he had avoided giving away to Ken that he knew anything of his decease and therefore was not unduly disturbed or very much different in the knowledgeable sense from when they both had met.

Now immediately he had to re-arrange Friday. He telephoned Helen and found her answer phone on. He was quietly relieved by this since it meant he did not have to have a protracted conversation with her about things and get into unnecessary tangled webs of deceit in giving her the bad news. Thus he merely outlined that due to meetings with locals vis a vis his new newspaper commitments he could not get away when he had hoped. He was, he explained, committed to a dinner with Andrew Pollard and some of his friends and therefore would be along as near to midnight as possible. He knew his soft tones and simple expressions in delivering the message would work subtley on Helen and she would not even telephone him to get more details. She was so trusting, he hated having to lie to her but he felt she was best out of this matter, though there was a strain of thought at the back of his mind that nagged away and indicated to him that just as he had got embroiled in these events so she, by implication and association, was already known to the omniscient powers that were following the whole scenario.

Friday being two days away he now concentrated his efforts on the home front before he had to take off but Friday dawned with the inevitability of all Fridays that had dawned before John had taken his place in the world and all Fridays that would dawn after he had made his departure from it.

He arose early that morning and dressed in a smart, casual fashion, suited but not tied, that he thought would be appropriate to the object of his journey south. He took a small bag of toiletries with him together with a clean shirt for he had decided to head off early and explore the town of Poole a little. He would find a suitable place to wash and brush up and change into the fresh shirt before going to the hotel in the evening.

It was a no man's land day, frozen between the very end of Autumn and the very start of Winter. As he drove south he noticed the last trees bearing dual coloured leaves like the shirts Norwich F C shirts, others with straggling remants of plum, cinnamon, auburn, amber and cupreous hued foliage that created wonderful, variegated blotches supported on the scaffolding of the branches against a canescent sky. The first sign of winter was for him the need to use the car heater and this he had to do on occasions for there was certainly more than a touch of lingering frost in the air. The roads were quiet and seemed worn to the greyness of pencil lead by the traffic that had no doubt passed over them during the Spring and Summer months. And so he headed south along the M27 that petered out into the A31 to lead to the resorts of Bournemouth and Poole.

He first recoinoitered the area in Poole into which he was driving and sought out the Harbour Heights Hotel so that he would have no problems in getting there on time that evening. As Ken had told him it was set magnificently on the hill-side and the view over the bay was similar to that over the Solent from the heights of Portsmouth scene but was not quite so engaging as that view in his eyes, but none the less it had the merit of being, at least on a small scale, one of the heights of Wessex for 'thinking, dreaming, dying on.' Having satisfied himself as to its location he drove on into the centre of town and parked in a multi-story car park above a shopping precinct relatively near to the Arts Centre. He had not left Portminster too early and had take just over two hours to get there driving as he did at a very steady pace. It was like when he went to play rugby in his college and after college days; on the way to a match he was full of apprehension and tension but once having arrived, changed and out on the pitch with the starting whistle having been blown, he was part of the game and all nervousness disappeared. So now, he had arrived in Poole, and though there was a tingle of anticipation about what was to come, he was ready for the fray and resolutely determined to face it. It now being just after midday, he decided to have a light lunch and therefore found a suitable sandwich bar in the synthetic, cosmeticised shopping mall that was an integral part of the car park in which he had parked. As he sat and devoured two tuna and prawn brown bread sandwiches washed down with a tasteless cup of frothy, khaki coloured cappuccino he just watched the world go by and thought how ordinary everything seemed. Seemed was the operative word because for him things were far from ordinary yet when people looked at him no doubt they concluded just as he was doing that everything was normal, there was nothing special going on his life just as there was in theirs. Perhaps, he reflected, we all made the wrong conclusions; everyone was actually not waving but drowning but it was inevitable that this was ignored.

He snapped himself out of his reverie and decided to walk around the town and see what there was to see, if anything. On exiting from the shopping centre he crossed over to the Arts Centre and looked at the programme. The cinemas were all showing the appropriate films that were advertised as being at a cinema near you and the Bournemouth Symphony Orchestra, the music group in residence so to speak, being local, had a series of concerts lined up including a forthcoming Christmas prom. Seeing this his mind naturally made the connection with Helen : maybe this was something they could take in together around the festive season? And he smiled to himself knowing that within 12 hours or so he would be with her once again. He had always had a knack of reducing everything in life to time scales and would particularly indulge in this habit when apprehensive. It would all be over in . . . . fill in the blank and respond accordingly. And it was true, time was the ever-flowing stream that always passed by and its inevitability was a reassurance in time of trouble. No need to whistle a happy tune! At the theatre he noticed that there was a small series of plays to be performed by the Oxford Theatre Company before the onset of the Christmas Pantomime starring a whole load of actors over from Australia who were cashing in on their temporary, Andy Warhol famous for five minutes, fame from the soap operas which pervaded the T V screens. Nothing special about all this. The building itself was fairly non-descript but it was good to see Art finding its way along the south coast!

He wandered off from here along to the old town which reminded him a little of Old Portsmouth but without the attractive pubs and cobbled streets and certainly without the panorama of the Royal Naval Dockyard across the water. All was fairly quiet, this being definitely out of season time and part of the town were looking decidedly tired and empty and in need of trade and custom. The end of the old high street curved round onto the water front and there were a few fishing boats and yachts moored alongside the key in the grey, lack luster waters. The harbour and bay stretched out quite pleasingly towards Brownsea Island and to the right there was a modern, opulent and filled yacht marina which even from this distance looked impressive. But the naked, stark whites and browns of the pointed, rib-like masts of the vessels both here and in the marina, the dry flap and snap of their pennants in the cold air and the slender creamy ropes latticing the craft, indicated a lifeless winter ahead before the spring cleaning, the hoisting of sails and the setting out on to the waters for another journey. John strolled along taking in the view and thinking how different it would all be in summer. At the end of the quay the road curved back again passing a building advertising Poole Pottery and clearly leading back to the town. There was also a pub on the corner and so John meandered in and seeing the most impressive beer to be a Wessex ale and this being Thomas Hardy country after all, decided to indulge. He reasoned that were he to have one now, the effect would have worn off well before his evening engagement when he had resolved not to partake of any alcoholic drink whatsoever. His reasons for this were twofold; simply he had to drive along the motorway to Portsmouth and above all he wanted to keep a clear head in his conversations with those with whom he was about to meet. The pub was warm, the bitter was certainly to John's taste and the atmosphere, although somewhat dank was quiet and peaceful enough and certainly John could relax in such surroundings. There were only a few customers; those who were here were clearly locals from off the boats or from the nearby shops. The décor quite intrigued John and the prints, mainly of Old Poole and the quayside made him think of the place and how it must have looked in and around the time of Thomas Hardy.

The day was thus passing away and it was close to three o'clock when John emerged from this tavern. He decided to collect his car and drive around the area probably to find a tea-shop in some neighbouring suburb or village and pass the next four hours in this way. Having collected his car he headed west driving slowly on the Dorchester road and heading towards Bere Regis. It was here he decided to stop and, luckily, he did find a small bakery which had an adjacent tea shop which made him most welcome as it would naturally do, he being an out-of-season customer and therefore a real bonus as far as they were concerned. There was little to see in this tiny village but he did linger as long as possible over the tea and cakes and then wandered to the church where he sat for sometime gazing at the D'urberville window and reflecting on that most famous of Hardy's heroines. The light had disappeared by the time he left this church and the time was now creeping towards six o'clock.

He drove back even more slowly than he had when traveling to this venue really elasticating the time as much as possible but he knew he was going to arrive extremely early anyway and he decided he would merely sit in his car in the hotel car park until the appointment time arrived. This he duly did and was rather annoyed to find that from the car park there was no view out over the bay as there was from the hotel itself, the area being below the hotel height and to the left of it and screened off by trees. He turned on the car radio and listened to the blank music and interviews on Radio Two which were broadcast between the twilight hours of 5.30 and 7.30 daily. At 7.25 precisely he took the shirt he had brought with him, his bag of toiletries and went into the hotel. At reception he introduced himself and was told that two gentlemen were in the bar awaiting him. He indicated his need to do a quick change and the receptionist pointed out the toilet facilities close by. Having completed his wash and brush up he quickly returned to the car, depositing the old shirt and toiletry bag on the back seat and heading inside again. The receptionist now asked one of the porters on duty to escort him to the bar and the reception committee that awaited him. They therefore went up a short flight of stairs, through a set of grand double doors and into a long, though not elegant bar. There were a variety of customers seated and standing in this area situated as it was adjacent to the carvery which was down a small flight of banistered stairs onto a mezzanine floor to the right. The porter indicated two gentlemen at the bar to John as being those who were expecting him.

John walked over and the taller of the two turned and greeted him, hand outstretched in welcome. They were both aged about late thirties to early forties. They were dressed, as was John, in smart, casual clothes, nothing too garish or ostentatious. The smaller of the two who was just receiving the drinks he had ordered from the bar had a moustache. They were hardly instantly recognisable, more like instantly forgetable. They could have been two colleagues in retailing enjoying an evening after work, or two members of a Sunday football team having a jar, or two teachers fatigued from a Baker-Day conference, or indeed just any two members of the public in any walk of life. And that was exactly what they wanted to be.

"John! Hullo. I'm Mark and this Luke," announced his host as he shook his hand. Luke turned from the bar and proffered his hand in greeting also and made his due salutations. To go with the non-descript appearances were two non-descript, received pronunciation accents and, as John was alert to note, the only Gospel writer not to be present was Matthew! A suitable choice of Christian names given the circumstances.

"What are you having to drink, John?" asked Mark.

"Just a slimline tonic water, please," and his order was acknowledged by a nod of the head to Luke who duly made the order to complete the round he was buying.

"Not wanting the fruit of the vine or the brew of the hops then, John?" enquired Mark.

"Driving later," was John's brief response.

John had clearly expected something different and his slight wonderment betrayed itself to Mark. As Luke received, paid for and handed out the drinks, therefore, Mark commented, "I note you're a little surprised, John?"

"A trifle astonished, rather than surprised," replied John.

"Semantic point taken," and now having the drinks to hand he added, "Cheers, then!" and they all three acknowledged the toast. "But, truly, what did you expect? That we'd be wearing green? Drinking *Guinness*? Talking in a lilting brogue with a touch of the blarney that geographically identified us? That we'd both be either the size of Willie-John McBride or rather of leprechaun stature and that we worked in the shoe industry? That we'd be carrying shillelaghs? That we'd have actors to speak our lines? That everything we said would end with 'so'? That we'd be spouting Yeats, Synge or whoever? Or we'd be pissed and enjoying the craich as they say?" he paused while the effect of this sank in on his guest before offering the conclusion of his argument. "Then how do you think we would keep our anonimity?"

John felt duly humbled by this sarcastic broadside.

"The trick," continued Mark, "is to blend in. To be chameleon-like. Really to be totally unidentifiable from the opposition." And then he smiled, "For all you know you could be talking to members of your own government's secret-service, could you not?"

And John had to admit that that indeed was the case.

"Then you have only my and Luke's here assurances that you're not."

"And I suppose I will have to rest content with that throughout the evening, won't I?" asked John who was certainly beginning to feel slightly confused. He had to acknowledge that to all intents and purposes there was no way he knew what was the truth of the situation and all he could do was to continue on the course he had planned and accept it for what he thought it was and had been led to believe it was. The Esher sketches flashed back into his mind at this point. A dual illusion indeed. If the senses could not be trusted what price empiricism? If the mind could not be trusted, what price rationalism?

"Well, let's make progress," said Mark. "We decided on a carvery meal. We order the starter and that's brought to us. Then we head up to the counter, so to speak and decide what we want there. I recommend the ham off the bone; one of the best things they do here. The sweet trolley comes at the end. Ordinary but satisfactory. Let's get started, shall we?" and he ushered John towards the small flight of steps leading down into the restaurant area. Luke, who had so far seemed the archytypal henchman, duly brought up the rear.

A waiter guided them to a table set near the great expanse of window that formed one wall of the dining room. It overlooked the bay and the blackness outside was stippled with illuminations from further down the hill and the jetties and a few boats out on the water. A bit like looking at the sky on a frosty, starry night but not quite so impressive. Their order for starters having been taken, Luke summoned the wine waiter and at last made a contibution to the evening.

"What would you prefer?" he asked John. "They do a good Mouton-Cadet here. Goes with most things."

John stuck to his resolve of avoiding alcohol and indicated to his hosts his reasons. They, therefore, agreed on an ordinary bottle of house red for themselves and a few bottles of *Perrier* for John. Thus the meal got underway and, as John recalled Ken Churcher's words, he had to admit even he found it quite tolerable.

The early part of the evening was spent in trifling talk mainly relating to interests focusing surprisingly enough on literature. John noted his hosts were extremely well read and, had it not been for the circumstances, he would have enjoyed the banter. But the serious business was inevitable and came most certainly by surprise when half-way through the main course, Luke interjected, "Well, now, and it seems you know about a mutual friend of ours, one Patrick Field?"

John paused. "I think so," was all he said.

"Think?" enquired Mark. "Either you do or you don't surely?"

"Let's say I have been led by a variety means to conclude that I do have information on this gentleman, but, even having said that nothing is definite." Still offering this vague and hopefully enticing bait, John then was quite forward and asked, "But if you knew him, how is it you need information from me?"

"That's a fair question," responded Mark. He looked at Luke and there was clearly an acknowledgement that passed between them like partners in a game of bridge. He then looked back to John and the eye contact between the two of them was the most intense it had been all evening. "It's only fair we reply to it. I will, therefore, let you in on a few details about Patrick Field. Details which may this time definitely surprise rather than just astonish you. Details which we want you to know because we believe you are in an ideal position to help us and we feel sure you will after hearing them. You are, after all, a journalist as we've been led to believe and as you've confirmed earlier. We have a scoop therefore to offer you but first just tell us whether the said Mr Field is alive or dead. Later you may fill in the background for us."

John's adrenalin was rising. He had taken the bait of the scoop. What journalist wouldn't? "He's dead and buried . . . ."

Mark cut him short. "Spare the rest." Again a look of acknowledgement passed between him and Luke and again he turned, determinedly towards John.

"Patrick Field. Terrorist. Born in county Cork, educated at Trinity College, Dublin and a teacher of Horticultural and Agricultural Science : or *gardening*, as he preferred to call it. Recruited by us in the late sixties, early seventies. Good worker. Learned very quickly, explosives and all that. Did some excellent early work across the border and was rewarded by being made head of a cell in mainland Britain whilst teaching over there somewhere near Deal in Kent. A standard C V for quite a few members of the organisation."

John's mind was starting to wander. He had heard this sort of thing before. *News At Ten* was more enlightening on membership of the I R A than these supposed insiders were providing to be. It was awkward. He desperately needed to concentrate because here he was in one of the most important meetings of his life yet he was already switching to the automatic pilot of his journalistic habits. He glanced out of the window. He continued eating. He sipped his drink. He looked at other diners and surmised histories about them : a standard people watching technique. These routine actions made greater impressions on his mind than what he was being told. Like skim-reading a novel, he was missing out chunks and hoping that his eyes would alight (or in this case his ears would hear) on the crucial bits.

". . . . til it came to the mid eighties and Brighton."

John's ears automatically tuned in.

"We always had designs on big targets and often thought about something like a party conference. But two factors dissuaded us. Security was the main problem. If you look at the record we've only managed a few biggies on that sort of scale—Mountbatten, The Marines in Deal (and that was a prime soft-target), the Airey Neve murder stand out and those over a period of about a quarter of century. Regardless of what may seem ineptitude on the part of security services, given their strength they are surprisingly effective at their job and certainly all terrorist organizations of any worth rarely underestimate their ability. But we are famous for the indiscriminate blast, sometimes, sadly, irrespective of public sympathy. And that was the second factor. We may well detest governments in office and the Tories in that respect probably elicited our greatest loathing but we are well aware that killings can have disastrous backlashes against what we are trying to achieve as much as promote them. Thus although such targets were mouted at the odd rendezvous of cell leaders together with administrators like ourselves they were invariably dismissed from the agenda. Interestingly enough, Patrick Field was a prime-mover in this respect. Based in the south he was forever raising this as an issue, as an objective, as a target for him and his forces." Mark stopped and took a sip of his wine.

"But you eventually went ahead and did it all the same!" wrily commented John indicating he was sitting up and taking note.

"That's what you and the rest of the population have been led to believe, yes," replied Mark putting down his glass but with such an authoritative air that it was clear something of great moment was coming. "Patrick did the bombing . . . ."

"But that's never been the verdict of our courts. One of your men is serving time for that even now as we speak!" interrupted and exclaimed John believing he was now being offered the real culprit as Salome was delivered the head of John the Baptist.

". . . . but he was not acting for us when he did so." Mark paused allowing this qualification of his subject to sink in.

John was slow. Patrick not acting for the I R A then he was going it alone. So? He was still a member and even if it wasn't at their instigation it was at their motivation! As he mused over this he noticed again Mark and Luke exchanging that knowing look of intimacy and privileged knowledge to which he, John, as an outsider was as yet not privy. His look betrayed his lack of understanding. Mark decided to lead him more gently through the intricacies of the matter.

He started somewhat obliquely. "I am sure even if you do not subscribe to the Christian faith, John, your Biblical knowledge is as good as, possibly better than, most believers, given that you have studied English literature! You will recall that one of Christ's most fervent supporters was Judas Iscariot; yet it was this same Judas that betrayed his master. And why? Being put down! No one likes their ideas being passed over no matter how strong the arguments against them. Patrick was like Judas. His ideas being continually spurned he sought a remedy for what he considered being overlooked. There are many precedents. Iago is such another from literature is he not? Mordred in Arthur's court? Edmund? Macbeth? And in the real world? Lee Harvey Oswald? Quisling? Perhaps we should alter the saying about *Hell hath no fury* . . . . ending it with like a believer or supporter scorned instead of allowing it cast aspurtions on just females. So, like all traitors, double agents, call them what you will, Patrick sold out. Sold out to his enemy. The British Government!"

John thought the whole idea thoroughly risible and therefore just sat back and laughed. He decided levity was the order of the day and commented, "Well, it's pretty clear that it's you who has been drinking, not me!"

This did not deter his hosts. "True," intervened Luke, "but I think it's you who is going to be desperate for the bottle when you give it all some more consideration." He paused and then in the most serious of tones and leaning over the table towards John in a most conspiratorial manner he continued, "Look at the facts. If we had got close enough to plant that bomb do you think we would have been so unlucky as not to have killed someone important? We would have ensured a 'name' target in those circumstances, not just smashing up a few rooms and maiming the odd nonentity. Think harder. How did the Iron Lady win her elections? Always she drew sympathy or managed to engineer or use events to her advantage. Do you think the Falklands War was an accident? And, indeed, why is it that we are searching for Patrick Field? As you asked yourself, being one of ours how is it we don't know exactly what happened to him? What we do know is he totally sold out and was spirited away by those he sold out to after fingering one of our own—one with whom he was a personal friend and whom he knew could easily be put in the frame and sent down. Greater love hath no man that this than he lay down the life of a friend for his own! Excuse the re-wording but it is highly appropriate."

John was beginning to take the whole scenario a little more seriously. Certainly the doubts they raised were genuine ones but the thought of a Government in office actually perpetrating such a crime on itself for election or political purposes hardly seemed possible. He voiced his doubts in duly incredulous tones yet again.

"A crime, you call it? How? Anyone die? A few casualties, non fatal at least at that time as I recall. On yes, a few fatalities and invalids after. But who were they? Remember any names? Now compare to our crimes. Yes, you can remember names can you not? When we want to make headlines we certainly make them. Do you think the government is above such skullduggery?"

The question was asked rhetorically but even so John considered it needed an answer.

"All very well but all you have presented me with is circumstantial evidence. You have offered no proof. None anyway that would stand up in a court of law! What you suggest is probably not without the remit of any politician but it does stretch the bounds of credibility." He paused and took a long drink of mineral water and then continued, "You know it reminds me of that book about the Masons and Jesus . . . . *The Holy Grail and The Holy Blood* . . . . or vice-versa . . . . great entertainment, would make a good thriller, suspense novel but that's where it belongs . . . . firmly in the realms of fiction!"

His audience, surprisingly, was quite receptive of his comments, Luke commenting, "We can't force you to believe us and we probably can't offer you the substantiation you require. O.K. So we've done our bit. How about you now filling in the details of your knowledge of our mutual friend?"

John was being led but he was oblivious to what was happening. He therefore launched quite airily into his tale and his summary was succinct and to the point, though omitting the emotive subject of Trevor's death, and closing the whole with, ". . . . and that's why we're having this meeting this evening!"

Mark and Luke thought the whole story thoroughly risable and therefore just sat back and laughed and as they did so, so it dawned on John that his story to them had sounded just as far-fetched as theirs did to him. Now what he had to come to terms with was whether they were both fooling each other or whether they were both telling the truth or at least what they understood to be as close to the truth as they could get. It was back to Esher again: the double illusion.

It was Mark who decided to go for the attack. "Don't you see that such an elaborate game, such an extensive cover-up could not have been just an accident? Why would anyone want to get rid of a priest unless he were Henry the Second the priest in question were turbulent? Why would anyone want to eradicate a school caretaker? Why would anyone want a person buried as damn near anonymously as possible? Who were the anonymous men in charcoal grey suits who attended the funeral and visited your Reverend Fergusson? Those are questions you can ask about your own experiences. Now add the questions that Luke put to you previously. Yes, it could be a series of bizarre coincidences but I can assure you, Patrick Field reneged on us, his fellow conspirators and we are glad he's gone to his death (if indeed he has!) though, to be honest, we would dearly have loved to have had a hand in it. We would not be surprised if he was quietly done away with anyway; having live evidence around is always a problem. Finally, maybe the burial was all a fake anyway. Our mutual friend being taken into an elaborate witness protection programme? You yourself are a witness to a burial which others told you was not a burial!"

John gulped. Mark's phrase of having live evidence around had many meanings and implications as far as he was concerned. He thought. He thought hard. All three of them used this lull in conversation to complete their main meals and drinks and Luke gestured to a waiter to bring over the sweet trolley and at the same time ordered another bottle of wine for himself and Mark. As John ate and ruminated Trevor's letter came to mind and in particular his reference to *Gulliver's Travels*. It was the passage in *The Voyage to Laputa* that distinctly stuck in his mind. Trevor had been fond of referring to it, part of his Irishness and always featured in his drunken quotes, but it was probably the best indictment of politicians and their kind and was worthy of being reprinted at regular intervals. It was significant that part of it had featured in Trevor's letter. As

John gazed out of the window, fragments filtered back into his mind almost as if they were being said with the soft tones and cadences of Trevor's own voice . . . . "'the royal throne could not be supported without corruption . . . . Perjury, oppression . . . . fraud . . . . were among the most excusable arts they had to mention . . . . some confessed they owed their greatness and wealth to sodomy and incest . . . . others to betraying of their country or their prince . . . . more to the perverting of justice in order to destroy the innocent . . . .'"

They were interrupted by the arrival of the sweet trolley. John decided on cheese and biscuits as did Luke but Mark indulged in profiteroles and cream. They ordered coffees at the same time and Mark insisted that John have a least one drink with them before he left so they agreed on good malt whiskys all round to go with the coffee and mints. There was an air of resignation as they had this, the last rites of the meal.

"Well, let us say I am inclined to accept your version of events if only that they dove tail with my own and the whole is either totally absurd or totally true. Whatever, it would be hard of me to use what you have said to any purpose apart from a work of fiction and, despite my journalistic background and the innuendoes that may be applied to much of our writings, I am not quite into that branch of communication. It may be other things will be unearthed either by me or by you and that might at some future date change the situation but until then . . . ." and John lifted his glass of Tamnavulin malt and pronounced, "your health," to his hosts almost as if he were concluding a prayer.

"But you could stir up things yourself, couldn't you? Given what we've said why don't you write to your local newspaper and ask the provactive questions about whose is the mysterious corpse, if indeed there is one, interred in the churchyard? Naming names would be something! How about putting your colleague, Ken Churcher on the spot? Forcing him into a corner would be an interesting move," suggested Mark.

"All very fanciful. There's no guarantee of publication. Indeed, I would suggest that there are people involved in the cover-up who would be in a position to suppress such publication anyway. As for further involvement with Ken Churcher and the like I would probably be putting myself in greater jeopardy that I have already done so! But there, I wonder could things be much worse? I'm in this mess stepped in so far . . . ." He did not have to complete his adapted version of the Macbeth quotation for it to be instantly recognised by Mark and Luke.

He saw they were somewhat chagrined by his rather negative, dismissive attitude towards the evening's proceedings. Apologetically, therefore, he felt it essential to add, "Look. I will try to think this one through. I realise that here we probably . . . ."

Mark and Luke chorused the correction, "Certainly . . . ." at this point as John continued.

". . . . have the most intriguing, Machievellian piece of political chicanery in this country this century but even you must see that a humble person like me cannot be expected just to expose it and trust to instant belief and being loved by the distracted multitude because of it. Moreover, I would, by revealing it all, be explicitly supporting you and, with respect, that's not a very good side to be on! I will do what I can, but I am making no promises, nor do I expect you to hold me to any. I really am not sure of the way forward but give me time. I usually can work things out and make headway."

"Well, that's better than the excuses you started with," concurred Luke and added with a look at Mark, "and in the parlance of the movies, 'you can't say fairer than that!'"

The meal was now over. John looked at his watch. It was 10.50 and he had reckoned to be on his way by 11.00 to make Helen's by midnight or just after.

"I must go," he said. "I have enjoyed the meal and the conversation though you are aware I am a bit perplexed by it all. I doubt if we shall meet again though depending on the outcome of things I assume other contacts may occur. Friendly ones, I hope, though I must say when I consider all that's happened I do shudder at times as to what I have got into." He stopped realising he felt awkward in offering a customary parting to two persons unknown who, were he to believe all he had heard, were members of an organisation which was certainly a threat to the National Interest. "Well," he hesitated. "Goodbye and thanks. That really is all I can say," and he rose to depart.

Luke and Mark also rose and, less embarrassed by customary partings, shook his hand and bade him farewell.

He walked out of the hotel and down to the car park. The night air was cold and sharp and being rather casually and lightly dressed it cut into him and made him hug himself together for warmth as he headed towards his car. There was a sprinkling of light dappling the hotel and its surroundings being cast from some feeble exterior lighting but much more so from the rooms of the hotel itself. He climbed into his vehicle and headed off on the boundary road east with its myriad roundabouts that leads out from the Poole-Bournemouth connurbation.

As he drove along he wondered where Mark and Luke were staying? Were they hotel residents? They could not be driving anywhere after all they had had to drink, surely? A chauffeur then? Yes, they would probably be spirited away somewhere. Who knows where? And what of their story and Patrick Field? Well . . . . it could be fabricated but even John had always entertained doubts about the current government and certainly would not put anything past it or the cabinet. Still . . . . Things nagged away at his mind despite the fact that he tried hard to focus on Helen and the delights of the weekend to come.

As he neared the outskirts of Bournemouth he noticed an increase in traffic. Certainly heading east the dual carriageways were slowly starting to become congested, then he found himself having to slow down his speed until he was the tail car in what seemed quite a long queue and he could only surmise there was an accident up ahead. He cursed at the delay but at least it concentrated his mind on different things and for that he was grateful. As the line of cars and lorries nosed forward he caught sight of the whirling, orange lights of the police cars up ahead flashing like demented lighthouses. As he got nearer again he noticed there was no accident but that the police, and there were a great deal of them, were doing some sort of routine check on the traffic leaving the area. Each vehicle was in turn being stopped and the drivers questioned and then allowed to go on. In some cases he discerned documents being produced and acknowledged before drivers were proceeding. He merely thought this was another case of officers of the law with nothing better to do. But then it was Dorset and that was hardly likely to be a seriously crime-ridden county and so their efforts were probably being reasonably directed.

It came his turn and a burly officer stood beside his car. He wound down the window and the officer asked for this licence and insurance documents. John reached into the glove comparment to produce the latter and handed it over and then extracted his wallet from his right hand inside breast pocket and produced his licence. The officer used his torch to illuminate what he had received and instead of returning them to John and ushering him forward which seemed that rules of this traffic game he walked away indicating he would be back shortly to return them. John felt like he had inserted his card into a cash till machine with a line of customers behind him all witnessing the said machine gobling up his card and refusing to return it to him. What an embarrassment!

He did not have to wait long, however, until matters were resolved, though certainly not in the manner he expected for he suddenly found his car being surrounded by police and a senior officer was asking him to step out of the vehicle whilst the traffic behind was being directed onwards and past him. He did not care to argue with the show of such force.

As he stepped out the senior officer immediately read him his rights and charged him of acting with persons unknown in a conspiracy to cause an explosion or words to that effect. In truth John was mesmerised by all that was happening. This seemed like a scene from out of a bad film. But just in that instant, just as the police had moved towards his car John had realised this was all connected with the events in which he had become enmeshed. It came upon him like Paul's conversion on the road to Damascus. This was all part of his destiny or the destiny that had been prescribed for him once he had made his initial inquiries. He had been allowed enough rope and now he was about to hang. This was the inevitablity for which he had been waiting. He was taken to the waiting police vehicle, his head was pushed down in the statutary manner as he was forced onto the rear seat. As he was driven away with sirens screeching in this standard Ford Sierra of the force complete with all the trappings of multi-wave radios and surrounded on either side by two burly officers and in front by the mute driver with the senior officer to his left, all he was now asking himself was where was he going from here?

CHAPTER 13

A Way of Looking at Things

"Everybody knows the deal is rotten: Old Black Joe's still pickin' cotton for your ribbons and bows. And everybody knows."
(Leonard Cohen: Everybody Knows).

John had never thought he would be happy to see the inside of a police cell but for such a place he was eternally grateful at the end of that night. The car had zoomed him and its occupants back into the Bournemouth-Poole conurbation and at the station he had been photographed, finger-printed, advised again of his rights, his pockets had been emptied and his belongings audited and taken away, been told he was being held under the Prevention of Terrorism Act or some such fabrication and then marched along a corridor of grey, steel doors and ushered inside one into the Spartan rooms that was to be his for whatever period they deemed fit. Once inside, having been subject to the final through-slit glance of policeman cum usher, John sat on the bed and just got his thoughts together before succumbing to the inevitable, sleep.

Strangely enough he was not frightened any more. It was if he had almost expected this scenario. He had not bothered to ask for a lawyer, nor for a phone call amidst all the kafuffle and shouting to which he had been subjected on arrival. He reasoned anyway that despite their statements about such issues he would have been denied these rights on some pretext or other for it was not in their interests at present to have him communicate with anyone beyond themselves. Furthermore, he suspected that within their plans and given their knowledge they would have looked after his car and would have contacted Helen with some story to assuage any fears and anxieties she may have through his not having turned up. He felt drowsy, it being now well past midnight and he had had a meal which had made him feel replete and although the quantity of his whisky sleeping draught had been less than usual, the quality had been superb and it was beginning to have the desired effect. He felt ready for sleep and the surroundings were not sufficiently gruesome to keep him from it. He therefore unrolled the coarse, battle-ship grey blanket, rolled himself onto the mattress and bedded down for the night. As he dozed off to sleep he felt warmly contented and the words of a hymn he remembered from his youth stole into his mind and seemed reflect how he felt . . . . "I trace the rainbow through the rain and know the promise is not vain that morn' shall tearless be . . . ." Mere optimism was his last thought before the transition from waking to sleeping.

He slept well and was woken by the clang of the cell door as it opened and a blue uniformed officer brought in tray of breakfast and put it down on the desk at the right of the cell before exiting. John looked up from his bed and viewed the action as if he were in a play. After the officer had departed, John rose and although feeling dusty from having slept in his clothes he felt clear headed enough and hungry enough to see what had been brought. He shuffled over to the table, pulled out the small wooden chair from under it and sat down. There was a plate bearing two rashers of pink, underdone bacon, with a jaundiced heap of watery scrambled egg surrounding them. Decidedly uninviting! There were two large slices of rusty, dry toast, a bit burnt at the edges but sufficiently edible with the slab of butter and marmalade that had been dolloped onto the edge of the plate on which they rested. Then there was a large mug of mud coloured tea, heavily sugared, which John certainly did not like but which he forced himself to accept as the only liquid which he was going to get at this point of his captivity. As he forced himself to eat and drink what he could, John smiled at the plastic cutlery provided along with the plastic plates and cups. It was peculiar his having come to this point, having come into direct contact with a situation about which he had only ever read or seen on films or on television. The reality was not as disturbing or shattering as he thought it would be when he had only the second-hand experience. Perhaps everything was like this. Things from which he recoiled in his mind were just imaginings; when they were for real, the mind could accept them with a due degree of equanimity! Like the terrors of the darkness of the night being dispelled by the new dawn. They had taken his watch so he unsure of the time but he surmise it to be about 7.00 a.m. for he felt he had had his usual amount of sleep; in this, he was not far wrong for it was, indeed, just after that hour of the morning that his breakfast had been served.

After eating he relieved himself in the toilet in the far corner of the cell and then rinsed his hands and face in the sink (minus a plug!) next to it. No soap, no toothpaste to make him feel more human but at least he felt he had done what he could to make himself seem alive given the circumstances and conditions. He then sat down on his bed to wait. Something would transpire, though he knew not what. He was thinking of literature connected with imprisonment but had not far when the door of his cell clanged open again and the same officer came in to retrieve the remnants of the breakfast tray. But behind him came a very smartly dressed man who, after the officer had departed with the debris, remained behind as the cell door closed to on them.

He was about 5ft 11ins in height, of slim build and was dressed in a finely tailored, dark blue striped, suit with a double breasted jacket. He had a striking but not overtly strident, small crimson rose, reminiscent of the Labour Party's adopted symbol, in his button hole and a college tie with its suitably coloured crest setting off the white shirt and the dark suit itself. His black, gibson shoes were highly polished indicating perhaps a military connection. He was finely built and elegant and though his hair was thinning on top it was still stark and there were no streaks of grey or white to suggest he was the wrong side of forty or so. He looked condescendingly at John and as their eyes met he smiled more in a manner of greeting than in a sense of victory that he was the captor and John the captive.

"John, John Ellis. I am David Sinclair." Thus he introduced himself. He made no attempt to shake hands to consolidate the meeting. His accent was definitely Scots but with the anglicisation of that of Glasgow's Kelvinside rather than with the guttaral sounds of the Gorbals or Cowcaddens. It was the type of Scots accent that sounds reassuring and that people like to hear; distinctive yet not threatening. Definable but not nationally characteristic, identifiable but not chauvinistic.

"Well," he continued, "to quote Gilbert and Sullivan, 'here's a pretty how de do!' A serious matter but one that can readily be resolved. Given cooperation, that is. I am sure you are aware of that."

He talked with such vagueness, yet with such an assurance that John understood him, that John was almost stunned into just sitting back and listening. What could he say? What could he do?

As Sinclair progressed, things smacked of clarity without necessarily becoming totally lucid, however.

"Trumped up charges of course. They may seem to you as if they would not stick. They could certainly be made to do so though. Most assuredly within the realms of possibility. Has been done before. More frequently than some would like to imagine, I'm sure, so no reason as to why they could not work again. However, we want to avoid such tangled webs if we can do so. Don't you agree?"

John decided his best reply was to answer a question with a question. He decided on the most banal one he could think of that would invoke a response which would bring a bit more light to the situation.

"Are you my lawyer then?"

His ploy worked.

"Good grief! Whatever gave you that idea? Hopefully you are not going to need one but should you do so I can assure you that will all come later! No. I am merely here in order to discuss matters with you which I hope will bring about a satisfactory solution which will avoid the niceties and nuances of the law; getting involved in those shinanagans I assure you is decidedly not in your, nor really in my interests. No, John. I want you to spend the day with me. We need a long chat. You have undergone an interesting experience over the last few months and it's in our mutual interest that we talk through all of this and resolve a way forward that will be useful for both of us. I am here, therefore, to make you an offer. It is this. I want you to come with me today to Blandford. Just up the road. To the Army's Royal School of Signals . . . ."

Then he was military thought John. Those shining black shoes betrayed him.

". . . . It will be an educational visit. Look upon it as a journalistic exercise. We will take your car," and noticing John's look of surprise at this point he explained, "Yes, it's safely out the back. I'll show you round the establishment and this evening there is a Officers' Mess Guest night so you may stay and enjoy quite a sumptious dinner in the company of myself and others. You may then stay overnight at the establishment and on Sunday head along the coast to your beloved." Again, by way of placating John's anxious look at this reference, David added, "Don't fret. She's been suitably informed that you will be arriving late. Everything's been verified and documented for her so she's not at all worried."

So it had all happened and was happening much as he had imagined! John felt quite proud that he had had sufficient insight into their machievellian tactics to have worked this much out! Yet he was not sufficiently etherised by all this just to play along.

"What's the catch?" he asked and as he did so immediately regretted his question since it was so clichéd, so obvious and he knew that was exactly what David Sinclair had wanted to hear.

"There is no 'catch' as you put it. Ken Churcher, whom you've met, indicated we would want to know how you got on last night. That's what I want to discuss with you. I also want to fill in some details about about which I know you to be blisfully unaware. If we talk today, we will, with your cooperation, I assure you resolve matters. It's very important that we do. Then we may all get back to a semblance of normality and you may get on with your life as you wish." He paused here and then qualified what he had just said. "Well, I suppose there is a 'catch'. I was being slightly less than honest when I said there wasn't. Quite simply the catch is the choice. Come along with me and talk or stay here, be charged and face trial and imprisonment. Not much of a 'catch' really!"

Again John was moved to cliche. Again he was being manipulated and yet he felt powerless to avoid it. "You said yourself they were trumped up charges. They would never stick. Anyway, what I would have to say, nay reveal in court, would ensure you would never bring me to trial."

"On the contrary, on the contrary. You will also recall I indicated that such charges had been fabricated in the past and had been made to work; no reason why they could not be used again. With regard to what you have to reveal as you put it, I hope that's something we could discuss today but in the meantime, just pause and think how what you have to say will come over in a courtroom situation. Will you tell them with whom you have consorted? Will that put you in a good light, do you think? You'll elicit the sympathy of the jury, will you? You'll show us to be perverters of the course of justice will you? Or rather won't what you say just seem the ravings of a lunatic about to get his come-uppance?"

John had to admit to himself that David Sinclair and the 'they' whom he represented held all the aces at this stage. There could be no harm in going along with what had been suggested. Perhaps it would all work out satisfactorily. Anything was better than remaining here. David Sinclair noted his resolve before he had noticed it himself. He therefore interrupted his thoughts.

"Good. Knew you'd see sense. We'd better get off then. Get you smartened up first. Bit more respectable." He knocked on the cell door which almost immediately opened. He ushered John out saying, "Don't get the wrong idea. I'm not military myself. Strictly civil service with responsibility for . . . . I'm sure you know the sort of thing."

At the end of the cell corridor John was greeted by the desk sergeant, his belongings handed over in unceremonious fashion the previous night were returned and he was also given a hold-all with a complete change of clothes and appropriate toiletries with which to freshen up.

"One of the few to go away with more than what you came with," quipped the desk-sergeant as John duly signed the acknowledgement note of receipt.

Along with David and a senior officer he was then taken to another part of the building where he was offered the facility of a private toilet provision whilst they waited for him to return to follow-up on the next part of his adventure. Just before he availed himself of what was a most welcome opportunity David remarked, "We know you to be an innocent, John: but we most certainly do not take you as being naïve!" Well aware of the implications of the words John went about his business, duly returned and was soon to find himself happily behind the wheel of his car and being directed by David, now his passenger, through the environs of Bournemouth and Poole and out onto the Blandford road, due north. As he looked in the rear view mirror he knew he was being followed but by a benevolent pursuer protecting not so much him as his passenger.

It was altogether a brighter day than it had been previously. The mellow, wintery sun lit the countryside rather than warmed it but brought with it sufficient glow to suggest heat in the rays that issued from it, though in truth the air temperature had hardly risen much above the zero below which it had been for most of the night. Skeletal trees lined the border of the road like a thin, pressed crowd of onlookers forced merely to observe the passing by of the equally thin streams of traffic. The neutral tones of the surrounding countryside were only offset by the shiny green of the occasional patches of clumpy grass. Flocks of rooks occasionally circled or perched above or on the taller trees and with their great black, flapping wings they seemed like satanic angels hovering in the sky accentuating the somberness of the day with a cawing, ominous chorus celebrating the opposite of the peace and goodwill which should be being broadcast abroad, the season nearing as it was towards Christmas. Before the car, to the side of the road John glimpsed the odd, solitary Jackdaw. One for sorrow . . . .

The journey did not take long and was conducted largely in silence but for David giving occasional directions. At the gates of the School of Signals itself his car was greeted and went through the customary and routine search and clearly the soldiers on duty were familiar with David given the acknowledgements and salutes he received. David directed John towards the officers' accommodation and within that block conducted him to a room where he could leave his hold-all and therefore be free of accoutrements during the day. This was clearly also to be his overnight guest room. It was comfortably furnished with appropriate en-suite facilities; a vast improvement on the accommodation he had left behind. In the room John noticed and David pointed out a suitable evening suit had been provided for the evening when he was to wine and dine in the officers' mess itself. He was also given a suitable top-coat, given the state of the weather, for their journey round the barracks and David himself collected a coat from a reception office at the front of the building.

At first David's tour simply pointed out, with appropriate illustrations as the camp's inhabitants were going about their routines, the functions of this service; communications in the theatre of war. The emblems emphasizing this arm of the forces dominated the decorations in corridors and offices, the hardware and software of the force, the uniforms, cutlery, tableware, furnishings; everywhere and everything seemed dominated by Mercury, fleet-footed on the globe, with the motto, *Certa Cito,* beneath and the imperial crown above. Impressive enough but the overall symbolism was not lost on the student of literature, John. Here was a communications service he could see; they were clearly operating an even greater one that he couldn't. What was not in a text was as important as, sometimes more important than, what was not!

They lunched alone in one of the many cafeterias in the complex and the morning had passed most satisfactorily from John's point of view because they had not touched at all on any matters relating to John's recent past that had been hinted at when David had introduced himself in the cell earlier that same morning. But again the student of literature knew the inevitablity that exists in the rich tapestry of life and early in the afternoon as they were being entertained in a large lecture theatre by a slide show illustrating the world-wide satellite communications network run by the Corps David inquired directly about what had transpired at John's meeting at The Harbour Heights Hotel.

John told him all. He reckoned, not quite accurately as it transpired, that this Corps of Signals had probably bugged the whole meeting anyway and any concealment on his part would be unwise if not downright foolish. David smiled as he listened to the narrative. At the end of it all he simply enquired, "And do you believe what they said?"

"I honestly don't know what to believe any more," sighed John. "On balance, though, and given my own experience, including the last 12 or more hours," he emphasized, "I must say, yes, I think I do."

"And what do you propose to do about it, may I ask?"

John was quick to pick this up. He knew he had been led in the past, perhaps was being led even now but decided to go on the offensive for what it was worth. "I have no doubt that that is what you intend to tell me," he cynically responded.

"I intend to tell you nothing of the sort," the host laughingly replied. "All I wish to do is talk through a few things with you, enlighten you perhaps and the final decision will rest entirely with you. We do not, after all, live in a dictatorship in this country. There is freedom of expression, freedom of speech, human rights and all that. You will not be coerced, badgered, made to toe the line, threatened, cajoled, made to confess or anything of that nature. You are free. That will always be kept in mind and what you do, provided it's within the limits of the law, is entirely down to you."

"Well, since I am a bit concerned about what you say are "the limits of the law" then I want to leave. To have time to think and then act . . . if that's all right by you?"

"Fine. But not just yet." David saw John smile in the semi-darkness in which they sat while watching this slide show as if he were acknowledging the first contradiction of what he had just been told. "Let's say you are free to go when you want. You want to go now? Then go." He paused waiting to see if his guest took up his offer, then he added. "But did you not agree you would stay and hear me out, enjoy a meal this evening and go tomorrow morning."

John did not move. In truth he was intrigued. He felt that in staying this final part of the course he might discover the truth; maybe it would confirm what Mark and Luke had told him the previous evening; maybe it would totally contradict that and offer some tangible proof in so doing rather than the vapid outpourings of those two which could only at best seem true. He realised that all the time he had been here he had hardly noticed what the slides were showing. For a brief moment he concentrated on them and noticed they were illustrating massive arrays of satellite dishes perched on buildings on the continent. David had realised he could use what was being displayed to his advantage.

"Marvellous, isn't it? You saw the works for the battlefield this morning. There's a much bigger battle, of course! Everything that's communicated between governments is potentially threatening to the state. Those dishes are our eyes and ears, our whole senses in fact, into that territory. Modern technology! As scientists invent new ways of communicating—faxes, scrambling machines, god knows what, so other scientists invent ways of intercepting those communications. It's an interesting game. An expensive one, too. We are exceptionally good at it. Probably the best in the world, in fact. Good source of income since Governments—even those on whom we eavesdrop, I must add—pay us to intercept things from others and notify them about it! All part of life's political tapestry!"

The show continued and the conversation became more serious.

"Our main aim, here and in other branches of the forces and the civil service is, of course, to protect everything that's been built up over the centuries. To that end, we have to go along with the political doctrine that the end justifies the means. I know that is universally disliked and even our mainline politicians in the House of Commons or the Lords for that matter would all disavow subscribing to it but I can assure you that it is the most effective means of operating and it is what has been responsible for preserving an enviable mode of life in our democracy which most of our inhabitants can be said to enjoy. We, the executive arm of government, may not always be proud of the way we do things but we generally take genuine pride in what we achieve." So far this had sounded to John like no more than a party political broadcast on behalf of any bureaucratic party. He wasn't hearing anything he didn't already know. His ennui both with David's diatribe and with the slide show started to become obvious. Sensitive as he was to dealing with such individuals in such situations, David snapped his fingers; the slide show terminated, the lights came on and he said, "It is a bit tedious in here, isn't it? Let's go for a walk in the fresh air. What I have to say might sound better there and there's more likelihood that we'll both stay awake!"

John mumbled an apology but was cut short. "No need, John. A bit of Socratic dialogue rather than a Browning monologue is called for; I sympathise with you," and together they exited the building.

It was a raw day but the undulating hills of green which surrounded the camp made a pleasant background for them to meander within as they tramped the heavy duty tarmac roads that bore the weight of the military caravanserais and that were laid out like a tartan across the camp itself.

"Tell me, John, do you do the football pools?" was David's opener in conversation as they started.

"Used to. Syndicate at work. No success, of course. Never bothered on my own. Too much trouble," confessed John.

"Do you know of anyone who ever won the pools?"

"Well, our syndicate won £2.58 or was .85p once?" he laughed.

"No. I was meaning a significant win."

"Why, yes. There was a lad a school whose father was in the Fire Brigade I think. Won a five figure sum back in the seventies and that was worth a bit then. Never thought much about that then. And, yes, one of the member's of the local rugby club's brother—there's a mouthful for you—won nearly quarter of a million only about 18 months ago I think. Close, but not close enough, eh?"

"Precisely. Yes, I imagine quite a few could give similar examples, wouldn't you?"

"Why yes, I suppose so." John was clearly puzzled: he had no idea where such a banal conversation was leading.

"What about premium bonds?" inquired David.

"No luck there either. Mind you I have only got a handful. One very old though, no numerical pre-fix would you believe. Bought for me at birth I think. AW242955. For some reason I have always remembered that number! Even used the numbers as a pin code! Since then I've accumulated a few, but as I said—there again, no luck!"

"And do you know anyone who has won on the Premium Bonds?"

"Well, legend has it my grandmother did! Couple of pals at university did as well I think I recall."

"And how much did they win?"

"Oh, only the modest amounts. £50 tops! But then that's all I do know of. Never have I discovered anyone winning a sum beyond that."

"Precisely!" repeated his host and then elucidated further. "And does it not strike you as odd that despite the number of years these bonds have been circulating and the prizes that have been awarded—now a million pounds monthly but before that £250,000, £50,000, £25,000s etc and yet we know of no one who has been so successful? But with the pools, a slightly different matter!"

"But more people do the pools, there's more prizes," said John as if issuing a self-evident truth.

"Even given the truth of what you say, were you a mathematician and were you to work out the odds involved you would definitely come up with an anomaly. The answer of course is far more simple. Control. When next you see the holder of the million pound bond 6ZW356198 or whatever lives in Chesire just remember such a bond and such a holder do not exist!"

John voiced his incredulity.

"Then don't believe me! But what we have done is create an illusion of winning that people believe. And that in itself is sufficient for the sale of bonds and for a small source of governmental income about which very few, if any, questions are ever asked. We even add to the illusion by stating there is a list of unclaimed bonds which people may inquiry about; few do and anyway the list contains no valid numbers so all enquirers are disappointed. Or are they? They will probably rest content that they tried. That is sufficient for most."

John shook his head. Such manipulation, such control of something like this he had never even considered. He still could not bring himself to believe it. David had sowed the seeds of doubt again in his mind, the doubts about who to believe, who was in control.

"Now think," continued David. We are prepared to control something as simple, as obscure as Premium Bonds, and, by the way, don't think we cannot determine the football pools as well. Maybe even the results? Who knows?" He gave a smile as he saw John shaking his head in continuing disbelief about what he was hearing.

"I want you to understand the point about all this, John, is that there is a tight control over many, many aspects of our daily lives which keeps the whole from becoming quite anarchic. It's a much better system than that of the former Communist block countries. Dissidents there who saw the situation for what it was were put on trial, sent to Siberia, declared insane or whatever. By getting involved in such actions against individuals a group grew up which was identifiable both outside the countries themselves and within. A clear case of political naivety for a Government so to create its own fifth column so to speak! Many people see through our control mechanisms here. You are such a one since you have become probably more enlightened about them now from your recent encounters and your meeting with me and you are naturally horrified, disgusted. Your British sense of fair play has taken a knock back. You want to expose what you have learned. You feel that behaving like the enemy or probably worse than the enemy we have demeaned ourselves, brought the country into disrepute or whatever the buzz phrase would be. Some people do go around doing this. I am sure you are aware that they are about as relevant as the flush on a dead man's cheek. They always remind me of the hot gospellers who stand on street corners announcing the end of the world is nigh and we must repent our sins. Most noble. Probably absolutely right. But they are eccentrics and that is the beauty of our nation. We tolerate, we indulge such eccentrics. Their frustration is then magnified for they are like Cassandras, unable to convince the populace at large as to the veracity of what they are saying. Rather sad really but our national characteristics accepts them as faintly amusing and acceptable. Such a political ploy works wonders."

"So you are telling me that what I learnt last night is indeed true. Just as you say you control a simple thing like the premium bonds, so you have indulged in vastly more serious matters—bombings, murders, framing people or persons unknown et al for political ends. The moral gap between the two is enormous, even I see that. I might even accept a bit of cheating in financial terms, we all like to dodge the tax man, but exterminations for political ends? Yes that appalls me. That surely cannot go unpunished? Cannot be tolerated!"

"Yes. Unequivocally yes—at least to the questions about what we have done. As for recriminations, assuaging the guilt or whatever, no that's totally unnecessary. *The greatest happiness of the greatest number*; that Benthamite principle is what we've used and preserved by what we've done however open to criticism it may be by political theorists or philosophers. It may be a somewhat arcane philosophy but, as I have said, tied in with our strategy it makes sense."

John shook his head and was about to mutter his bitter recriminations at the loss of Robert Fergusson and others but David, with his sixth sense of what was coming—John later thought how brilliant this man was for the job with which he was entrusted!—anticipating his very utterances continued, "and now you're angry and upset. And you want to expose all you know not so much for the political games being played but for that worst of all motives, revenge!"

"'Revenge should know no bounds!'" quoted John defiantly.

"Quite so. Well let's see if I can explain. The Reverend Fergusson. A splendid fellow indeed. But sadly he was caught in the moral trap of having to decide between God and his country and sadly, but inevitably for him he chose the former. Well he was a man of the cloth. An idealist. A martyr probably but one that will never be listed in Fox's book of the same! Heart attacks are easy to induce . . . . or should I say fake as an excuse for an untimely death? Tom Barber? You must admit if ever there was expendable cannon-fodder, Tom fell into that category precisely? Tom was marvelous. He was straight out of the World War One trenches ; he wouldn't even have needed a tot of rum to go over the top to his death. Stupid he most certainly was. Couldn't see a good deal when it was presented to him. Pity really. *'Tis but another man gone,* as they say. Then, Mark and Luke with whom you met last night should never have hired that boat to cruise round Poole harbour this morning ; most definitely wrong time of the year, don't you agree?"

John was flabbergasted. David was so matter-of-fact. How could he be so dismissive of human life? And what about Trevor? He hadn't mentioned Trevor? Why was he expendable? After all, wasn't he on their side, whoever they were? Yet again, David divined his thoughts.

"Trevor. Yes Trevor! 'Fraid you can't pin that one on us, John. No he was a good, if not useful operative. Did his fair share of work for us, indeed he did. But he made one inquiry too far, so to speak : and I am sure you know what that inquiry was. It happens. I R A got his measure and that was that. A definite loss there!" and while he got thus close to offering condolences on one of the deaths he added by way of undercutting anything John might now fire back, "Bet you're glad Mark and Luke went the way of all flesh by way of revenge, now, aren't you?"

John was repulsed. Repulsed partly by David's attitude, his in-built suaveness and his treatment of death as part of a job as naturally as if he were an undertaker or as if he were the appointed executioner or hangman. But repulsed even more by the fact that even he at least had to admit to himself there was something satisfactory in this eye for an eye doctrine. Trevor had been a friend, romanticized by the aura of youth and studentship and that had been very much part of John's life so his death was thus more pertinent to John himself. "*I am a part of all that I have met*," as he would have said to himself. A loss that had been adjusted by or perhaps compensated for by the death of these two. But were they not just victims like Trevor had been? Just like he now was. Pawns in the game. He could see David's logic, terrifying and Satanic though it was. O.K. So it could be justified perhaps ; but it could never be excused.

The light was beginning to fade in the sky over Blandford and the cold, white lamps at the camp were being switched on to light up the perimeter fence. The sky was becoming a deep, azure blue in colour, absolutely cloudless and appeared like a newly matt-painted, plastered wall into which the paint was soaking to which new layers were being constantly added to darken it up. They had slowly walked probably 2, maybe 3 miles, perhaps more, during their conversation and neither had felt the cold for sometime since they came out into it. Now, as the day diminuendoed into evening, the chill came back. To John it seemed like a pathetic fallacy in the light of what David had been talking about. As he mulled over all he had heard and let it sink in, somehow he had always known this was what had happened. All he was doing now was having his own suspicions confirmed and coming to terms with them.

"You are too young to have fought in a major war, John. So am I. However, any doubts I ever had about what I was doing were obliterated when in talking to a senior colleague who had been on the destroyers in the Second World War about the loss of the *Belgrano* and subsequently the *Sheffield* during the Falkland War I was told quite simply, 'That's show business!' And indeed it is." David stopped here. He felt he had said enough. If John wanted to come back at him he could do so. He surmised, rightly, however, there was nothing John wished or wanted to say. He had enlightened him as he said he would. Was it enlightenment or a mere sermon for the almost converted? He directed his and his companion's footsteps towards the interior of a cafeteria yet again where they could have tea.

They were glad to unburden themselves of their coats once inside the building. There was as smattering of personnel, army and civilian in the cafeteria probably enjoying afternoon tea-breaks which they had earned. David might be said to have earned his, as for John he needed tea as the natural remedy for shock, the prescription in time of crisis.

They drank and ate the two toasted tea-cakes David had purchased in silence. At the end of the refreshment John looked up at David and with an almost spaniel like expression just asked, "Well, where do I go from here?"

"I could be frivolous and say back to your room to have a rest and get ready for tonight's dinner," responded David. "Instead, having said it, I am going to be equally frivolous and say that's entirely up to you! Actually," he corrected himself, "that's not frivolous. You are a wise, intelligent man, John. What I have told you I am sure has not landed on deaf ears. You're not religious like Robert Fergusson so you won't choose the God option : and your education certainly puts you out of the league of the Tom Barbers of this world. You may have some tendencies of a different political direction to Mark and Luke but whether you have the same fervour about your beliefs as those two only you can tell. I personally think not. You're much more like Trevor; naturally since you were undergraduates together! You may draw your own conclusions and act accordingly.

Remember though, in Kantian terms, to employ the categorical imperative!" Then finally, intriguingly he added, "Perhaps by dinner tonight your ideas will be more focused. Perhaps the dinner tonight will help you finalise that focus!"

With that he took his leave reminding John that it was 7.30p.m for 8.00p.m.; drinks before the meal.

John was alone. He looked around the cafeteria swathed in artificial neon lighting which reflected off the stainless steel and formica surfaces. It was slowly becoming deserted as the occupants left to go home or go back to work or whatever. It was like watching a performance of Haydn's *Farewell Symphony*. Now might he run away if he wanted. A short walk to his room to get his keys. Collect the car and then exit. Telephone a national newspaper and sell his story. It was possible, certainly. That was one form of action he could take. Then again, there was the dinner. He could equally well desert tomorrow and do the same thing. No need to forgo a free meal. Something about the dinner excited him. He had never been to a Mess Dinner and he imagined it to be like a college dining night. There would be plenty of drink and the food would be of a good standard and there would be plenty of it. Maybe the conversation, the company would not be so amiable, but the formalities would be of interest. Yes, it was worth waiting for and going to and it would give him more time to think about things. Very little time, he admitted to himself, but time enough perhaps.

As John walked out of the cafeteria he suddenly realised he had lost all sense of direction in this camp. He had trudged in and out of offices and workshops in the morning and trod the tramaced roads in the afternoon but he had not kept his eye on the geography of the place. As he now surveyed the surrounding brick blocks with large rectangular eyes of yellow light glaring forth they looked all the same and he had no idea in which direction he had to go to get to his quarters and subsequently the Officers' Mess. Down the end of the path leading from the cafeteria was a large, illuminated board with the mandatory Corps of Signals emblem at the top. This had a series of letters and arrows in red but since they merely designated the directions of 'A', 'B', 'C' and the rest of the first 7 letters of the alphabet blocks it was not very useful. John paused. Should he strike out hopefully? Being of a somewhat reserved nature, John decided to return inside and ask directions. This he duly did and was told to follow the signs for 'D' Block and once there the specific areas of quarters, mess etc would be revealed.

After a short walk therefore John found himself back inside the room to which he had first come in the morning. It was really warm inside the building and inside his room. They certainly cosseted the officer class, he thought to himself. But the warmth was pleasant after the cold of the exterior and it gave him a feeling of reassurance, safety, security even. He looked at the time. It was a few minutes past 5 p.m. He decided to lay on the bed and watch some television or at least let whatever was on wash over him. He had too much to think about to concentrate on fatuous programmes at this time of the evening. Despite his thoughts and especially his lingering internal anxieties, the television had the usual soporific effect and that, combined with his healthy walk in the fresh air for most of the afternoon and the ambience of the room temperature, contrived to make him drowsy and he slipped into one of those most pleasant of dozes that just helped to take him away, albeit temporarily, from the world of reality. He felt himself going, lingeringly making the transition from consciousness to unconsciousness, but the pleasantness of just letting it happen, of being sans care, made the progression from waking to sleeping that much more enjoyable and the temptation to slip away was temptation that could not, that should not, that would not be resisted.

He was more tired, perhaps the true word was exhausted, than he had imagined and he did not wake until just before 7.00p.m. The television was broadcasting the tail end of some local south-west news item or feature and for a few minutes after coming back to consciousness John watched this to try to register what it was about. Once he had worked that out and therefore assured himself that he was fully with it he rose and went to have a shower. This was most refreshing and just what was needed to add that edge of awareness after sleeping for so long in the afternoon-evening period. The invigorating shower over, he wrapped a towel around himself and looked at the outfit provided for wear that evening. Both the clothes they had provided for the day, and now the dress suit and appropriate accoutrements for the evening, were exact to size and very much in keeping with his own choice. It all served to emphasise how much they knew and thereby how much control they exercised. They had even provided him with toiletries which again were among ones he would, in fact did, use himself. But then, they had visited his house on at least one occasion that he was aware of and gleaning such facts at least about preferences and size would not have been difficult.

John dried himself off slowly and then prepared himself for the dinner. Once completely suited out he viewed himself in the cheval mirror in the corner—a necessary for officers, clearly!—and considered that he looked most elegant and presentable. Certainly he would pass muster. He had only to walk through a small labyrinth of corridors to the bar which was an ante room to the Officers' Mess dining area and at 7.30p.m. precisely he headed off for the first round of drinks. As he did so and negotiated the route he realised that far from focussing on his problems he had done nothing towards resolving a way forward at all. But then, maybe that was focusing in itself; perhaps what he had to do was forget it all. Learn to live with it and carry on as normal .... if normality in the future now was possible.

He approached the doors to the bar. The lights seemed brighter here and the atmosphere of chit chat bubbled down the corridor as he neared and was now at a crescendo as he entered. He saw David over near the bar. To his right was a tall, obese gentleman and to his left an officer of the corps. In front of him and with his back towards John was the figure of a demure lady and to her left the back of someone he instantly recognised, even though he had only the briefest acquaintance of the man, Ken Churcher. Well, he should have expected as much, he thought as he went over. As he moved towards them, brushing past other groups with mumbled apologies on the way to make it to someone he knew, he also imagined that the female figure was in some way familiar. He was not to be disappointed in his powers of recognition even though they had not come up with the answer by the time he arrived: indeed, here was Caroline Hobbes, the Headmistress whom he had met in Cambridge. He tried not to look shocked when he renewed her acquaintance.

Through David he ordered a beer and while this was being got for him Caroline Hobbes introduced him to the large, dominating figure of Nigel Stafford, whom she mentioned was one of the school governors and whom she assumed and hoped would be the next chairman thereof in the next academic year. She also reminded him that this was the gentleman who so kindly had housed Donna Barber in her time of need: John did not need such a reminder as he had already grasped this to be the case. The officer of the corps was also introduced and they shared the normal trivial chat of pre-dinner drinks. A few other persons joined their group and left and Caroline and Nigel went and came also. At just before 8.00p.m. a sergeant announced that dinner was about to be served and the group, headed by the appropriate heirarchy of the barracks headed towards the dining room. As they assembled together in order to dine together, John's party was joined by one more guest who had probably either arrived late or been lurking at a distance. It was none other than the ubiquitous David Hart.

They marched to their allotted table and took their places, cards having been duly laid out to assign the positions according to rank or just a prescribed guest order. As they stood for the playing of the national anthem, piped out by a small, army military band tucked over in the corner of the quite huge dining area, John surveyed the company with whom he was dining.

To his right, the fat Nigel Stafford, a god-father-like figure, truly a pig satisfied! Then in anti-clockwise order, David Hart, now in John's eyes taking on the insidiousness of Uriah Heap. Was it coincidence they had arrived at his house absolutely together on that day after Tom Barber had shown up? Then Caroline Hobbes, not so much school-marmish as school-smartish. Obviously she had completed the toadying ladder necessary to climb to headship in these days of the managerial master—there was no need for the feminine gender any longer, politically correct language had seen to its demise—of the school. She made an ideal partner for Nigel Stafford; what collusions could they not get up to if and as required or requested? Then a Major John and a Captain Hardy from some or other branch of the army; well, they were paid to defend the realm and take orders, certainly not to think, however, high their rank! They were no better than the ordinary squaddies of whom they were in charge! Flanking them was Ken Churcher, the thinking man's chameleon. John recalled a titled family he had come into contact with at University and had been to its stately home for some party or ball or whatever. On the walls were the family portraits stretching to times well before Henry V111's reformation. At the time he had reflected how such a family would have survived by constantly changing religion and politics in order to keep itself as flavour of the month with whatever monarchy, dynasty or whoever was in office and was therefore dictating the required religion of the times. So, too, Ken Churcher and his ilk. John recalled the one slip Ken had made when he met him; he had used the past tense, but had immediately corrected himself when referring to Trevor. Was it a slip or was it deliberate? Strange, or was it so strange, that such a fine detail should come back to him now? Then David Sinclair, the brains, the mastermind of this small play into the action of which John had stumbled. And amazingly versatile, erudite individual; he should have been Irish given his blarney! Finally, John himself. How did he now see himself and, more importantly, his future? The evening would help finalise that focus.

The band had completed the anthem. The royal and loyal toast was given, taken and they sat down. The band then discretely struck up excerpts from Gilbert & Sullivan. It was going to be live background music. How John hated Military Bands. Brass bands, fine; they had the sonority of grand and great pipe organs. Orchestras quite acceptable; they had the sentimental vibrato of strings coupled with the warbling reediness of the woodwind and the solid, steel bass of the brass and percussion. But the blending of the reeds and the brass for John did not gel; it was like a hermaphrodite, neither one thing nor the other.

Still, in this context it was purely background music and it was being played appropriately pianissimo so they could converse over the strains. Strains indeed, such a highly appropriate word though John.

The room was not brightly lit but what light there was sparkled off the highly decorative and elaborate silverware which abounded on the tables and on the decorated chests of some of the military might that was assembled. On those chests too the gold took on a more amber appearance and the variety of ribbons gave a kaleidoscopic effect against the red or black military dress uniforms being worn. The sound of conversation bubbled through the air virtually, but not quite, drowing out the musical melodies swirling around seeking attentive ears in what was a squeaking tread across the parquet flooring of the waiters and waitresses—again, thought John, was there any need for the femine gender or should all such words be deleted from the dictionaries a la Orwellian Newspeak dictionary?—as they went about serving food and wine and wine and food with the discretion of priests taking confession. On the cutlery and on the plates John noticed yet again the logo, such a commercial term being as appropriate now to the army as to the other forces and education and health for that matter. The winged god, Mercury, carrying communications. Here then was an appropriate sound of revelry by night in which John could converse, carry forward his communications and focus, as he was clearly meant to do on the future that lay before him.

As he ate, therefore, they talked; and as he talked, therefore they ate. But above all he listened, marked and inwardly digested all that was being said.

CHAPTER 14

Envoi

> "... it is among communities such as these that
> happiness will find her last refuge on earth,
> since it is among them that a perfect insight into the
> conditions of existence will be longest postponed."
> (Thomas Hardy: The Dorsetshire Labourer).

May day, bank holiday. It was early morning and John slid softly and undisturbingly out of bed, leaving Helen, his bride of nearly eight weeks sleeping the slumber of the quiet conscienced. For a moment he paused at the edge of the bed and surveyed her form, the gently curve of her back from the nape of her neck, the peach blush and softness of her skin and her coiffeured, blond hair undisturbed even by the bedclothes and pillows. She seemed to be an ethereal imprint on or in the bed itself. His being suffused with love for her and he was tempted to stroke her gently into life and enjoy with her a most sensuous love making. Yet he was not one for destroying what was inherently beautiful and so he refrained. She was a work of art at this point for him, like one of the figures on

Keats' *Grecian Urn* not to be defiled. He smiled to himself and remembered Keats' vocabulary and with that in mind he thought how he would ravish her later.

He slipped into his dressing gown and tiptoed through the bedroom door which as always had been left ajar. He walked across the living room to the long sliding windows which opened out onto the balcony of his flat here in Port Solent. Going to the left of the windows he pulled the curtain rope and drew back the slatted, vertical, fawn-coloured blinds which covered them. The thin rays of what promised to be a bright, effulgent, warm spring day cascaded into the room. John turned the key in the windows and slid back the centre panel to his right; it moved with silently oiled ease. He walked out onto the balcony and sniffed in the sea air as if it were essential, like the winding up of a clockwork toy, to give him life for the day ahead.

The sun sparkled on the water and reflected off the fibre-glass, plastic, shining gloss painted hulls, brass and metal fittings and the glass of the potholes and cabins of the many yachts bobbing on the gentle tide lapping in the marina below. The light zephyr in the air shook sweet music from the masts' ropes and their metallic accoutrements and a few gulls chorused a rather discordant accompaniment to these pleasant chimes that heralded the day. A few keen sailors were out on some of the decks or at the side of the quays getting ready, no doubt, to release their craft on the tide for a day or more's sailing out on the inviting Solent. As John surveyed them quietly going about their business he felt a slight touch of envy that sea-faring had never been for him and in part, that attraction of this most wonderful of seaside venues, was a little lost on him. Yet he was happy to watch and internally applaud the skills with which these mariners maneuvered their vessels in and out of the smallest of narrowest of niches which were allotted to them as berths.

Looking at the other flats he saw a few individuals like himself taking the morning air and some in anticipation of himself breakfasting comfortably on the dining furniture which amply filled their balconies. That's what he would do, prepare a light spring breakfast for his wife to enjoy after she woke. Before re-entering the flat to carry out his mission he glanced around the buildings that circled below. The heavy, sienna timbers of the shops, restaurants and cafeterias were offset by multicoloured pennants softly swaying in the light breeze and further away shone the colours of the few parked cars which were, even at this time of the day, flowing in to fill up the car park. Later that area would resemble a paint manufacturers brochure of colours as the flags would cheerily wave greetings to the myriad of visitors which would troop here on such a day as this.

John re-entered the flat leaving the window-door open behind him. Even in the short time he had been up and out on the balcony the light had got brighter and the air had got warmer. He hoped this was a harbinger of a good summer, what would be his first summer, here in the environment that only last year he could only dream of finding himself in. But since then he had aspired to chief features editor for the Portsmouth News group of papers, his salary was appropriately commensurate with such a position as was his British racing-green, '5' series, B M W parked next to Helen's Peugot in their massive double garage below. And Helen herself had received promotion subsequent to her German sojourn within the Chemical Corporation for which she worked. Times that had seemed so hard, especially for John in the winter had indeed turned round. Spring, Summer, Autumn, Winter and then again Spring he smiled to himself as he went into the large, fitted kitchen and went about his task.

He took two large, Edinburgh crystal glasses, two mugs and two cereal bowls and small sideplates and appropriate cutlery from the kitchen out onto the balcony. He placed them on the table and went in to retrieve what he should have got in the first place, a small, sea-blue table cloth to spread over the mahogany table itself. Having sorted out the tablecloth, receptacle and utensil problems he proceeded to squeeze some large, Outspan oranges to make the freshest of orange juice which he then put into the fridge to give the semblance of a chill at least. After this he took four, small, croissants from the bread bin, and placed them on a large plate, and grabbed two boxes of cereal and the container of the polyunsaturated low flat spread which seemed to have universally replaced butter and margarine and he now added to what he had already placed on the table. Once more back inside he found the Kenyan coffee beans, ground them in the Moulinex grinder and then transferred the ground coffee to the percolator and switched it on. He then took the jar of clear honey to add to the food already placed outside. All was going well, so as he waited for the percolator to bubble away, he finally poured milk, splashingly white into a large jug and took that together with the jug of orange juice outside. His final operation was to take the small, battery operated transistor radio and place this also on the table; they could not have piped music but at least they would have something in the background to listen to as they dined. Satisfied that everything was in hand and that the coffee, the piece de resistance, would be suitably ready for when he and Helen came out to breakfast, he switched on the radio and went back into the bedroom.

His wife had since his departure turned over and perhaps even awoke but registering his absence had not made her anxious to arise and seek him out, rather she had clearly enjoyed having the bed to herself and gone back to sleep. Gently he drew the duvet back from her shoulders and peeled it off her back as if he were removing her coat. His hands subsequently moved over her naked form and softly caressed her back and the cheeks of her bottom which he gently, ever so gently squeezed. She moaned as she came to consciousness and as he his tender palms skilfully and secretly found their way to even more erogenous zones. She smiled, her eyes still shut in a drowsy sleep, as she turned in exquisite enjoyment of erotic awakening. Her arms stretched out and she caught him in them and entwined him close to her with the duvet between them. He kissed her on the mouth and kept his lips pressed firmly against hers as they rolled over together enjoying the sensuosness of the duvet which kept their bodies from touching intimately. Rolling like lovers under the covers as the song says. It was an act of loving self-denial on themselves but it added to the eroticism of the moment and was indulgently satisfying. As they paused, clinging together on the bed and she asked the time he merely told her what a beautiful day awaited and how he had prepared breakfast to make the ideal start. She loved him for such simple sweetness and caressed him even more and kissed him ravishingly.

"Come on," he whispered. "Get up. Let's greet the day."

"Don't you want to . . . . ?" she asked.

"Yes, but later. I want us both to enjoy this day, the herald of a delightful summer ahead. We'll celebrate sexually tonight after we've discussed what we're going to do, unless . . . ."

"Make love to me now," she urged, "and we'll celebrate tonight as well," and she gently maneuvered him over to the side, hurriedly stripped away the duvet, undid his dressing gown and brought him to her. She devoured him sexually like the air he had taken in when he first stepped on to the balcony that morning. Their union was perfect and they lay briefly at the end of it, silently side by side on the bed together. Then he leapt up, grabbed her by the hand and just laughed and said, "Come on! before the coffee stews and the milk and orange juice reach undrinkable temperatures!"

He pulled her out of bed, and he grabbed his gown and she hers and throwing them on they went through the lounge out onto the balcony not forgetting to grab the percolator on the way. As they sat down, John switched on the radio tuned in as it was to Radio 2, music very much for easy, perhaps really non listening!

She shook her head soaking up the air and surveyed the scene and smiled first to herself and then to her husband, John. She, like him, reveled in this newly wedded bliss and in their recent change of fortune. It was, indeed, what they had both dreamed of; that it should come so soon made her feel indeed that the gods had most certainly smiled on them. And, she felt, moreover in the light of John's brief troubles, deservingly so.

As they breakfasted and discussed their plans for the day, the radio played on in the background. The disc-jockey had put on Don Quixote's song from *The Man of La Mancha*. It's opening monologue wafted away over the idyllic scene hoping in vain to find discerning ears . . . .

"I will impersonate a man . . . . the problem : How to make better a world when evil brings profit and virtue none at all. He lays down the melancholy burden of reality and conceives . . . ."

And it floated away on the breeze and inexorably, inextricably mixed in with the music of the air in the harbour below and the chatter of the conversation of this and other balconies and on the quayside and in the car park and out, out across the whole geographical globe.